THE
GRAVE
THIEF

DEE HAHN

PUFFIN CANADA
an imprint of Penguin Random House Canada Young Readers,
a division of Penguin Random House of Canada Limited

Published in hardcover by Puffin Canada, 2022

1 2 3 4 5 6 7 8 9 10

Text copyright © 2022 by Dee Hahn

Jacket design by Emma Dolan

Manufactured in Canada

Library and Archives Canada Cataloguing in Publication

Title: The grave thief / Dee Hahn.
Names: Hahn, Dee, author.
Identifiers: Canadiana (print) 20210094567 | Canadiana (ebook)
20210094583 | ISBN 9780735269439 (hardcover) |
ISBN 9780735269446 (EPUB)
Classification: LCC PS8615.A3646 G73 2022 | DDC jC813/.6—dc23

Library of Congress Control Number: 2020951910

www.penguinrandomhouse.ca

Penguin
Random House
PUFFIN CANADA

For Michael:
You're the Gumpus to my Gertrude.

CHAPTER 1

NIGHT WATCH

The graveyard lay damp and still tonight, just the way Spade liked it. No wailing women tossing limp flowers, no undertakers. No one at all, except for him. And Ash, of course.

The raven sat perched atop a scraggly elm tree beside the open grave. Head cocked, the bird uttered a soft croak.

"I know," Spade sighed, a familiar ache creeping up his leg. "Back to digging. Yer not much help, you know. Sitting up there like a king."

The raven ruffled his feathers.

One shovelful of dirt after another flew over Spade's shoulder. He paused to catch his breath at ten shovels, glancing up at the engraving on the tombstone. He stood level with it now, five feet deep in the hole.

Bagman Grute, the stone read. Tax Collector, Wyndhail. Or at least he was pretty sure that's what it said. He wasn't great at reading. Tax collectors were a good choice: not a single mourner had attended the burial that afternoon as Spade hid behind the crooked elm. And not a soul came later to pay their respects that whole, starless evening. Likely a cantankerous old crotcher when he was alive, and greedy too. Both good signs.

Clouds obscured the moon tonight, the tombstones silent gray sentinels casting no shadow. His lantern's dim flame flickered. Another foot to go. He wiped his forehead, muscles aching, then dug the shovel in deep.

Thud.

His shovel struck hard wood, and he grinned.

Spade dropped to his knees and scraped the dirt away. Digging around the edges of the casket, he hooked his fingers under the smooth lid, feeling around for any trigger latches or booby traps. Nothing. Slowly, he pried the lid open.

Withered, sunken skin in a bearded face greeted him. Curious, he peered down at the old man for a moment. Spade had seen hundreds of dead bodies, but it wasn't the dead part that was the creepy bit. A body was nothing but a shell, his great-uncle Malachi liked to remind him. But every once in a while, a stiffer had a look to them. Bagman Grute had it—that uncanny look, like he hadn't been quite ready to go. His blueish lips, maybe, pulled down in a slight scowl. The twist to his waxen chin.

Ash crowed from his perch on the elm and peered into the coffin.

"I know, I know," Spade said. "I'm hurrying."

He poked around in Grute's clothes, but there were no

telltale lumps. The old man's wrists were bare of gold charms, the cold fingers empty of rings.

Most citizens of Wyndhail believed you took your riches with you to the afterlife, stuffing their coffins with everything from silk underwear to silver cutlery, but Grute's was clean as a toothpick. Spade sat back, frustrated. His dad wouldn't be happy if he arrived to find him with an empty sack.

Ash cawed again, a short, sharp sound.

He had to hurry. The night watchman would arrive at the stroke of midnight, and Benji wasn't the most reliable guard—his younger brother was likely sitting by the gate taking a nap instead of watching the road.

Maybe the shoes, then? His fingers swept the narrow ankles, searching the socks first. He untied the laces with deft fingers, pried them off the corpse's rigid feet and shook them.

A single smooth pebble rolled out. Spade sighed and plucked it up, turning it over in his fingers. He couldn't imagine how anyone walked around with a pebble in their shoe all day. He held it up to the lantern light, and for a moment, it seemed to glimmer. He turned it, but the thin glint was gone. Odd. He shoved it in his pocket. At least it'd make a good stone for his slingshot.

He jimmied the shoes back on, tying the laces neat— more respectful that way—then sat back with a frown. His gaze landed on a ripple in the fabric lining of the coffin and he spied a thin, sewn-up tear. Fingers smoothing over the ripple, he tore it open to reveal a spring-button latch hidden underneath.

"Bingo," he murmured, and pressed it.

A drawer slid out containing a few rings and a modest silk bag. He weighed the small bag in his hand: silvers, by the clank and feel of it. No gold or large gems. Disappointment settled in his stomach. His dad was sure the old coot had been wealthy, but it wasn't the first time he'd been mistaken. Shoving everything into a drawstring sack, he tied the knot tight, then glanced down at the corpse.

The stiffer's face was the same, but Spade liked to imagine the old man felt less burdened now. "Silvers would be too heavy fer yer pockets in the ever-after, anyhow," he told him. "You an' I both know it. Besides, what're you gonna spend it on up there?"

Ash flew down to Spade's shoulder and the boy lowered the lid, then climbed out of the hole. Now to cover the pit. He'd have to work quick. He dug down hard, feeling sweat drip down his forehead as he scooped dirt into the hole. Half-full. Three-quarters full.

Hoohoo, hoohoo. Benji's barn-owl call cut through the night air—once, then twice.

Spade froze.

The creak of rusty hinges carried up the hill.

Night watchman.

Spade snuffed his lantern and hid the shovel behind the nearest tombstone. He grabbed the bag of dead leaves beside the hole and shook them over the mound of dirt, then limped to the crooked elm that drooped across the path.

Dim lantern light spread its fingers over the hill as a tall man ambled into view. Spade cringed; the leaves would only do their job from a distance. The night watchman climbed the hill and swung his lantern higher, his heavy tread crunching over the pebbled path. He paused at the fork, then turned, taking the one to the left. The one that led right to Grute's grave.

Something had to be done.

Spade signaled Ash with a nod. The sleek raven took to the air, circled once, then swooped low over the graves, diving across the night watchman's path.

"Gah!" the man cried out. "Get back, filthy creature!"

The raven circled overhead, releasing his best guttural caw. The big man crossed his hands over his heart, blood draining from his face. "This here's sanctified ground!" he cried out, though his voice wavered. His hand reached up to clutch something strung around his neck—a token, no doubt. "Be gone with you!"

But Ash floated lower, hovering with dramatic flair, then dove. The bird's swift talons reached for the night watchman, plucking his hat off his head.

"Demon bird!" The man's hands flew up as Ash circled, dropping the hat at Spade's feet, then dove again, aiming for the man's tufted hair. The night watchman yelled a garbled curse, hands covering his head. He fled back down the path and the slam of the old iron cemetery gate echoed up the hill.

Ash landed on Spade's shoulder and puffed his chest out with a gleeful squawk.

"Okay, you were good," the boy admitted as he picked the hat up and dusted it off. He plopped it on his head. "Couldn't have done it better if I were a raven myself."

Pulling a cracker from his pocket, he held it up. Ash nipped it out of his hand, then spread his dark wings and launched to the top of the crooked elm to eat his prize.

Spade retrieved his shovel and turned back to the grave. All was quiet from the other end of the cemetery, which was a good sign. Mist rose in the cool air, the chill creeping into his bones. He buttoned up his tattered jacket. Time to hurry; his dad would be back within the hour.

The grave was almost covered when he heard it.

Shhhhhh, th-thump. Th-thump.

Spade froze.

He scanned the cemetery hill, squinting into the dark. Silence steeped the gathering fog, soft wind rustling the dead leaves at his feet. The tickle of the damp breeze crawled down his spine.

"Ash?" he whispered, glancing up. But the crooked elm was empty.

Shhhhhh, th-thump. Th-thump.

All the whispers he'd heard in town the last few days crept into his thoughts. There'd been rumors: more people gone missing in the dead of night. "The Woegan," they'd said in hushed voices. "It's returned."

Spade whirled and spied the raven perched on a tombstone several feet away, staring into the dark.

A shadow appeared through the gloom, not twenty paces from the tax collector's grave.

CHAPTER 2

GHOSTS IN THE GRAVEYARD

The hairs on the back of Spade's neck rose. The hunched shape crept closer, lugging something behind it.

Shhhh, th-thump, th-thump.

Spade stood like a statue beside his sack, breath caught in his throat.

Who would visit a graveyard in the middle of the night? And how had they slipped past Benji?

A tremulous voice drifted through the night. "Are you going to help me, boy? Or just stand there, watching?"

The bent-backed figure turned, and a sliver of moonlight washed over the wrinkliest old woman Spade had ever seen, her spectacles three times too big for her face, lips like prunes. Puffy white hair crowned her head like a ghostly halo. A mangy, one-eared tabby peered up from beneath her skirts.

Spade's heart stalled in his chest. His dad would kill him, getting caught out in the open like this.

"Well?" She tilted her head, one veined hand perched on her bony hip. "Or don't gravediggers speak English anymore?"

Gravedigger . . . Of course, she thought he was just a graveyard worker! His chest expanded a notch, relief sweeping through him. Right. Now to act like one.

"Yes, ma'am, 'course," he said, clearing his dry throat. He reached for his lantern and lit it with clumsy, nervous fingers. "How can I, uh, be of service?"

She gestured behind her. "I've a big bench here. I need to place it somewhere . . . where was I going? Oh yes, the top of that hill."

His gaze followed her long, spindly finger to the top of the cemetery rise. He glanced over his shoulder, nervous. Where was his brother?

"Don't worry, young man." She chuckled. "It'll take no more than a moment. And then I'll let you go back to your work, and we can pretend neither of us saw each other here at this unusual hour."

Her eyes were trained on him from behind those big silver spectacles, and he glimpsed a cunning gleam. The tabby meowed, a sound like a rusty hinge, and the woman narrowed her eyes at the lumpy sack on the ground beside him.

"Right. Sure thing. Let's go," he heard himself say. Anything to redirect her gaze. And the gaze of that ugly, ugly cat.

She smiled, wrinkles bunched in the corners of her ancient face. "My thanks to you."

Spade lugged and pushed, huffed and hauled the thick

wendigo wood bench up the hill, muscles trembling. The mangy tabby perched on top, watching him work with a bored air as the old woman shuffled along beside him, humming to herself. Ash circled overhead with one beady eye fastened on the strange procession.

Gritting his teeth, Spade wondered how an old lady had hauled a heavy bench all the way into the cemetery. He glanced at her out of the corner of his eye, and she gave him a wink. "Wonderful," she crooned. "Almost there."

At last, he hefted it over the crest of the hill, and she beamed as he dragged it next to her, wheezing, his bad leg cramping.

"If you don't mind me asking, what's the bench for?" he wheezed.

"For sitting, of course!" The old lady chuckled. "Take a look." She sat down on the bench and patted the empty spot beside her. "You'll love the view."

Exhausted, he slumped onto the seat and followed her gaze. The clouds had cleared, and they could see the whole town from the top of the hill. Nestled in the shadows of the Craiggarock Mountains, the houses and shops lay hemmed in by farmland on the north side, deep forest to the south. Wyndhail castle rose up on a steep hill to the west, its towers silhouetted against the mountains behind it.

"Beautiful, isn't it?" she murmured, her spectacles glinting in the moonlight. "A good sitting spot helps one to think."

"Uh, sure." He had to admit it was nice, though his aching leg disagreed.

She began to hum again. He was wondering if he might just slip away when she turned her strange eyes on him. "How long have you had that limp?" she asked.

He hesitated. It wasn't something he liked to talk about. But this old lady had a way about her, and for some reason he heard himself saying, "Long as I can remember. I was born with it."

She nodded, her gaze drifting over the town once more. "I was born with a peculiarity too," she murmured. "But it turned out to be useful."

Curious, he wanted to ask her about it, but she'd bent over and was rummaging around in her pocket. She drew out a small tin box. "Biscuit?" she asked.

His stomach grumbled at the sight. He hadn't eaten since the watery soup his family had shared the night before. But what if . . . what if she'd done something to the biscuit? After all, every story he'd heard about witches said they lured you in with goodies.

She waited, hands trembling with age as she held out the tin, and the smell wafted up his nostrils.

He couldn't help himself.

"Thanks," he mumbled. He bit into the biscuit, and its buttery goodness rolled off his tongue.

She passed a crumb to the one-eared tabby, who sniffed it with disdain. "Nitpicky thing," she commented. "At least someone appreciates my baking." Her gaze traveled over Spade. "It's not so often I see a helpful young person anymore. And not even wearing a luck token, I see."

Without thinking, he glanced down at the empty spot on his collar where his token should have been. Before he'd ripped it off and buried it several digs ago. "I'm not really a charm kinda person." He shifted in his seat, the ache shooting up his hip. "They've never brought me much luck."

"Unusual," she said. "Most parents encourage them, especially since the creature's reared its head in these parts."

"Oh, my parents wear them," he admitted. They were too superstitious to speak of the Woegan, of course, but he saw it in their glances, sometimes. The way they'd stoke their campfire higher at night. "But I don't think a trinket will stop a creature like that."

She nodded, thoughtful. "Wiser than you look, for someone only twelve years of age."

Wait. Had he said how old he was?

Before he could ask, Ash's sharp caw rang out from the tree above, and the sound of carriage wheels rumbled up the cemetery hill.

Spade leaped to his feet. *Crud.* "I've gotta go."

"Of course, young man," she agreed, reaching out her hand for him to help her up. He took it and was surprised at the strength of her grip—like wiry steel. "We all have our secrets." She winked at him and grinned.

A tingling warmth spread through her fingers and into his, traveling up his arm. He jolted, about to jerk away, when she released him and smiled, patting him on the cheek.

He stared down at his fingers, trying to figure out what she'd done, but they looked the same as usual. Who was she? *What* was she?

He looked up, and his breath caught.

The bench sat empty, the hill quiet.

The old woman had vanished.

CHAPTER 3

IMAGINING THINGS

Spade flew back down the winding path, limp-hopping between the tombstones, nerves jangling.

He'd never seen an old woman move so fast. How had she disappeared like that?

He jolted to a stop at the old elm where he'd left the small sack of goods from Grute's grave. Hefting it up on his back, he headed down the path and through the tall, metal spiraled gate as Ash flew overhead, keeping close on his trail.

The carriage clambered up over the rise just as he reached the road, breathing hard.

A scrawny boy stood up from where he'd been leaning against a tree, tossing a little stone figurine up and down in his hand. "What took you so long?" his little brother demanded. "I did the bird-whistle, but you didn't come. The watch came running out of the cemetery like a spooked ghost, an' you were nowhere to be seen."

"That's because of the old lady, Benj!" Spade jerked his chin over his shoulder. "Where'd you go? You were supposed to stay by the gate an' warn me!"

"What old lady?" Benji's green eyes narrowed, and he shook his tousled blond head. "I was watching the gate the whole time. There weren't no old ladies sneaking through."

Spade stared at him. "No one could have missed an old woman like her. You were napping, weren't you? Or snacking?"

"My eyeballs were glued to the gate, Spade. Not even a weasel could've snuck by. You sure you weren't imagining things? You took forever."

"I know what I saw, Benj!" Spade stared at his brother. The old woman had stood right beside him. He'd spoken to her. She'd touched him, for jewels' sakes. His mind crept to all the campfire stories his Joolie relatives told at night . . . but no. She was no ghost. She was real. He was certain. Mostly certain.

The clatter of the Joolie carriage interrupted them as it came down the hill. Their dad, Garnet, sat at the reins of two stubborn-looking mountain yaks.

"There's my fine, strapping gravediggers!" he called out, his green eyes eager, a smile on his broad, golden-bearded face. "How'd it go?"

Spade hesitated. He glanced back up the hill to the cemetery, but the darkness obscured any sign of the bench.

Benji scowled. "Spade was daydreaming, Dad. Something about old lady ghosts."

"If you weren't dozing, you would've seen her," Spade retorted. Garnet pulled the yaks up beside them, and

Spade tossed the sack of coins to him, bracing himself for his dad's disappointment; the haul had been especially light tonight.

"No jewelry?" His dad grunted, weighing the small sack.

"Not much."

"An' nothing else?" Their dad was always interested in gemstones, especially the larger ones mined from the Craiggarock Mountains: they brought a fortune on the black market.

Spade braced himself. *Here it comes,* he thought. Their father's specialty lecture. "Nothing but dirt, Dad."

But Garnet laughed. "Never mind that now, boys." He chuckled. "We'll do better next time."

Spade and Benji both stared at him, startled. He'd seen the lack of coins, hadn't he?

Their dad looked down at them then, a slow grin spreading across his face. "We've got bigger things to worry about, my boys. Because tomorrow's the day. Tomorrow's the day we make a name for ourselves."

CHAPTER 4

A FAMILY OF THIEVES

G arnet sang the whole way home, past windblown farmers' fields and ramshackle barns, humming a song he'd made up:

> *The Joolies know what others don't.*
> *That common work's a waste of time.*
> *When all you'll make's a grubby dime,*
> *You'll fare much better if instead*
> *You barter pickins from the dead!*

Spade and Benji exchanged glances, curious. Their dad was downright jolly. And he was never jolly, unless it involved the getting of gold. He urged the plodding yaks faster, and his voice echoed over the swaying wheat and barley as they clopped along the lonely country road and up to a bridge.

"Deep breath, boys!" he demanded, grabbing some salt from his pocket and throwing it over his shoulder. Spade rolled his eyes, and he and Benji pinched their noses as they bumped over the bridge. Their dad had strict superstitions, like carrying pepper ("To keep the demons away, my boys, never be without it") and stinky cheeses ("Nothing bad ever chases you if you smell like fungus"), and holding your breath over a bridge ("The ill-luck can't catch you if it can't hear you").

A familiar rickety white schoolhouse stood in the field opposite the bridge. The carriage bumped past the schoolyard, an abandoned ball lying in the grass. Spade craned his neck to try and catch a glimpse inside like he did each time they passed. He'd always wondered what it would be like to read and write and learn stuff all day.

"Never you mind that place, Spade," his dad's stern voice interrupted his thoughts. Garnet frowned and flicked the yaks' reins. "Joolies weren't made fer book-learning an' rules. Not when they've got freedom an' thieving at their fingertips, the best things you could ever want outta life."

But as they passed, Spade couldn't help but let his eyes linger on the small white door. He thought of the grave markers he was surrounded by each evening, the intricate inscriptions etched in their stone. Malachi had told him once that often the best stories could be found on a tombstone. Stories that Spade wished he could read.

The carriage jolted forward through an overgrown field of stony soil. A group of colorful yurts stood amongst the tall grasses beside a few lone, stubborn trees that clung to the ground like scarecrows in a cornfield.

The yak-skin doorway of the nearest yurt drew aside,

and Spade's mother ducked out. She sauntered across the field, chocolate hair piled on her head, long skirts swirling about her. While Benji was fair like their father, Spade resembled his mother with her deep olive skin and brown eyes, though their personalities were opposite.

"Well?" Opalline crooned, her gaze narrowed. "How'd it go?"

"Smoothly oiled as a casket's lid, Opalline my dear. Fortune smiled on us tonight." Garnet bent to give her a mustached kiss, but she swatted him away.

"What sort of fortune?" she demanded.

He jumped down, drew the small sack off his shoulder and plopped it at her feet. She gazed down at it with a critical eye. "Well, my love, fer a grin as wide as the one on yer face, that's not the fortune I was hoping fer."

"But my sweet! I haven't told you the best part."

Their mother glanced up. "No? An' what is that?"

But their dad shook his head. "You know the rules, darlin'. A good plan spoken before its time is a good plan jinxed." He leaped back onto the carriage.

Opalline pursed her lips. "An' now where're you off to, Garnet?"

"I've some errands to do." He winked, turning the yaks around.

The carriage rattled into the night, away from Opalline's frown. She turned to Spade and Benji, leveling them with a look. "Boys? What's this about?"

They shrugged. "Dad's been singing again," Benji said. "That's all we know—he ain't told us nothing."

"Singing, hmm?" Their mother considered this, a hungry gleam flashing in her dark eyes. "Well, yer father can sniff out gold better than a troll, I always say."

She ruffled Benji's hair. "Go eat some porridge, Benitoite, darlin'," she said. Benji scowled at the use of his full name but trudged away obediently, shoulders slumped at the prospect of yet another bowl of the mush they ate when gold ran low. Opalline turned to examine Spade and her crimson lips drew together in a thin line. "Spade Archer Rustle. Where is yer token necklace?"

Spade sighed. Not this again. "I . . . uh. Lost it."

His mother's scowl deepened. "And how come you didn't get another?"

"I don't really like luck tokens, Mum. They get in the way when I'm digging."

"Easy fix," she trilled. She rummaged in the pocket of her tattered cotton skirts, then pulled something out and placed it into his palm: a thin chain with a lucky clover dangling from it. How she always managed to find him a new token, he didn't know. "Tie it on yer ankle. No decent son of mine should be without it. Even Benji's got his frog-stone."

"Benji only keeps it 'cause he likes frogs."

Opalline crossed her arms. "Yer not yet a grown man, Spade, no matter what yer father says. An' even yer father doesn't tempt fate."

Spade swallowed a groan. He bent and pretended to tie it on but stuffed it in his sock instead. "Mum, has anyone in this family ever actually . . . seen the Woegan?"

His mother's wrist snaked out and she clapped a hand

over his mouth. "Don't utter its name, darlin'," she hissed, her eyes darting about. "It could be listening. Truly, Spade, what's gotten into you? I've told you time an' again about the dangers, an' my poor heart!" She straightened, pressing her hands to her heart, as if it might fall out of her chest. "You wouldn't want your mother to die of fright now, would you?"

"'Course not, Mum." He sighed under his breath as she whirled and strutted across the firelit circle, clutching the small sack. Uncle Topaz and Aunt Ermine looked up from the fire, and Grandma Flint hobbled over. Everyone crowded around the rings and silvers, Grandma Flint shining each one with her spit, holding it up to the firelight, her cracked golden teeth visible as she grinned. Often, the smaller trinkets were left for Benji and Spade, but Spade knew the meagre haul meant there'd be nothing for them today.

Well, not quite nothing.

Spade reached up and ran his fingers along the brim of his stolen night-watch's cap. And then he remembered something else: the small, gray pebble he'd found in the dead man's shoe. He pulled it out of his back pocket and sat down by the fire, turning it over in his hand.

For a brief moment, it seemed to catch the firelight with an unnatural sheen. He blinked and held it up, peering closer, but it had become cold and lifeless once more.

Strange, he thought, and rubbed at his eyes. It had been a long day, and he must be a little paranoid. He shoved it back in his pocket.

His mind wandered to the old woman in the graveyard. She'd appeared so suddenly, with that weird gleam in her eyes and her strange, steel grip. He knew Benji didn't believe him, but he'd talked to her.

Spade got up and left the circle of yurts, leaving the noise of his family's chatter behind. Ash flew off his perch from the tallest yurt's smokestack, lighting down on his shoulder. Spade fed him some stale bread crumbs and sat down on a tree stump while they watched the grass bend in the wind, listening to the rustle of weasels darting between the stalks.

A quiet *thud, thud* sounded nearby, and his great-uncle Malachi came into view, his cane crunching over the pebbles. He sat down beside Spade on another stump and lit his pipe. His gray eyes crinkled in the corners, looking up at the golden moon from beneath his weathered black cap.

Malachi always knew when Spade needed to think. Other than Ash and Benji, his great-uncle was the only one who understood him.

They sat in silence for a while, listening to the crickets. A weasel darted out from the grass and snatched a cricket in its teeth, disappearing with a flick of its tail.

Malachi puffed a curl of smoke into the air. "Anything wrong, Spade? You seem extra quiet tonight."

Spade brushed his dark bangs out of his eyes and glanced up at his great-uncle. "I saw something funny in the grave-yard tonight. An old lady. She came out of nowhere. An' I thought . . . well, maybe . . ."

"She was a ghost?" Malachi finished. The older man sat for a moment, tugging at his short beard. "Could you touch her?"

"Sure. She took my hand, an' her grip was like iron. An' I felt this strange feeling go through my fingers."

"Could you see any tokens on her? Any gems?"

"Nothing. Not a single piece of jewelry."

A fleeting look of surprise crossed Malachi's face. "The old magic," he muttered.

"The old magic? Like the kind the mages in yer stories use?"

"Not quite, boy." A spark flickered in the old man's gray eyes. "It's something even deeper than that."

Spade frowned, remembering the tales his great-uncle had told him around the campfire at night when he was younger. Stories of mages and witches, of trolls, ice giants, or even stranger creatures, once said to have roamed the land. "You don't mean fairy tales, Uncle?"

"Every fairy tale has a seed of truth." The lines in his uncle's face deepened. "They say that the old magic was common once. It came from inside a person, and it was mighty useful; it could help things grow, mend things, even heal. But over time, people began to forget how to use it. It took time to learn it, see, and a steady patience. Around that time, some peculiar gemstones were found in the mines, carrying a different breed of magic: a kinda magic that was quicker to wield. If you had one of these stones, you could change things, twist the old magic into an unnatural sorta magic. You could cause flowers to turn to weeds, turn fresh milk sour, or even manipulate rocks an' water. 'Course, even they had a limit to their power."

Spade's thoughts churned. "Are those the kind of stones that Dad's always looking fer?"

Malachi nodded. "Yes, boy. But there's more to the story. You see, there was one miner that dug deeper than all the others, and he broke through the shaft into an odd sorta tunnel. He followed it all the way down to a vast cavern." Malachi took a long drag from his pipe and puffed the smoke out into the night. "That miner found some gemstones in the cavern that were stranger than all the others. He hauled them back up to the surface, an' it's said that the royal family claimed most of 'em and dubbed them the deepstones. The rumor goes that the magic of the deepstones was far beyond that of any others found in the mines. Some said they could bring their bearer incredible fortune . . . or endless sorrow." Malachi's gaze slid up to the stars. "No one knows if it's true, of course."

"But what's this got to do with Dad?"

Malachi scratched his whiskers and sighed. He turned to meet Spade's gaze. "The royal family claimed most of 'em, as I said. But not all. An' yer dad, well, he happened to come upon an unusual stone in his travels. At the time, he didn't know what it was. He traded it to someone who offered a handsome sum, only to later hear these strange rumors about deepstones. So yer dad got it in his head that his stone was one of them and that he let it slip through his grasp. He's bin looking for it ever since."

The information sunk into Spade's brain. "What would Dad want with a magic stone like that?"

"What all men want them fer: power, wealth, magic. Protection against the Woegan."

"I'm guessing it'd be more useful against the Woegan than a luck token," Spade said. He scowled down at the sock where he'd stuffed the clover token his mother had given him.

Malachi snorted and gestured out to the tall grass where a weasel popped its head out of its hole. "How does that critter catch his prey?"

Spade narrowed his gaze as the weasel slunk toward the cricket. "He traps it, of course."

"An' that's what fear does to you." Malachi gestured. "The weasel counts on it. His prey gets all panicked an' wobbly, an' then bingo—it's dinnertime! Easy pickings."

"But what does that have to do with magic deepstones? Or the Woegan?"

"People go relying on stones an' luck tokens to protect them from dark creatures like the Woegan. They get lazy an' fearful an' forget to use their noggin."

A shiver snaked down Spade's spine. "An' the old magic? What happened to it?"

Malachi shook his head. "I don't know, my boy. But I reckon there're those out there who do."

"Spade!"

His mother appeared around the corner, eyes narrowing when she spotted Spade with his great-uncle. "It's dinnertime," she said curtly. "I've scrounged up some more broth. An' Mal, no more stories from you tonight."

"Sure thing, Opalline." Malachi nodded, and tipped his hat. Under his breath, he murmured, "Be careful tomorrow, boy."

Spade frowned as his uncle stood and ambled away. What was his dad planning?

His mother turned her hard gaze on Spade. "Off with you, then. You must be starving." Eyeing Malachi's back, his mother whirled, shoes clipping across the dirt, skirts swirling behind her.

Spade cast one last glance at the fields, glimpsing the weasel as it pounced, snatching the cricket up between its teeth.

CHAPTER 5

STOWAWAYS

Wyndhail's market square bustled with the calls of vendors and the smell of fresh-baked bread as Spade and Benji followed their father into town that morning. Ash circled high above so as not to attract attention, but even so, a few townspeople stopped and eyed them with suspicion, their whispers floating close to Spade's ears.

Spade ignored them, forcing himself to walk faster despite his stiff leg. He'd had trouble sleeping the night before—he'd dreamed of old ladies, ghosts, and weasels and had woken at the first glimmer of light, leg aching. He wished they could have driven the cart into town, but of course he'd never ask. When Garnet had a mission, they always entered town on foot so that they would blend in and their colorful Joolie carriages wouldn't give them away.

Not that a Joolie boy with a limp was very good at blending in. Remembering the village boys who'd hounded him in the last town where they'd lived, Spade did his best to smooth his gait. Benji glanced up at him as they walked down the dusty lane, and Spade knew he was remembering too. Benji was a fighter, and he always stood up for Spade.

"You keep your fists to yerself, okay, Benj?" Spade caught his brother's eye. "I'm yer older brother an' I can take care of myself."

Benji's freckled nose crinkled, and he kicked at a few pebbles. "I know. But . . . I'm yer back-up. You know. If you need it."

"I know it, Benj." Spade glanced down at his new clean-pressed shirt and pants, which itched and smelled like soap, and he wondered how the nobles could stand them. His dad had brought them to him that morning, beaming, no doubt having stolen them the night before as a disguise. Villagers always disliked Joolies. It was the same everywhere they went.

Most Joolies dealt in trading gemstones, charms and jewelry, hence the word *Joolies*, the name most people called them. Of course, many of these items were stolen, though Spade's family was the only Joolie family that traded in what was known as "deceased goods." "More honorable that way, son," Garnet always said. "Nobody's missing it, certainly not the corpse."

Spade knew nobody else saw it quite like his dad did, of course. Garnet had a way of making everything sound good, like the year they'd almost starved, and he'd convinced Spade that fried grasshoppers were delicacies, or that time he'd insisted a sixty-foot drop into a lake while escaping from a guard was just "a little splash."

Garnet glanced back at Spade. "Walk tall, boys," he said. "Keep yer head high an' yer eyes out."

There were strict rules about thieving in Wyndhail, and Spade had heard of Joolies who had served sentences in jail—or even been hung—but Garnet never batted an eye. "Confidence," he loved to say, "is what's saved my neck all these years. It's what separates the best of us from the dead of us." Then he'd chuckle and wink at Spade and Benji like they'd shared a good joke.

Garnet led the way into the market square, his best blue hat on, one of Ash's feathers perched jauntily in its brim. His bright green eyes missed nothing as Spade and Benji walked just behind him, weaving between stalls of flowers and skewered meat, pottery, leather workers and shoemakers. Garnet had insisted that they go to the square that morning to stake out their next job, though he still hadn't said what they were looking for.

The mouth-watering smell of cinnamon sweet dough drifted in the air as they neared the town bakery. Spade's stomach rumbled as he watched the baker's cart being loaded. He glanced up and saw Ash light down on the church steeple, examining the cart with a greedy eye.

"Dad," Benji whined. "Can't you just tell us the plan? I don't see what we're supposed to be noticing about the square. An' I'm starving—"

"Benji." Garnet's eyebrows drew downward. "Ignore yer bottomless stomach fer just a moment, an' take a good look around. If you can use yer smarts, there'll be a sweet dough in it fer you."

Spade observed the crowd. Several of the wealthier merchants were dressed with black hats today, and vendors' stalls were packed with marketgoers. Flowers were bought up by the dozens.

"It's a funeral," he said. "An' not just fer anybody."

"That's right." Garnet grinned and tipped his hat at a pretty woman as she walked by carrying a basket of cheese buns.

Sniffing the air hopefully, Benji followed the basket with his eyes. "Does that mean we get sweet loaves?"

"You haven't used yer brain enough yet, Benji. Now, tell me. Who's fancy enough to garner a crowd like this at their funeral?"

Benji looked up at the castle. "I dunno. A wealthy person, maybe."

"A *very* wealthy person," Garnet corrected, and his teeth glinted yellow in his wide grin. "The Baron Archibald Downfer himself, to be exact. Died of a heart attack just last night."

"You want us to rob the royal cemetery," Spade said with a dim realization, his stomach churning.

"Now yer thinking! There's no dig so rewarding as one in the queen's graveyard. Especially as I've heard the baron might be in possession of a particular sort of treasure I've been looking fer."

Benji stared at their dad, mouth falling open. Spade gazed at the line of carriages trundling up to the castle gates, thoughts clicking together.

"You think we're gonna find one of the deepstones!" he said, excitement leaping up his spine. "Like the one you sold so long ago."

His father's brows raised, his shrewd eyes inspecting his son. "You've been talking to Uncle Mal, I see."

"He was just telling me stories." Spade didn't want to get his great-uncle in trouble for sharing family secrets, but his dad read him anyway.

Benji looked between them, confused. "What are you talking about?"

Garnet ignored him, his gaze on Spade. "Anyhow, it's a fine opportunity fer my two wily boys."

"But, Dad," Benji muttered. "We can't just ride into Wyndhail castle. Our carriage gives us dead away."

"You won't be takin' our carriage, son. You'll be riding in something more suitable, of course."

"What?" Benji paled. "But what if we're caught, Dad? Aren't there a load of guards checking the carriages? An' I haven't ate any breakfast."

"Never you mind yer breakfast, Benj. You'll be getting some soon enough." Their dad pulled a small map from his pocket and whispered the plan to them, his eyes gleaming.

Spade and Benji exchanged looks. The plan was risky, crazy even. But no one said no to Garnet once he had an idea in his head.

A clatter of wheels made them look up, and a large bread-laden cart pulled up next to them, a big-bellied baker at the reins. He nodded once, nervous, and Garnet slipped his hand into his jacket and handed the baker a small sack with a wink and a nod.

Spade sucked in a quick breath. His dad had just bribed the baker with the sack of coins he'd stolen from Grute's grave the night before. The money that was meant to last them two months.

"Dad," he whispered. "Are you sure about this? I mean, what if the baron's not as wealthy as we thought, or what if—"

"Hush now, boy. I know the real thing when I see it." Garnet silenced him with a steel gaze, lowering his voice. "You're a Joolie's son. We named you Spade, didn't we? You were born to dig graves, to be the best thieves this side of Wyndhail."

Almost unconsciously, he glanced at Spade's leg. "You an' yer brother, I mean. Working as a team."

His father pulled his gaze away, but Spade had seen the shadow of doubt in his eyes, if only for a moment. He was reminded of a conversation he'd heard between his mother and his Aunt Ermine once when he was very small.

"Why'd you call the boy Spade, Opalline?" his aunt had demanded. "It ain't a proper Joolie name." His mother had frowned and looked down at Spade, who sat playing with lock-picks near her feet. She lowered her voice, thinking he wasn't listening.

"The stars told me he'd be unusual," she murmured in a hushed tone. "And when he was born with that leg . . . it didn't seem right to give him a Joolie-luck name, so his father chose Spade. Claimed it was an auspicious name fer a gravedigger." She sighed. "At least it won't jinx the boy further."

Spade hadn't understood all that his mother and aunt had said just then. But it wasn't long before he did.

"Ready, boys?" Garnet clapped a hand on Spade's shoulder and drew Benji in close, jolting Spade back to the present. Spade blinked and swallowed the painful memory.

He didn't believe in luck, anyway.

"Ready." He reached into his pack and tugged out his usual clothes, then ducked into a narrow alley to change. When he emerged, his father scanned him and nodded, satisfied.

"I'll need a couple of aprons," Spade said, forcing a grin to his face.

"You've heard the boy." Garnet turned to the baker, eyes gleaming. "My son's as clever as they come."

The baker hesitated, then rummaged around in his cart, unearthing a bundle of fabric.

"It's finally time fer yer pastries, Benj," Spade said, and his brother's eyes lit up. "In fact, yer about to be sick of them."

CHAPTER 6
THE BAKER BOYS

Hard sourdough loaves squashed Spade's face, Benji's elbow jutting into his ribs.

The baker's cart trundled up the steep hill, layers of bread jostling on top of the two boys as the carriage made its way to Wyndhail castle.

Spade had always wanted to see the castle up close, dreamed of it since he'd first spotted the towering, locked gates. But he hadn't planned on seeing it like this, squished between rye and pumpernickel like a piece of salami.

Benji groaned softly, and Spade knew he'd taken too many bites out of the sweet loaf pressed against his cheek.

The horse slowed, and the loud creak of hinges sounded. A guard called out from the gate. "State your business!"

"Making a delivery," the baker replied, his voice deep and robust. The cart rumbled forward, and then the horse's hooves clopped across paving stones.

We must be in the courtyard, Spade realized. The cart jolted forward, then rumbled to an abrupt stop. Benji belched, clutching his stomach. Voices rang out in the distance, and Spade clapped a hand over his brother's mouth.

Eyes wide, Benji clutched his little lucky frog carving in his fist, face pale with fear. Spade's chest tightened a little at the sight. Sometimes he wished that he and Benj could spend just one afternoon skipping rocks or swimming in the pond. Something normal, for a change. Something that didn't involve digging up dead bodies or hiding in cramped carriages.

The voices grew louder and loaves rustled overhead, interrupting Spade's thoughts. His heart pounded as a hand reached for the sourdough covering his face.

A sharp caw sounded, followed by men's shouts. Spade breathed out in relief. Thank dirt for Ash. He tugged at some loaves lining the wall beside him, pressing his eye up against the peep hole. Ash circled high above to the left of the cart, a long sourdough loaf in his claws. The raven hovered, then dropped the heavy bread over the baker's head. The portly man cursed and leaped out of the way, yelling profanities at the bird.

"Let's go." Spade pulled his cap low and gestured to Benji. They slipped out of the cart, bags of loaves over their shoulders, and lunged behind the wine barrels lining the castle wall. One of the kitchen boys glanced their way as they ducked, noticing something out of the corner of his eye. He took a step toward them, but Ash spotted him, swooping low over the courtyard. The boy shrieked and brandished a loaf of sourdough at the bird while Spade and Benji darted around the corner of the castle wall.

"That was close," Benji whispered. They hid in the shadows, breathing hard, and Ash joined them a moment later with a chunk of bread in his beak. He circled once, and at Spade's signal, soared up to perch on one of the turrets and eat his prize.

"Remember to walk normal," Spade reminded Benji. They shouldered their bread sacks and straightened their baker's aprons and caps, then stepped out onto the path.

The narrow route led behind the kitchens, veering out along the western wall of the castle. Flecks of light caught their gaze, and Benji craned his neck back, his green eyes widening. "What's that stuck in the walls, Spade?" he asked.

Flecks of fool's gold reflected the late afternoon sun, and up close, they could make out dozens of small, pearly stones embedded in the mortar high up on the wall. A few glowed faintly in the shadows, their opalescent hue catching his eye.

"Moon-gems," Spade muttered. "Dozens of them."

They looked impressive placed along the castle wall, he had to admit. He'd mostly seen them in women's jewelry and lanterns, but never used to light up a wall before.

"Probably brought from the Quaren mines," Spade guessed. "Only royalty could decorate a whole castle entrance with them."

Benji stopped beneath the wall and gazed up at the closest moon-gem nestled high above him. "Maybe we should just try an' steal these," he suggested. "Forget the old baron."

But Spade shook his head, dragging Benji away. "They're well out of reach," he said, "an' the rest is just fool's gold. They're not stupid." He thought of the excitement on their dad's face that morning. "It's the baron's grave that'll have the good stuff. Real gold an' silver, an' maybe even some gems we can actually get our hands on."

Spade's eyes skimmed the grounds, spotting green hedges in the distance, tendrils of ivy curling up the castle wall. "This way," he said.

They walked along the path and passed under a wide arch, stashing their aprons behind a bush as they strolled into the most lavish garden either of them had ever seen. Groups of nobles, laughing and talking, strolled by exotic rose gardens, fruit bushes and trees.

Pulling their caps low, they hurried toward the groundskeeper's hut. Spade listened as the nobles veered down another path, their chatter fading. He reached out and tried the latch.

It swung open on creaky hinges and Spade sighed in relief. Inside, cobwebs clung to the rafters and a rusty wheelbarrow sat propped against the wall beside three shovels and a dusty lantern. He dropped his sack, emptying all the loaves on the ground with regret. Stuffing them in various plant pots, he kept two in his pockets for later. Spade grabbed two of the shovels and shoved them in the wheelbarrow, the lantern alongside them. Then he bent and held the sack open. "Time for part two of the plan," he said, gesturing to the bag.

Benji scowled. "Don't see why I can't be the one that does the digging," he muttered, but he climbed inside while Spade held it open. He stretched out across the ground while Spade tied it up tight, making sure to poke a few holes here and there with a garden fork.

"Ouch," Benji complained, his voice stuffy. "You stabbed me in the butt cheek."

"Sorry," Spade said. "I was giving you some air."

"My butt don't need no air."

Spade smothered a grin and hefted the Benji-sack into the wheelbarrow alongside the shovels and lantern. The boy's covered feet poked over the edge.

"Smells like cinnamon buns," Benji groaned from inside the burlap. "Mixed with moldy 'taters." He sneezed.

"Could be worse. Could smell like ratwart cheese. Or rotten eggs."

A muffled grunt replied.

"Now be quiet," Spade whispered, "an' act like a dead person."

CHAPTER 7
A BARON'S FUNERAL

Spade bumped the wheelbarrow along the winding path
that led toward the small gate at the western corner of
the castle. He spotted the gate guard and lowered his cap
as he approached the guardhouse.

"Got a burial," he called, trying to deepen his voice.

The guard squinted down at him, and Spade was glad
for the shadows of the late afternoon. "Where's old
Alfred?" the man asked, peering at the Benji-sack. "Or
did he finally get himself an apprentice? You're a bit
young to be a gravedigger, aren't ya?"

"Yeah, well, I've had lotsa experience." Spade's father
had assured him that the castle gravedigger was sick and
wouldn't be showing up today. He didn't know how his dad
knew that, but he hoped it was true.

The guard clucked his tongue and nodded. "Ah. His
arthritis is acting up, I'll bet."

"I'll bet," Spade said.

"Funny, I didn't hear of no deaths this week other than the baron himself," the guard said around a mouthful of chewing tobacco, eyeing the Benji-sack. "Who's this poor sod?"

"One of the gardeners," Spade said, thinking quick.

"Oh, really? I didn't hear about it. How'd he die?"

"How'd he die?" Spade repeated. Out of the corner of his eye, he saw Ash swoop overhead and perch on the roof of the stone tower. "Well, they say he fell right over, hand clutching his heart when he saw a raven swoop overhead, big an' black as a ghoul. Died on the spot."

The guard stared at Spade, then shook his head. "Little odd, isn't it? Two fright deaths in one month? Anyway, you've got your work cut out for you this afternoon, digger."

Spade nodded. Two fright deaths? He wondered what could have scared the baron to death but couldn't ask. He was supposed to be the replacement gravedigger, after all.

The guard grunted and glanced over his shoulder at the dozens of nobles gathering at the bottom of the hill, the cemetery gates open to let them in. "You'll need to be quick about it. Don't interrupt the baron's funeral."

"Quiet as a mouse." Spade nodded, then hefted the wheelbarrow once more. "Afternoon," he said, tipping his cap at the guard. He wheeled it down the narrow path, his legs shaky with relief.

"We did it, Benj," he whispered. "Almost there."

"Can't breathe." Benji's voice was muffled, annoyed. "An' I need a snack."

"You made yourself sick on bread an hour ago! No one can eat more than that."

"Says you. My stomach is talking."

"Then tell it to be quiet," Spade grunted, rolling the wheelbarrow around a curve in the path. Soft green hills extended before him, the royal cemetery gate glinting in the sunlight. Its wrought iron metalwork gleamed in swirls and eddies, depicting Wyndhail's mountains and foothills.

A breath of wonder stuck in his chest as he peered through the gate. The grandest cemetery he'd ever laid eyes on spread before him, not so much a cemetery as a piece of art. With a small shove, the gate creaked open, and he wheeled Benji in past marble statues of angels and monuments so haunting in their fine detail, Spade found himself slowing to take them in. An arched pathway of great weeping wendigo trees led him along the smooth-stoned path, the scent of their pollen blooms cloaking him as he passed beneath their branches. At last he reached the small royal chapel, lonely in the shadow of Wyndhail castle's northern wall. It was a gray, hunchbacked building that seemed old and tired compared to the beauty around it.

A colorful group of nobles, bedecked in lavish outfits, stood around a grave near the old church. Silken shawls were draped across the women's arms, while the men wore polished black boots.

A slim woman with a feathered hat laughed loudly, standing amidst fairy statues and marble nymphs. Her titter carried across the garden as Spade pushed the wheelbarrow closer, pausing on the other side of the statues. "I wonder if the queen will actually make an appearance," she mused.

"They say no one's seen her all day," one of the men remarked.

A second lady snorted. "Not terribly unusual, if you ask me. She's been this way since you-know-when."

"It's no wonder they call her the Stone Queen," feather-hat woman muttered.

"Lower your voice," another man said, glancing over at Spade as he ambled by. Spade pulled the brim of his cap lower and quickened his pace. "You know she doesn't like it spoken of."

"It's time someone did. She hides in the castle all day and never comes out—not even for funerals."

"I still can't believe it about the baron," said another woman. "He was in the forest, hunting. Heart attack from pure fright, they said. The creature's getting more brazen, and yet the queen does nothing."

Spade stumbled while pushing his wheelbarrow, sur-prised. The nobles glanced over their shoulders, and Spade busied himself examining the shovels. After a moment, the man spoke in a lowered voice. "She's tried—sent all her best guards to stop the beast. It doesn't seem to have worked."

The funeral music faded, and the priest stood up. The nobles fell silent while the drone of his voice filled the graveyard. Spade found an out-of-the-way wendigo tree and pushed the wheelbarrow to it, seating himself under the low-hanging branches.

"What were they talking about, Spade?" Benji's muffled voice came from inside the sack, and he wiggled a bit. "You think the Woegan got the baron? An' why does the queen hide inside?"

"Stop squirming." Spade looked around, but nobody paid attention to them. A faint memory came back to him of hearing his parents talk about it. "I dunno much about the queen. But they say she stopped leaving the castle after her husband went missing several years ago."

"Where'd he go missing?" Benji whispered.

Spade called up the memory, sifting through it. "He went on an expedition to the Craiggarock Mountains but never came back. They think maybe an avalanche got him. Uncle Mal says it was ice giants, but you know him an' his fairy tales." He shook his head. "Anyhow, you were too little to remember. But they say something happened to the queen when she found out. She became all cold an' silent."

"Huh." There was silence inside the sack for a while, and then the sack wiggled again. "Spade?"

"Stay still, Benj," Spade hissed. The sack fell still, and he sighed. "What?"

"D'you think it's real? The baron dying of fright? Just from seeing the Woegan?"

Spade straightened, uneasy. "I dunno," he whispered. "But don't you worry," he added, forcing a light tone. "Yer too bony for it to chase, anyway."

The priest finished at last, and the nobles began to disperse. The sun sank lower on the horizon and a cold wind picked up, a funny, stale scent on the air. Soon, they were the only ones left. He untied the sack and Benji's tousled blond head poked out.

His little brother's eyes widened at the sight of the royal graveyard. "Holy shovels," the boy breathed. "Looks more like a fancy palace than a graveyard."

Several exquisite statues surrounded them, a large, ancient mausoleum casting a shadow across the graves.

"What's that?" Benji breathed.

Etchings of strange, mythological creatures were carved into the mausoleum's walls, its heavy door made of wendigo wood and inlaid with iron, the handles an unusual shape.

"It's a tomb-house," Spade said, eyeing the ivy-covered structure. "A place where they bury someone important, though this one looks kinda abandoned."

"Creepy." Benji's shoulders hunched, as if to guard against a chill. A lonely, haunted sort of feeling hung in the air, and Spade suppressed a shudder. He backed up a step, eager to leave the mausoleum behind. "C'mon," he said. "Let's keep moving."

They wove along the path, passing statues of angels and cherubs and a small stone deer, its details so fine Spade almost thought it was real. It stood several feet away beneath a wendigo willow, a little wren perched on its back. A statue of a hooded nymph sat on a bench near the deer, shadowed in the evening light, as realistic as the deer, perhaps even more so. He took another step toward it, wanting a closer look, when Benji's hand gripped his arm, tugging at his sleeve.

"Can I have my snack now?"

Spade rolled his eyes and turned, heading back to the baron's grave, Benji following. He searched his pockets and handed Benji one of the stale loaves he'd managed to stuff into there earlier.

The grave lay open, several bouquets of flowers tossed beside it. Spade swung the lantern over the hole, and the gleam of embossed gold shone in its depths. A thrill ran through him. Maybe this was it at last: the grave his dad dreamed of, loaded with coins and jewelry. They'd have more than enough to buy Benji decent clothes so he wouldn't have to wear Spade's ragged hand-me-downs anymore. Their mum could wear fancy dresses, and the hungry look in their dad's eyes would be satisfied. Malachi would have medicine for his cough.

Spade had even heard once that, for the right price, you could hire a fancy doctor to fix a leg that isn't right.

"Spade? You okay?"

Spade shook his head, running a hand through his dark hair to clear his thoughts.

"The signal," Benji prodded.

"Right," Spade murmured. "Anyone comes, you do the night thrush call."

Benji swallowed his last bite of bread and nodded. Spade turned to grab his shovel.

"Spade?"

Spade glanced at Benji. His brother stood with his gaze on the baron's open grave, his lucky frog carving clutched in his palm.

"Yeah?"

"I think Dad may be right. I think tonight is the night everything could change." He brought the lucky frog carving to his lips and kissed it, then slipped into the dark.

CHAPTER 8

AN UNEXPECTED VISITOR

The casket shone in the depths of the grave, black and gold lines glittering across it.

Spade stood at the edge of the hole, his lantern light illuminating small diamonds inlaid along its smooth surface, and his heart skipped a beat. The baron himself was likely just as decorated.

He dropped down and landed on the casket with a quiet thud. Balancing on its edge, he reached out for the casket's thick silver handle and heaved—it weighed a lot more than he was used to. The lid cracked open an inch and he ran his fingers along the inside. The light click of a latch sounded: a sound Spade knew well. A booby trap. Excitement jolted through him at the challenge.

Taking off his thick-soled shoe, Spade removed a thin metal rod from a small leather pouch he'd sewn inside the lining. He slid the rod into the crack, then lay down on his back beside the coffin. Covering himself with dirt, he pulled the rod down and levered the lid open with a *pop!*

A cloud of dust exploded in the air, spraying the casket and everything around it with a fine layer of ink powder—the stuff wouldn't come off for weeks, even with several baths. Which made it pretty easy to identify the thief.

Spade grinned and sat up, shaking the ink-soaked dirt off him. He cracked the lid open, spotting a pair of long, white hands, gold rings on each finger. He frowned and peered closer. The gleam wasn't quite right. Reaching in, he slipped one off and brought it to his mouth. He bit it.

Fakes, he realized. The real ones must be concealed inside the silken lining of the casket. He leaned forward to push the lid open farther, when a sudden cascade of dirt rained down on his head.

"Spade!"

He jerked upright. The lid slammed shut.

"Benji—what happened to the bird call—"

"No time," Benji hissed. "Guard switch. He's already at the gates!"

Spade leaped to his feet and stabbed his shovel into the dirt wall, using it as a step. Benji threw out his skinny arm and Spade gripped it while Benji heaved him out.

"Quick," Spade breathed. "Into the sack."

Benji scrambled up into the wheelbarrow and shimmied into the burlap sack, and Spade tied it tight. He leaned down into the grave and pulled the shovel out of the dirt wall, then dug hard into the dirt pile, sending a few shovelfuls flying into the baron's grave. Rigid bootsteps sounded on the wendigo path and a lanky guard appeared through the drooping branches. His arms swung stiff at his sides, nervous gaze flicking around the cemetery.

The guard spotted Spade pretending to fill the Baron's grave, and the man jumped, startled. Spade straightened and tipped his hat.

"Didn't know Alfred the gravedigger hired a new apprentice," the guard said, his voice hoarse.

"Yup," Spade replied, keeping his face in shadow. "He needed a break."

"Oh, right." The guard nodded, glancing nervously around the graves. "You haven't seen anybody come down this way, by chance?" he asked. "You'd save me a trip down the other side of the cemetery."

The man disliked graveyards, Spade realized. Likely a gate guard, forced to patrol the area—a job that most superstitious folk avoided.

"Not a living soul," Spade replied. "But now that you mention it . . . maybe a funny moaning on the wind, an' once, I thought I heard a growl. Nothing I'm not used to, of course. Graveyards are full of those kinda noises."

The man paled, and Spade glanced up at the steeple, eyes flicking to Ash. He nodded with a slight tip of his chin.

The raven's caw broke the silence as Ash launched himself off the steeple and circled slowly above them.

A muscle in the guard's jaw jumped, his arms going stiff at the sight of the bird.

Spade allowed his jaw to fall open, his eyes to widen in exaggerated fear. "They say the raven is a warning! An omen of bad luck to the person who sees it," he said, forcing a rasp into his voice.

"Right," the guard breathed, eyes glued to the bird. "I'll be going then, got to finish my rounds." He whirled on his heel when a faint noise sounded, hanging on the still air.

A sneeze.

Hand at his sword belt, the guard froze.

Crud, Benji, Spade thought. *Of all the times.*

The guard turned slowly, his eyes going to the sack in the wheelbarrow.

"Did that—was that—" The tall man fumbled. "Did you hear that?"

Spade's mind churned fast. He lowered his voice. "Well, that's the sound of the spirit leaving this poor sod's body, of course. Sometimes it hangs around a bit." He gestured at the sky. "Ravens can always tell. I'd better get the body buried quick. After I finish the baron, of course."

The guard's gaze darted to the sky, his jaw working, face pale. "I'll let you get to it, then, gravedigger," he croaked.

A soft chuckle rang out, drifting across the graveyard, startling both of them. "A clever tale, grave thief. You almost had even me believing it."

Spade whirled. His gaze landed on the deer statue, then moved past it to the seated nymph statue he'd seen before.

The nymph shifted, a pale hand reaching up to draw her hood back, revealing a living, breathing woman. Her blue eyes pierced him as she stood, tall and slender, to her full height.

She stepped out of the shadows, the moonlight filtering over her fair face. A silver circlet crowned her golden hair, a sapphire pendant at her throat. Spade's heart stalled, then plummeted.

The guard drew in a sharp breath, bowing his head.

"Queen Carmelia."

CHAPTER 9

THE STONE QUEEN

Spade had heard stories of her, of course. But people rarely saw the Queen of Wyndhail, which is why her sudden appearance left a hole in Spade's mind, a spot where the gears stuttered to a halt.

It ain't possible, he thought.

But it was. She'd been seated there the whole time. She'd seen everything.

His brain began to chug, then ramp into full-blown panic as the Stone Queen walked forward, dark green cloak trailing between the tombstones.

He stood frozen as she approached, her long fingers entwined together, ice-blue gaze locked on his.

"Do you know," she said, her low voice crystalline, "I don't think I've seen thieves quite so adept at weaving stories and taking advantage of my hapless guards. A remarkable talent, really, as my night watch are supposed to be superior protection." She peered at the young guard, and he blushed a deep crimson.

"Thieves, my lady?" he stammered. "But—"

Her gaze moved pointedly to the sack in the wheelbarrow.

The night watch's eyes sparked with understanding, then wrath. "Filthy Joolie," he growled, and lunged for the sack.

Spade was used to this kind of reaction from a guard seeing a Joolie. And so he did the first thing that came to mind.

He leaped forward and plowed into the man, yanking at his belt buckle and pulling his helmet over his eyes. The night watch yelled, his pants sliding down around his ankles as he stumbled forward. He drew his sword and attempted to hitch up his pants while swatting wildly in Spade's direction. Spade seized the moment. Dropping to his knees, he ripped open the sack.

Benji toppled out and clambered to his feet. His startled gaze darted to the queen, then the guard.

"Run, Benji," Spade hissed, shoving his brother toward the wendigo trees. They darted between the trunks and were racing for the path when Benji grabbed Spade's arm. "Look!" he hissed, voice taut with fear.

A massive man appeared on the path, blocking their escape. His tall black boots and black uniform told Spade he was a guard, but the belt buckle at his waist bore the royal crest, inlaid with a glittering red ruby—the color of the Wyndhail monarchy. The queen's personal guard.

The guardsman lifted a bow off his shoulder and

notched an arrow. Before Spade could move, the guard fired. Spade's hat fell to the ground, and his gaze dropped to the hole bored straight through the fabric.

"If you move," the guard growled, "it'll be your head next."

Spade and Benji froze.

An angry screech tore through the graveyard and Ash plummeted from the sky, talons extended. The guard looked up in surprise as the raven hit him full force in the face, then arced up into the air. Roaring in pain, the man shielded his eyes, trying to locate the bird.

Spade whirled to Benji. "This is our chance, Benj!"

They dropped and rolled behind the tombstones, then sprang to their feet, darting toward some low-hanging branches. "To the left, quick," Spade gasped over his shoulder, then froze.

Benji had stopped, turning back.

"Benj!" he hissed. "What are you doing!"

"My lucky frog carving," Benji whispered. "I dropped it in the grass." He darted behind the tombs, lunging for the carving.

"Forget yer lucky frog!" Spade whirled and limped after him.

A shadow detached from the trees in front of him, slipping up behind Benji.

"Benji!" Spade yelled. He sprinted forward, but his bad foot caught on a rock and he fell, sprawling on the ground.

He pulled his face out of the mud to see the night watch standing with a sword to Benji's throat.

Benji froze stiff as a corpse, his lucky frog carving dropping from his hand.

Spade's heart slowed. The man looked madder than a hornet, which probably had something to do with Spade's earlier pants-dropping trick.

The night watch raised his wide eyes to the skies. "Don't you dare, you cursed demon!" he shrieked at Ash, circling above. "Or he's dead!"

The raven lit down on a tree overhead with a sharp squawk. Spade saw a slight movement and looked up to see the queen's guardsman aiming an arrow at Benji's chest.

"Now, just hold on a minute," garbled Spade. "You've got the wrong kid. Just look at him! My brother's barely outta diapers—" Benji scowled despite the arrow. "An' he doesn't do any of the stealing, not really, he's just the watch!"

"Enough." The queen spoke quietly, and everyone stilled. "Stay your hand, Henchcliff."

The massive guard paused, the arrow still notched. The queen walked toward Spade, twirling her sapphire pendant in her fingers, brow furrowed. She stood staring down at Spade for a long moment, then turned to the guard. "Take them to the dungeons. I will deal with them myself."

The night watch rustled around behind Spade, then held up the baker's sack.

Just as the sun was coming up, darkness enveloped Spade's head, along with the smell of pastries and moldy potatoes.

CHAPTER 10
MOON-GEM

"Spade?"

Benji's voice sounded in the stillness, broken only by the plip-plop of dripping water somewhere in the dank, subterranean cell.

"Yeah?"

"I hate the dark."

Spade inched closer to his brother on the small, hard cot, and put an arm around his shoulders. "Don't worry, Benj," he said. "I'm sure they'll light a torch down here soon. Besides, it's a nice break from the scorching sun back at camp, right?"

His brother was silent at his half-attempt at a joke.

Spade sighed, feeling the darkness seep into his bones. "How about I tell you a story?"

He could feel his brother shift in the dark. "Okay," Benji said, his voice faint.

"Once, there was a boy named Benjini," Spade began. "An—"

"Benjini!" Benji interrupted. "Sounds an awful lot like me."

"It's not," Spade said. "It's about a famous magician called Benjini. An' he don't look anything like you. Well, he likes sticky toffee pudding like you, but that's it."

Benji was quiet. "Fine," he grumped. "Hard to blame him. Who wouldn't like sticky toffee pudding?"

"That's right. Now where was I?" Spade continued. The words began to come to him as he went along. Right when he'd reached the climax, where Benjini used his dazzling skills to trick the wicked witch into falling off a cliff, Benji interrupted.

"Spade," he said. "Do you think bad guys always have bad endings?"

"Why do you ask?"

His brother shifted in the dark. "'Cause I think we're the bad guys. In the real story, I mean. Being thieves an' all."

This story wasn't going the way Spade planned. "Maybe bad guys an' good guys aren't always easy to tell apart," he said at last.

Benji was silent a while. "Maybe there's a bit of good an' bad in both sides?"

"I'm thinking so."

Somewhere in the dark, a faint *scratch, scratch* sounded, and Benji stiffened next to him. "What was that?" he whispered.

Spade stilled, listening. Silence, and the drip, drip of water. "Just a mouse," he said, though he couldn't be too sure.

They stayed like that for a long while. Eventually, Benji's head drooped against Spade's shoulder. "I'm sorry, Spade," he muttered, half awake. "I shouldn't have gone back fer my lucky frog carving."

"It's okay, Benj."

A moment later, a soft snore reached Spade; Benji had fallen asleep, gripping his hand.

Spade leaned back and sighed, and a small twinge of heat spread through his pocket. He startled and drew out the pebble he had stolen from the tax collector. As he examined it, warmth spread through his fingers. A faint light rippled across the surface and it began to glow.

It wasn't just any pebble, he realized. It must be a moon-gem. He held it up, twisting it this way and that. At certain angles, it shone with an opalescent glimmer, just like the stones he and Benji had seen embedded in the castle wall. That must be why Bagman Grute had hidden it in his shoe; it was valuable if it really was a moon-gem, Spade supposed. It wasn't the casket of gold or gems they'd dreamed of, but it would still buy them full bellies and some security for a while. He could spend a day or two fishing at the pond with Benji and Malachi, even. And maybe, while sitting on the bank, Malachi could go back to teaching Spade how to read.

Benji mumbled something in his sleep, and Spade stared out into the dark. There was one problem: they'd have to get out of here first.

He tucked the pebble in his pocket once more and leaned back, listening to the faint sounds of scratching somewhere in the dark.

Creak.

The sound of the main prison door opening echoed in the distance, followed by heavy, purposeful footsteps. Spade jerked awake, confused. How long had he been sleeping? It was impossible to tell in the dark cell.

"Who's coming, Spade?" Benji's voice was thin with fear. Spade stood, bracing himself.

Lanternlight blinded them as a guard walked toward them, bootsteps ringing out in the dungeon corridor. His face was cast in shadow, but the crested ruby belt buckle glittered in the dim light. Henchcliff.

He unlocked the door and looked hard at them with his granite black eyes, his mouth set in a grim line. "You," he grunted at Spade. "Come with me."

He grabbed Spade's arm and pulled him out into the corridor, but Spade wrenched around. "What about my brother?" he demanded.

Benji stood pressed against the bars, his face ashen and his lip trembling, though Spade knew he was trying to be brave.

"He'll stay here for as long as Her Majesty wants," Henchcliff spat. "No more questions."

He prodded Spade with his club, but Spade clung to the bars for a moment. "Be brave, Benj," he whispered. "Finish the story while I'm gone, an' tell me the ending when I get back."

Benji jerked his head in a wobbly nod.

Henchcliff herded Spade through the dark twists and turns of the corridor, Spade limp-hopping to keep up. With each step, he felt himself being dragged farther from Benji, and his legs felt like lead. Henchcliff pushed him up a narrow flight of stairs and through a heavy oak door at the top.

Spade's eyes widened as the dim lantern light played across several beautiful tapestries lining the walls of a grand hall. Muddied browns and deep greens portrayed the moorlands to the east of the castle, while stark blues and grays showed the Craiggarock Mountains to the west and the mines at their base. His gaze darted over them as Henchcliff marched him past. He'd heard tales of these places, stories of the lonely boglands, of gem mines dug ten stories deep, of mountains that hid their peaks in the mist, so vast your echoes got lost.

The royal portraits came next, and amongst portraits of queens, dukes, princesses and barons, Spade noticed the queen's husband, Weston, who'd died seven years ago in the Craiggarock Mountains, leaving the queen a widow. He had kind eyes and stood tall and straight.

Next to him was a portrait of King Alistair, the queen's father, at his crowning ceremony. He held a small chest clutched in his hands, his gaze trained on it.

"Keep moving, Joolie," the guard barked behind him, and Spade hastened his steps.

They rounded a corner, and a slight movement at the end of the corridor caught Spade's eye. Henchcliff stiffened and bowed his head. A young girl with crimson hair and freckled cheeks stood at the far wall, looking closely at one of the portraits: a painting of a miner, covered in dust and grime, a pickaxe in his hands.

The girl glanced up as they approached, curious hazel eyes lighting on Spade before moving to the guard beside him. Her gaze darkened and she whirled on her heel, hurrying down the hall. Henchcliff grunted, his eyes narrowed as he watched her go.

They passed the painting of the miner, *an unusual painting to have on a wall of nobility,* Spade thought. Up close, Spade caught the shape of a dark sack in the man's hand, though his face was covered by a cap. Malachi's story came sharp to mind, the tale of unusual stones discovered in the mines.

Henchcliff reached out and grasped Spade's shoulder, dragging his gaze from the painting. The guard pulled up short in front of a pair of double oak doors. "You'll be on your best manners, thief, or your punishment will be severe." He turned and knocked once, and the doors swung wide open, held by a nervous-looking servant. Henchcliff gave Spade a sharp push, and he stumbled inside.

A vaulted room spread before him, with stained glass windows lining the length of it, revealing the early-evening sky. A chandelier of crystals hung at the room's center, catching the light of the firelit sconces along the walls. Spade blinked—he and Benji had slept all day in their windowless prison.

Queen Carmelia sat on a raised dais at the far end, four royal guards stationed along the wall behind her. She turned her head from the window and fixed her gaze on him. Against her a pale gray gown, the queen's skin appeared faint and almost translucent, the blue sapphire like a shard of ice at her neck. Spade could see now why the villagers dubbed her the Stone Queen: she sat as still as a rock, her face unreadable, cold. It was difficult for Spade to judge her age; her skin was that of a young woman, though her eyes were heavy, with dark circles beneath them. Beside her stood a thin, reed-like man, a scowl tugging at his long jowls at the sight of Spade.

Henchcliff took his place along the far wall beside the guards, hawk-eyes trained on Spade's every move.

The queen beckoned him with a long, thin finger. Spade hesitated, then limped toward the dais.

She studied him with her light-blue eyes that reminded him of a winter's pond, her pale cheekbones sharp and defined. The townspeople said she'd been beautiful once, though now there was something weary and hollow about her face.

"Well? What do you have to say for yourself, grave thief?"

Number one rule, son, his father's voice rumbled low in his ears. *If yer ever caught, play dumb. A Joolie's life an' family depends on the secrets he keeps.*

"Well," he began. "I've been told of the beautiful architecture in the royal cemetery, an' who could really blame me fer wanting a visit—"

"Enough." The queen's gaze hardened. "I will tell you what fate awaits grave thieves. They are punished. Regardless of age."

Spade's heart stuttered, the blood in his veins slowing. "Wait."

He shoved his father's words down. He'd had enough of Joolie rules—Benji's life was on the line.

She raised an eyebrow.

"My brother, he's got nothing to do with this, Majesty." He swallowed, thinking fast. "Maybe—maybe I can work for you, somehow? Be your, um, servant of . . . something.

I can earn his freedom! I can do anything you ask, just try me."

She laughed, a scornful sound. "And what use would I have for you?"

He met her gaze, thinking fast. "Everyone's got use for a thief, Majesty, ain't they?"

She stared at him for a moment. Slowly, she turned to the tall, thin man standing near the dais. "And what do you think this impertinent boy's punishment should be, Spinniker? You are my chief advisor, after all."

The gray-haired man cleared his throat, spectacles slipping down his long nose as he examined Spade and tugged at his wiry mustache. His mouth turned downward.

Spade swallowed, his throat chalky and tight, his hands clammy. Then something caught the corner of his eye: a small, frail old woman standing in the corner of the room. She slipped between the rows of guards, a shawl draped over her head and shoulders, but they paid her no attention.

Spade stared at the woman, then glanced between the queen and Spinniker, but neither reacted; they didn't even blink at the bent figure's approach. She hobbled around the dais and drew up beside the advisor. The old woman raised her head and cast a sly smile at Spade, her shawl slipping back from her face. Light glinted off a pair of full-moon spectacles.

A jolt of recognition shot through Spade. The old lady from the cemetery! Eyes twinkling, she leaned in, bringing her lips to Spinniker's ear. She murmured something, and the advisor's brow scrunched into a puzzled frown. He stuck a finger into his ear, twirling it around like a bug had lodged in it, then blinked several times.

The old woman winked at Spade, then teetered away, meandering unnoticed past the guards once more.

"Well, Spinniker?" the queen demanded, and Spade's eyes snapped back to the queen. "I am waiting."

"Hmm?" Spinniker shook his head, as if clearing it. "Oh yes. I have an idea, Majesty," he mumbled. "Just came to me."

Spade stared at the advisor, then whipped his gaze back over the massive room, scanning every nook and cranny for the old woman, but she'd vanished. How did she keep doing that?

The queen gave him a doubtful look. "Go on."

"Why don't you put the boy's dubious talents to use? Assign him a task that none would ever wish to do. Something . . ." Spinniker paused meaningfully, "in keeping with his abilities."

Queen Carmelia leaned back in her throne, tapping her fingers on her armrests. She narrowed her eyes, considering. "Perhaps I do have use for a thief, after all."

CHAPTER 11

ROYAL SPY

The queen stood on the balcony of the throne room, looking out over the town of Wyndhail. Spade waited just behind her, palms sweating. His neck prickled with the stare of Henchcliff at his back, standing just outside the balcony doors. The queen turned to Spade, her brow wrinkled in thought.

"It is more private here," she said. "And I can speak freely. But first, what is your name, thief?"

He hesitated, then swallowed. "Spade Archer Rustle, Yer Majesty."

"An interesting name," she said. "Appropriate for a grave thief's son, I suppose."

"My father thought it was lucky." Spade shifted on his feet. The queen's cold gaze swept over him, and Spade began to wonder if his father might have been mistaken.

She folded her hands at her waist, scrutinizing him. "And how old are you?"

"Fourteen."

Her eyes flickered.

"Give or take. Maybe closer to twelve."

She sighed. "So young to be living the life of a seasoned criminal. And your brother, just a babe, yet."

Spade's throat tightened, his heart thudding hard at the mention of Benji.

The queen cocked her head. "Ah. Your brother is a touchy subject, I see. You must be very devoted to him." She sighed and crossed her arms. "Let us try a different topic. Have you heard of the monstrous creature that stalks my land?"

He met her gaze, surprised. Everyone knew of the dark beast that had reared its head a few years back, casting a shadow over the kingdom. A shiver ran down his back and twisted around his spine. Most of the stories he'd heard described a massive, hunched-over shape that resembled an old, grizzled bear on its hind legs. It had horns, some said, while others claimed a tail. But a common thread ran through the rumors: grotesque, wide jaws. Soulless eyes like deep black pools.

He nodded slowly. "Yes, Yer Majesty. It's one of my uncle's favorite bedtime tales. You speak of the Woegan."

Her pale eyebrows lifted, her face unreadable. "I haven't heard too many brave enough to say its name."

"Pardon, Majesty, I'm not sure it's brave." Spade shrugged. "I just thought we might as well call it what it is."

A glimmer of something sparked in the queen's eyes. "True enough. Give the darkness a name, and it loses some of its hold over us, or so they say." She glanced toward the gray sky, where stars were appearing on the horizon. "Nevertheless. The creature has wreaked havoc on our kingdom, stealing villagers who are never heard from again. My people live in fear. And our usual methods of hunting down beasts aren't working."

She paused, bringing her piercing eyes to his. "So it seems I'm in need of someone bold and inventive. Someone who isn't afraid to get their hands dirty." She brought her hands together and tilted her chin. "This is your chance to prove yourself, thief."

Spade's stomach tightened, but he shoved it down, forcing confidence into his voice. "I won't let you down, Majesty. An' what would I be stealing, if you please?"

"A magical object that's fallen into the wrong hands, I'm afraid." Her gaze moved to the countryside beyond the town. "There are only a few people in this kingdom powerful enough to create such a beast as the Woegan. And one such individual has been hiding himself away for half a century now. A man who possesses a dangerous stone."

The queen turned back to him. "You've heard of the Moor Mage, I take it?"

"Fer sure I have, Yer Majesty." Spade had heard the rumors, whispers on the streets. "But I thought he was, well . . ."

"A fairy tale?" the queen suggested with an inward laugh. "No. Though he's so reclusive he may as well be. However, his powers are some of the oldest in the kingdom. You'll steal the stone and bring it back here to be destroyed, hopefully ridding us of this Woegan."

This whole thing sounded a bit more complicated than Spade had hoped.

"Of course, Majesty," he said. "But, um, if you don't mind me asking, what does the stone look like?"

"It's not just any stone, boy. It's something known as a deepstone."

Spade started. A deepstone! So the stories were true.

"This particular deepstone is the emerald green of a forest glade. The mage is never far from it; we know at least that much from the guards who attempted to retrieve it before you."

Spade paused. "An' if you don't mind telling me, Majesty, what happened to those guards?"

The queen started to reply, but a sharp croak rang out behind them. Spade whirled at the familiar sound. "Ash!" he cried as the bird swooped through the double doors, across the room and out onto the balcony, a black fury of wings and feathers. He lit down clumsily on Spade's shoulder, nursing one leg. An angry, low squawk rumbled in his throat.

Henchcliff's club was out in an instant, ready to strike, when a girl burst through the doors after him, red hair flying behind her.

"Wait, Henchcliff!" she cried. "It's just a raven. And it's my fault. I found it hurt and hobbling around the gardens outside—I've been feeding it."

Spade stared at the girl he'd seen in the hall. Her clothes were rich satin, beautifully embroidered, though her hair was unkempt and messy, her expression fierce. A spoiled noble, to be sure. But an unusual one, too: most folks would have tried to kill Ash, rather than take pity on him.

"Ember," the queen's voice was stern. "You've been spying."

"I couldn't help it, Aunt Carmelia," the girl replied. "We never have guests. Besides, the raven kept trying to get into the castle, and I supposed it was his pet."

The queen sighed. "The boy is no doubt grateful you've been feeding his accomplice. But don't worry, I don't intend on harming the bird. Go to your rooms now, Ember. The corridors are no place to be at night." She turned to the big guard. "Henchcliff, escort her."

The girl's eyes burned with mutiny. "You can't lock me up there forever, Aunt," she said. "Eventually you'll find me withered away in a heap."

Queen Carmelia's lips pursed. "Dramatics. You have plenty to do. You have a riding lesson tomorrow, and etiquette class. What more could a girl want?"

"Maybe some friends," Ember muttered as Henchcliff ushered her out of the room, his face as immovable as ever despite the girl's deep-cut scowl as she stormed away.

Despite himself, Spade felt a twinge of sympathy for her—he knew what it was to be lonely. Being a Joolie didn't exactly help you make friends.

The door slammed behind them, and the queen's eyes darkened, her gaze turning on Ash. Spade tensed. "He can be quite charming, Majesty," he began. "An' occasionally he does take a bath, an' he has a melodious voice. When it's on key, I mean."

The queen's mouth twitched. Ash held her gaze with his glittering black eye, feathers ruffling.

"The bird does appear clever," she said at last.

Spade dipped his chin. "Indeed, Majesty. A fair genius, I'd say."

"And he has been your loyal help in your nefarious business, I assume."

He hesitated, wary now. "Um. On occasion, Majesty."

She narrowed her eyes, considering. "The bird may remain here tonight in the hawk tower and join you in the morning. One of my guards will show you to your room, and a maid will bring you a meal so that you have your wits about you for the journey."

"Th-thank you, Majesty," Spade said, surprised. "For my raven, an' the food. But do you suppose I could stay in the dungeon this last night before I leave, so that I can be with my brother?"

"I think separation between the two of you is best." Cold returned to the queen's voice. "Motivating, in fact."

Spade swallowed. "'Course, Majesty."

"If you succeed in bringing me the deepstone that controls the Woegan, boy-thief, I shall release your brother and send you home with a worthy reward."

A worthy reward. The queen's words whirled in Spade's head. A royal reward could mean a new life for Spade, for his family. Nervous jolts shot through him.

The queen paused, her jaw hardening. "But know this: if you do not succeed, you will have seen your brother for the last time."

Her guards bowed as she swept through the balcony, across the room and out the great doors. Spade stared as they swung shut behind her, and his stomach turned to lead. He couldn't fail. Not if he wanted to save Benji.

CHAPTER 12

A CHANCE ENCOUNTER

The castle grounds slumbered in velvet darkness as the clock tower struck midnight. Spade turned away from his narrow window on the second floor and took in the soft, comfortable bed, the plush rugs and fine tapestry on the walls.

His own small Joolie yurt was barely a quarter of the size. At home, he and Benji shared a bunk bed and they didn't have dressers, only cubbies where they stashed their few clothes. They ate outside on tree stumps around bonfires, except for Grandma Flint, who ported her cherished rocking chair everywhere they went.

Quiet filled the room, strange and unfamiliar. Around this time of night back home, his father's legendary snoring would begin, the sound carrying from the carriage next to his and Benji's yurt. Benji often snuffled, his nose a bit stuffy. Spade was accustomed to the night sounds of his family, an odd sort of lullaby he'd grown up with.

His chest throbbed with a dull ache. Was Benji all right? His brother was terrified of the dark. He glanced around the room again, a world nicer than the dungeon Benji sat in, with its rich tapestry and soft bed. He suspected the queen had put him here on purpose to remind him of his brother, cold and alone.

Guilt ate at him. If only he'd been faster in the cemetery, been able to run as quickly as someone with two normal legs. He could've helped Benji escape.

Spade's memory shifted to when he'd been eight years old, his brother five. A few older town kids had spotted Spade going into a village bakery to buy bread. He was carrying the bread home, humming to himself, when he came upon the bridge at the edge of town where they'd been waiting. Taking his bread and trampling it in the dirt, they'd dangled him by his feet over the bridge, taunting him about his limp. Benji came flying at them, painfully accurate with his slingshot and then his fists.

Benji, his constant defender, despite the fact that Spade was older. And now, when it had been his turn to protect his brother . . .

His throat tightened as he thought of Benji in the dungeon. He wanted to yell, to scream.

Closing his eyes, he took a deep breath. *Panic gets you nowhere*, he reminded himself. *You can't help Benji by sitting here moping.*

He looked around the room, eyes coming to rest on the tapestry on the far wall. His father would have gawked at the threaded picture woven in the deep browns, greens and grays of the lonely moor to the west of the castle.

It was easy to picture Garnet sizing the wall hanging up, totaling its worth on the black market in mere seconds. But it wasn't its value that drew Spade's attention. Malachi's campfire stories trickled back through Spade's memory:

The Moor Mage is clever, he'd said. *Lots o' folks have tried to find his house only to get lost on the moor.*

The clock tower chimed again, marking the quarter hour. Crossing the room, he tried the door handle. Locked, of course. He pushed against the wood and the door creaked open an inch before it caught. A padlock rested snug through the handle.

It was one of Spade's favorite kinds. Unlike other children who were given wooden cars for their birthdays, Spade had been given locks, and this kind of lock was one of his earliest birthday gifts. Kneeling, he slid the long, hair-thin metal rod out of his shoe and unfolded it, angling it through the crack. He maneuvered the lock toward him, then inserted the rod into the keyhole. He tugged it left, then right, left, right. A sharp click reached his ears. The lock fell open, and with it, the door.

He allowed himself a small grin.

Spade crept through the castle with padded footsteps—a difficult feat with a limp—keeping to the shadows of the corridors, slipping in and out of alcoves.

He wasn't about to try and escape; Henchcliff would be lurking nearby, and guards were at every gate. But maybe he could find a way down to the dungeons. No one could stop him from visiting Benji if they didn't know.

Walking a little faster, he rounded a corner that opened up to a large balcony overlooking the grounds. He stepped out into the cool night air and took a deep breath, his chest loosening a bit. The night, the crisp air, the stars: this was familiar. This was what he knew best.

He was about to turn when his eyes landed on a tall tower on the far side of the courtyard, open windows encircling it. The hawk tower, he realized.

Ash.

Maybe he could get a message to his family. The castle was dark, and no one would notice a raven leaving. Cupping his hands, he croaked low in his throat, then waited. Silence, no answering croak. This time, he tried a low whistle, but the hushed night seemed to swallow the sound.

Maybe Ash couldn't hear from this distance. He leaned out and peered down at the fog-cloaked castle grounds. His gaze drifted across the courtyard, coming to rest on the thin stand of trees near the stables, and he paused. Something large shifted in the shadows between the spindly trunks. He peered closer, but the shape melted into the dark, blending back into shadows. A strange, stale scent drifted upward, and he wrinkled his nose.

A soft footstep fell behind him. He whirled.

The queen's niece stood in the doorway, one hand on her hip, the other holding a dimmed lantern.

"So." Her hazel eyes narrowed in her freckle-dusted face. "Are you planning an escape?"

She gestured to the courtyard behind him. "I read about it once," she continued, before he could say anything. "Where the character called his dog and the dog brought him the keys he needed to break out."

"Ash ain't a dog," Spade muttered. "An' I'm not trying to escape. I'm just getting some fresh air."

She looked skeptical. "I saw the padlock on your door open when I passed. And it sounded like you were signaling someone just now."

"Sometimes I whistle to myself. At night. You know, like a . . . lullaby."

"A lullaby, huh." She gave him a look that said she thought he was full of dung. "What's it about?"

"Um . . ." He glanced outside. "Stars. An', uh . . . sheep. An' pie."

"Pie?"

"Pie calms me."

Her mouth twisted up in the corner. "Wonderful. I can't sleep either. Can you whistle it for me?"

"Sure." He was terrible at whistling music. "But it might attract attention. An' I'm pretty sure princesses ain't supposed to wander around at midnight."

She narrowed her eyes, but before she could say anything, a low croak echoed through the air and a black shape flapped through the sky, bulleting downward.

The girl jumped back with a muffled cry, but Ash landed safely on Spade's shoulder, nibbling affectionately at his ear. A tattered rope hung from the bird's foot: the raven had pecked his way through it.

"I'm not a princess," the girl corrected. "I'm the queen's niece. And you're a terrible liar." She glanced at the bird, and Ash cocked his head, giving her a friendly croak.

Her lips twitched despite her glower. "He's a canny pet. How did you bewitch him to obey you?"

"With a little sprinkle of fairy dust an' a magic wand an' such."

Ember crossed her arms.

Spade chuckled. "Just kidding. He ain't bewitched—I don't got any magic. My great-uncle found him in an abandoned nest when he was a fledgling. He gave him to me to raise, an' he's been hanging around ever since."

The girl reached out to touch the raven's neck, and Ash let her stroke his feathers, ruffling them up a little to impress her. She laughed. "He's charming."

"An' sometimes annoying," Spade said, but he smiled in spite of himself.

She sobered then, glancing at him. "You're a Joolie, aren't you?"

He nodded.

She sighed, her eyes getting a faraway look. "I've always wondered what it would be like to be a Joolie, to sleep under the stars and hunt for my food, live like an outlaw."

"We don't sleep under the stars, we sleep in yurts," Spade corrected her. "An' we usually eat stale bread from the market and eggs from our chickens. My dad's a terrible hunter."

"Oh." The girl looked a little crestfallen. "How about your horses? I've heard Joolies have the fastest horses in Wyndhail, as swift as the wind when you're racing them away from manors or castles that you've robbed."

"Uh, we have a couple of woolly yaks named Gumpus and Gertrude. They pull my parents' wagon."

"Oh."

He shoved his hands in his pockets, looking out into the darkness. "Maybe we don't have racehorses, but we do get to travel places. An' looking at the stars away from the lights of town is like nothing else. Sometimes, the wolves howl at night, singing all together like a ghost choir."

The girl brightened. "That would be pretty neat," she admitted, a wistful sort of look in her eyes. "I'm Ember, by the way."

"Spade."

She laughed. "That's a funny name."

"Yeah. My parents thought it suited me."

"Perhaps it does," she said, and cocked her head. "You dug up the baron's grave. That's what got you here, right?"

He nodded. "More or less."

"How did you get caught? The guards?"

"The queen."

She whistled low, shaking her head. "Well, if you'd heard anything about the queen, you'd know she goes to the cemetery often."

"Now that information would have been handy, fer sure." Definitely a tidbit he wished his dad had researched.

"You don't know much about things here at the castle, do you?"

"Nope. I mean, I hear stories. People gossiping, that kind of thing."

A sigh escaped her, and she crossed her arms. "I overheard the guards say you're the 'new royal thief.' And that the queen's tasked you to go to the Moor Mage and steal his stone."

He glanced at her. "You're pretty good at eavesdropping."

She snorted. "There's not much to do around here." She gestured around. "So what are you really doing on the balcony? And don't bother lying—I can always tell when someone's lying."

He considered making up an elaborate story just to see if her claim was true, but he was exhausted. "I wanted to send Ash to my family," he admitted. "Let them know Benji an' me are . . . all right."

"That you're alive, you mean." She glanced down. "I'll bet you were also trying to find a way to see your brother."

He stiffened. "If I happened to come across him, then maybe."

She wrinkled an eyebrow.

He shrugged. "You can't blame me for trying."

Rolling her eyes, she looked pointedly at his pockets. "Well, do you need something to write on? For the note?"

For the first time, he began to feel nervous.

"Uh, no thanks . . ." He'd planned on sending Ash back with a piece of his shirt tied to the bird's leg, a sign they were okay. But she had already turned and disappeared down the hall. Within a moment she returned, holding a writing quill with a bottle of ink.

"Here. You must want to say something."

"All right, I guess." He took it from her, fighting the heat that rose up his neck. He could write even less than he could read. Malachi had taken stolen moments to try and teach him using the tombstones when Spade was younger. But then Spade had taken over digging for his dad, and the lessons had been cut short.

Spade turned and went to the windowsill, where he laid the paper out, away from the girl's prying eyes. He pretended to write something, moving the quill over invisible words. Instead, he did the only thing he could think of—he drew a picture of himself, Benji and Ash, safe. Then signed it with a drawing of a spade.

"What's taking so long?" Ember asked.

"Well, I'd think better without you breathing down my neck," he retorted, though he hunched forward to avoid letting her glimpse his doodles. He folded the note quickly and tied it with the piece of frayed rope, attaching it to Ash's foot. Stroking the raven's back, he whispered into the bird's ear, and Ash took off into the sky, his black wings blending seamlessly into the dark night.

Heavy bootsteps sounded in the hallway, and Ember shot a look at Spade as they both froze.

Henchcliff rounded the corner, his wide face hard, two guards flanking him.

CHAPTER 13

MUD AND MUCK

"Miss Ember," the royal guard grunted, black eyes flashing. "You must not be out alone at night. Especially with a Joolie prisoner." He turned to Spade.

"Joolie," he said, his voice low, a snarl brewing just underneath. "If you leave your rooms again this eve, I will make it so that you can't walk."

It was an ironic threat seeing as how Spade limped in the first place, but he wasn't about to mention it. Henchcliff didn't seem like he liked jokes.

Ember scowled as Henchcliff locked Spade's arms behind his back, then signaled to a guard to hold him. Henchcliff reached for Ember, but she leveled him with a livid stare. "I can escort myself back," she hissed. "I don't need a captain of the guard nursemaid." The big guard's scowl deepened as Ember turned and walked stiffly down the hall, and he nodded for the other guard to trail behind her. Henchcliff took hold of Spade and marched him in the opposite direction.

A minute later, Spade stood on the other side of the door of his room once again, a new padlock placed on its handle and a different guard stationed outside. "See that you don't take your eyes off this door," Henchcliff's rough voice commanded the guard. "And keep the lanterns lit tonight."

Spade stood in the grand foyer the next morning, tattered jacket buttoned up against the chill of the morning air.

A rush of wings made him look up. Ash soared in through one of the alcove windows and landed on his shoulder, a small slip of paper tied to his leg. Spade glanced around to see if anyone was watching, but the guards standing outside the great doors hadn't moved.

Spade unraveled the paper with deft fingers, then frowned. A brief message was written there, but it would take him too long to try and sound out the words—time he didn't have at the moment. Malachi had made his mark at the bottom, a wobbly *M*, and Spade wondered why his uncle would send him a message he knew he could barely read.

Then again, his uncle had always been a bit odd like that.

Rustling skirts sounded behind him, and he shoved the note in his pocket as he turned to face the wide staircase that descended into the foyer. Queen Carmelia stood at the top, formal black gown trailing behind her, the thin crown at her forehead gleaming cold in the morning light. Spade's nerve were strung taut as he watched her descend, Henchcliff on one side of her, her advisor, Spinniker, on the other.

A servant scurried forward and handed Spade a small pack with the buttery smell of fresh baking.

"For the journey through the moors," the queen gestured, stopping at the last stair. "You'll need it. The mage isn't easily found."

Spade bowed and took the pack. "Thank you, Majesty."

She nodded at Spinniker, who produced a slip of fine parchment sealed with the royal wax stamp. "Present this to the Moor Mage," the queen instructed as a servant brought the letter to Spade. He glanced down, confused. Why was she sending her enemy a greeting note?

"It's a riddle," she said, amused at the expression on Spade's face. "You'll need it in order to gain an audience with the Moor Mage—if you happen to make it to his door alive."

Unease washed over him. The queen didn't know he couldn't read—most citizens could. But he could hand it to the mage. Surely that would be enough.

"I'm looking forward to meeting him, Majesty," Spade lied, and gave her his most confident smile.

Spinniker looked Spade over, obvious doubt in his eyes, jowls drooping even farther than usual. "Good luck, boy," he said, his voice flat.

But the queen laughed, a crooked, sad sound. "There's no such thing, Spinniker," she said. "Only fate."

Spade found her icy gaze upon him, before her eyes flicked to Ash.

"One more thing, boy. Unlike Joolies, I keep my promises. If you even think of abandoning your mission or breathe a word of this to anyone, including your family, know that your brother will suffer the consequences."

"Yes, Majesty," he forced out, her threat lodged hard in his throat.

The queen turned away and climbed slowly back up the staircase, long dress trailing behind her. Henchcliff stepped forward, black eyes glittering, and gestured for Spade to follow.

Falling in behind the guard, Spade limped across the foyer. As he turned to the door, he caught a glimpse of flaming red hair and a pale face watching from the balcony above.

"Move your legs, boy," Henchcliff's gravelly command carried through the grand doors, jolting Spade around.

He shuffled down the steps to where the guard stood in the courtyard, impatient. A tall stable boy dressed in fine clothes led a sleek gelding toward them, its coat white and speckled with gray.

Spade's eyes widened as the boy handed him the reins.

"Your horse," Henchcliff said. "A gift from the queen. Take care of it."

Spade took hold of the reins with a clumsy grip. He didn't know how to ride a horse. Joolie mountain yaks were for pulling, not riding—Gumpus would try to stab you if you tried. And Gertrude would simply roll over with the rider on her back. But no matter. How difficult could it be?

Henchcliff gave him a dour look. "You have three days, boy. You'd better hurry. It'll take you half the day just to get to the moors."

Spade steeled himself and swung up onto the horse's back, sitting a bit lopsided. The stable boy looked at him, amused.

"Okay, horse," Spade said in his most authoritative, prince-like voice. "I'm commanding thee to go, steed."

The horse didn't budge.

"Giddy-up, you lazy sack-a-bones," he tried again.

"His name is Pronto." The boy chuckled. "And when you want to go, you just lean forward and give him a little nudge with your heels."

So that was the trick.

"Thanks." Spade leaned in, squeezing hard with his feet.

The horse bolted forward through the castle gates, and his stomach launched into his throat.

This was no woolly yak.

Ash took to the air from the castle gate, screeching in excitement.

And then Spade was flying, galloping down the cobbled road and out into the countryside, Ash a streak of black above them. He clutched the horse's mane with a death grip, the castle falling away behind him, his teeth rattling in his head.

Villagers stopped to watch, taking off their hats and shaking their heads as he flew by. For a brief, wondrous moment, Spade forgot about his limp, forgot about his mission, even forgot about the Moor Mage. He whooped out loud as the wind whipped at his clothes, Pronto's hooves pounding beneath him as they headed east.

The crumbling manor appeared as quickly as it faded—a funny, crooked shape nestled between two distant hills on the moor, one moment distinct, the next, shrouded by curling mists.

Spade peered into the gloom, blinking. After a couple hours of riding the moors and spying nothing, he'd finally spotted the silhouette of a castle-like house in the distance, though only for a moment. Ash circled high overhead, urging them on, and Spade gave Pronto a nudge. The horse picked his way through the thick, thorny brush, ears laid back against his head, snorting nervously. They rounded a tussock when Pronto stumbled, tripping over a rock embedded in mud. Spade jerked up on the reins, the mist and shadows so deep he couldn't see the ground.

There was nothing to do but make camp and wait till morning. Spade slid off the horse's tall back and led him to a stand of scraggly trees, his bad leg aching. Ash settled on one of the branches, hunching his feathers up against the damp of the evening.

Pronto nickered softly, his warm puffs of breath hanging in the cool air as Spade unsaddled him, his numb fingers fumbling with the straps and clasp until at last he'd managed it. He'd need to practice that. Leading Pronto to a tree, he tied him to a low branch. Pronto bent and munched on blades of prickly, sparse grass, his eyes wide and darting about. Spade paused and looked out into the mist.

A slight breeze whispered through the brush and spindly trees, carrying the chirp of crickets, the low hoot of an owl. Nothing else. He returned to unpacking, draping the saddle and saddle blanket over a branch, then huddled underneath. He took out his water canteen and a bun and chewed slowly.

The bread was the best he'd ever had. If Spade survived the queen's task, he might even ask for unlimited bakery buns as his reward—Benji would fall over with excitement at the thought.

He checked his other pocket for a pastry he'd swiped at breakfast, and his fingers brushed against the pebble from Bagman Grute's shoe. He drew it out and rolled it absent-mindedly between his fingers, thinking.

Ash croaked from the tree branch and Spade looked up at the raven, head hidden in his wings. "Yer right," he said, and dropped the stone back into his pocket. "Time to make a fire."

A chill hung in the air as he gathered some branches, then searched his pack for matches. After several attempts, he coaxed a weak flame from the smoldering sticks. It flickered in the night, casting dim shadows across the lonely bogland.

He was reaching for another bun when a *snap* sounded in the dark. Then the soft thud of approaching horse hooves, the sound hovering in the gloom.

Who would ride out on the lonely moors after dark?

Spade doused the fire—best not to draw whoever it was to him. He bolted to his feet, scanning the dark shapes of the bushes, the trees. Pronto whinnied, sharp and fearful. Ash cut to the sky, a black streak, scouting for the source of the sound.

The snap came again, nearer.

Spade bent and felt around for a pebble. He plucked one from the ground and straightened, pulling his sling-shot from his belt.

Another twig snapped, followed by a snort.

A small figure broke through the thin trees leading a big black horse, several wild tendrils of red hair escaping her hood.

Spade lowered his slingshot.

"Ember? What are you doin' here?"

CHAPTER 14

THE RUNAWAY

Ember's scared eyes lit on Spade, and she pressed a finger to her lips.

"We have to hide," she breathed in a ragged whisper. "It's coming—it's been following me for a mile. And it's as fast as my horse."

He stared at her, then tilted his head to listen. Silence filled the night. He glanced at Ash, who seemed unperturbed.

"Please," she urged. "I'm not imagining things. Something's out there, I swear. I thought it was Henchcliff— that he'd followed me. But there was no sound of horse hooves . . . and it doesn't sound like a man."

Spade stood and peered into the thin brush, but the bramble leaves were still. He sighed. *Just great*, he thought. *An escaped princess who's afraid of the dark.*

Then he noticed something: a strange, creeping sort of mist at the edge of the circle of firelight, spreading across the ground. Ash uttered a low croak, ruffling his feathers.

Crunch.

The crackle of a breaking twig sounded, faint and distant. But he'd heard it.

He glanced at Ember. She'd heard it too, her hands clenched white around the reins of her horse.

The mist crept closer, and with it, a strange, rank odor, pungent like rotting meat.

They couldn't hope to outrun whatever it was on their horses in the dark—the ground was a mucky bog, rife with holes and rocks. And Spade couldn't move quickly enough on foot with his limp. But endless evenings spent outwitting the night watches had taught him something else: how to hide.

"Let's go," he whispered, thinking fast.

Spade raced to his horse and untied him, then slapped his rear. The horse whinnied shrilly and stumbled out onto the moor.

"What are you doing?" Ember hissed.

"Whoever or whatever it is, it'll follow the sound of the horses an' buy us some time. Let yer horse go."

He yanked her away from the camping spot, out onto the moor in the opposite direction. They stumbled over the uneven ground, scrambling through the mist.

"Spade," Ember hissed, "my foot!"

He whirled to see her stuck in mud up to her ankle. The mist spread, the air thick and moist, and another sharp snap of a twig rang out in the night. Ember's eyes widened, but to Spade's relief, she stayed silent, working feverishly to free her foot as he bent to help. At last they pulled her out and pushed farther into the boggy ground, water now up to their calves.

A rotting tree stump rose before them on a small hump of dry land and scraggly brush, the fallen trunk leaned against it. They lurched toward it, then dropped to their hands and knees and crawled beneath the fallen log.

Ember's breath came short and fast, and Spade crouched down, waiting. A strange noise drifted over the bog: deep, heavy sniffing.

A wild boar? But how was it following their scent? They'd moved through swamp and sludge, and animals couldn't track across water.

Another long snort sounded, and then a low groan rose in the air. The hair on the back of Spade's neck stood up. This was no wild boar.

The quiet snap of a branch sounded next to him, and a thin sliver of moonlight revealed Ember, brandishing a stick in her hands.

Spade's heart raced, and then an odd, warm jolt spread up his thigh. He startled, then stuck his fingers into his pocket and drew out the moon-gem, staring at it.

Its glow filled the dark space beneath the rotting trunk, casting light across Ember's astonished face.

"What is that?" Ember hissed, her wide eyes on the stone.

Spade shoved it back in his pocket, and the light immediately died. "A moon-gem," he hissed.

The snorting circled the bog now, and a long, low snarl sounded at the edge of the water.

Ember's breathing sharpened, and Spade's own heartbeat thundered in his ears.

They held their breath, listening.

A moment passed, then another.

Spade edged forward, peering between the tree's roots.

A hulking shadow stood at the edge of the bog. It raised its snout, and Spade swore he could feel it staring into the dark, searching for him. Spade froze, his blood going cold, and the breath stilled in his throat. After a long, terrifying moment, it turned and lumbered into the darkness.

The chirp of the bullfrogs returned. A fleck of dark circled overhead, cawing once, sharp.

Spade crawled out from under the log, water sloshing over the tops of his boots, something wriggling around by his ankle. Ember crawled out after him, grimacing, her hair a wild, untamable nest.

"That thing . . ." she whispered. "Was it . . ."

"The Woegan? I've only heard stories, but I'm pretty sure nothing else sounds like that."

Ember's face paled in the moonlight. "I guess we'd better get somewhere safe."

Spade nodded but couldn't help glancing down at his pocket. She followed his gaze.

"I've never seen a moon-gem quite like that one," she commented. "Are you sure that's what it is?"

He wasn't sure, but he didn't want her to know that. "'Course," he said. "What else would it be?"

She frowned. "Well, where'd you get it?"

He couldn't tell her the tricks of his family's trade. She'd probably be shocked, anyway, at the gritty details of robbing dead men's clothes. "None of yer business."

"Fine," she muttered, rolling her eyes. "I don't care about your Joolie secrets anyways." But her gaze darted once more to his pocket.

She marched past him, and Ash chose that moment to light down on her shoulder. She jumped with a cry of surprise.

"Don't worry," Spade chuckled. "He's just being friendly."

She reached up to pat him with a tentative finger, and the raven cocked his head, then nipped a big black beetle out of her hair. He crunched it in his beak and it slid down his gullet, his eyes closing in satisfaction.

Ember grimaced in disgust.

Spade stifled a quiet chuckle.

And after a moment, a reluctant grin crept across Ember's face. She plucked another beetle out herself, pinched it between her fingers and flicked it at him.

They trudged through the bog, their boots and socks encrusted with mud and slime.

Spade glanced back at the girl, her fine dress now splattered with filth, swamp flies lodged in her hair. "So, are you gonna tell me what yer doing out here?" he asked.

Ember's sharp gaze flicked to his and she sighed. "I followed you, of course."

He squelched to a stop. "And why would you do something dumb like that? I'm going to see the Moor Mage, not to the market."

"I know," she huffed, pausing to scratch at some mud on her arm. "I'm tired of being stuck at the castle and never allowed out. I want an adventure," she said, emphatic, rubbing harder at the mud. "I want a—wait—" She looked down and noticed the mud was actually long, skinny and black. "Argh!" she shrieked. "A leech!" She ripped it off and flung it through the air, then stumbled backward, landing in the mud.

Spade looked down at her, her dress now so brown she looked like a bog-person. She glared back, smoothing down her filthy hair. "As I was saying. I want a chance to prove myself."

He sighed and reached out to help her up. "I'm not sure yer gonna like this kinda adventure."

"How do you know?" she demanded. "Anything is better than the castle. Aunt Carmelia thinks I should be kept under watch at all times." She straightened, and her voice rose. "I've read a hundred books about the kingdom and its creatures, and she still ignores my ideas. Instead, she sends her supposed strongest men to find the Woegan's master."

Face flushed, she kicked at a clod of mud. "And do you know what? They all failed. So then what does she do?" She trembled with anger, her eyes burning like coals. "She asks you. You! A scrawny boy—a *Joolie!*—that she sends to go do something her most well-trained guards couldn't. And she tells me I am no help?"

Her face was a couple inches from Spade's now, her nostrils flared, eyes flashing. "I'll bet you haven't even read a single book about the Moor Mage, have you?"

She'd spat the word *Joolie* at him, like it was a curse. He'd heard it all before, of course, but for some reason, this time made him angrier than all the others. He straightened and met her gaze, anger burning in his stomach.

"I may be a Joolie, an' I may not know much about the Moor Mage, but it don't take fancy talk an' nice manners to know how to track something down." He grit his teeth. "An' I don't know what you got to complain about. If I lived in a castle an' had three full meals a day, wandering about riding fancy horses with servants an' the like, you wouldn't catch me running off to a bogland, moaning about my life."

For a moment, she seemed taken aback by his words. Then her lip curled in disdain. "You don't know anything about my life."

He snorted and turned his back to her, plodding toward dry ground. She followed behind with quick, angry steps.

They marched back across the moor to the small stand of trees and found the horses had returned, nickering softly. Spade patted Pronto on the neck, calming him, then took off his pack and rifled through it. Ember went to comfort her stallion, steadfastly ignoring Spade.

A moment later, tiny flames sparked to life with Spade's match, and Ember whipped her gaze toward the trees, eyes nervous.

"Don't worry," Spade muttered. "I don't think it's gonna be back tonight. An' I'm pretty sure it doesn't like fire."

"How do you know?" Ember asked, doubtful.

"I haven't read all the books you have, but I've listened

to the stories my great-uncle tells me, an' I notice things others don't. The Woegan likes to keep to dark places. If I hadn't heard yer horse approaching, I wouldn't have doused it in the first place."

A faint look of surprise crossed the girl's face. "Oh. Right."

"Besides, Ash will tell us if anything's coming."

They crouched by the fire, trying to dry their mud-soaked clothes, and Spade remembered something. The letter from Malachi! Jumping up, he reached into his pocket and felt the slip of paper, damp and crumpled, at the bottom. He pulled it out. The edges were blurred, but he could still make out most of the letters.

"What's that?" Ember gazed at the paper, curious.

"Nothing. Just a note from my family," Spade said, quickly folding it.

"Do they say anything important?" she asked.

He hesitated. "See for yerself." He shrugged at last, handing it to her as if he'd read the note a hundred times. She skimmed it, then read it out loud:

Spade,

Don't lose hope, my boy. At last, it's time to use the talents you've been given. Remember: take the winding path, even if it costs you. Some things are worth the trouble. Don't believe first appearances, and never underestimate a friend.

—Malachi

Ember looked up and handed him the letter. "Your uncle seems like a wise sort of person."

"He is."

She fell silent for a while, staring into the fire. "You can't read, can you?"

He stiffened. "Not much."

Garnet had always liked to say, "Reading's fer those with plump behinds an' wasted minds." But even so, Spade spent hours by tombstones, trying to discern their meanings. It ate at Spade to think people like Ember knew about a whole world he didn't.

To his surprise, she didn't make fun of him. They sat quiet for a few moments, and then she looked up. "You may not be able to read, but you're pretty good at fooling people. And I may have lots of books up here—" She pointed to her head. "But I don't know much about, well . . ."

"The real world?"

"Yeah."

He looked up from the flames and saw a glimmer of hope in her face. *Maybe she's right*, he thought. But Benji rose to the front of his mind, sitting cold and alone in the queen's dungeon, and Spade knew he couldn't do anything to mess up. And "kidnapping" the royal niece was probably tops on the list of things not to do.

"Listen, I'm sure you've read tons. But yer the queen's niece. Half the kingdom will be searching fer you, an' if they find you here . . ." He shook his head. "You have to go back in the morning."

She squared her shoulders. "I will. After I visit the Moor Mage."

He clenched his jaw. "You'll never make it! The guards will be gaining on you by now; you've been gone a whole day."

"I told my maid I have the stomach flu. She'll tell my aunt I won't be at dinner; my maid's terrified of contagious things." She shrugged. "Plenty of time still before she works up the courage to open my door. And even if she does, the fake me is bundled up in my bed, in a deep, sickly sleep."

"The fake you?"

"A mannequin I borrowed from the guards' target practice shed."

Spade glared at her. He hated to admit she would have made a good Joolie. "That's real clever, but it don't change a thing. Yer not coming."

She was trouble. And he didn't want anything to do with trouble, not to mention how much of it he'd be in if they found her there with him. His brother's life was on the line, and he couldn't afford any more of the queen's anger. He stared into the fire, ignoring the girl.

She shrugged. "Of course, everyone knows that even though you can see the Moor Mage's house, doesn't mean that you can find it."

He glanced up despite himself. "Why?"

"Because he casts a spell on the moor path to make it confusing. You have to take the small animal trails toward the house. They won't lead you astray."

Always take the winding path. Malachi's words came back to Spade, and he paused. "Thanks," he grumbled.

"No problem. I read it in *Myths of the Mages*, of course."

"'Course you did." He turned away, muttering under his breath.

"I heard the last royal guard was magicked right on the front doorstep," she continued. "He likely didn't say the riddle right. The Moor Mage makes you read it to him in person, you know."

Spade stared at her.

She knew very well he didn't know what the riddle said. "Yer not gonna tell it to me, are you?"

Ember pursed her lips, arms crossed.

He sighed. He couldn't think of anything more dangerous than bringing a runaway royal niece with him . . . but on the other hand, it was equally dangerous for Benji if he came back empty-handed from the Moor Mage.

"Maybe we should go together," he forced through gritted teeth.

Ember brightened. "What a good idea!" she said.

Spade glowered and curled up with his head on his lumpy pack, certain it was not a good idea. That it was, in fact, a very bad idea.

Exhaustion tugged at Spade, his eyelids heavy and dragging. Ember's loud snores reached him within a few seconds.

He was drifting to sleep when he caught a slight movement in the brush just beyond the circle of firelight. He snapped awake.

A pair of small, shining eyes glinted in the dark, watching him from under the tangled branches of a bramble. They blinked at him, then disappeared, the whisk of a tail slipping away into the brush. Spade sat up and stared into the darkness.

The bramble bush stood silent, and despite himself, his eyelids began to sag once more. The flames flickered bright, dancing in the night, and he could have sworn they looked like they were laughing at him as he fell into a dreamless sleep.

CHAPTER 15

ONE-EARED CAT

Spade's stomach grumbled as the horses trudged along, traveling for the last hour through thick-crusted mud and treacherous bogland. The mists parted every once in a while, and they'd catch a glimpse of the manor. Spurring their horses toward it, they'd arrive at the top of a hill, breathless, only to find it swallowed up in fog once more. Spade grew irritated, and not just with bogs and disappearing houses.

Ember rode beside him, eating a baguette.

The smell tickled Spade's nose, making his mouth water. He didn't want to admit he'd eaten most of his food the night before. Ash crowed from his shoulder, also eyeing the bread.

Ember nudged her horse closer to him. "Want some?" she asked around a mouthful of bread.

He shrugged, trying to act uninterested. His stomach groaned.

Ember shot him a sideways look. She broke off half the loaf and tossed it to him. As he reached out to catch it, Ash snapped it up in his beak, gulping it down.

Ember chuckled. "Such a clever bird, aren't you?" she crooned. "You love treats, I can tell."

Ash croaked and opened his beak, asking for more, and Ember giggled.

Traitor raven, thought Spade as he glared at them both.

But he found himself happier when she tossed them two more baguettes. She may be stubborn and reckless, but at least she was generous.

They plodded on, weaving down into a valley that approached the hills they'd seen earlier. The horses sloughed around tangled bush, and Spade scoured the grass slopes for another glimpse of the manor.

"So, what's the story with the queen?" he asked at last. If they were going to ride for hours, they might as well talk. He could learn a few things about the castle and the queen that might come in handy.

She glanced over at him. "She keeps to herself a lot of the time. I don't see her much, never have. She's been sad ever since I can remember."

"Since her husband went missing?"

"Yes, but there's . . . more." A shadow crossed her face. "When my uncle was lost to the mountains, my aunt was pregnant. Two months later, the baby was born, but there were complications." Ember shook her head, her eyes sad. "Her little daughter only lived a few months. My aunt doesn't allow anyone to speak of her. That's when she became the Stone Queen."

Spade thought about what it would be like to lose every-thing all at once. He wasn't sure what he'd do if he lost his family. The thought of never seeing Benji again . . . he remembered the queen's threat, and a shudder traveled through his body.

"Look," Ember said, drawing her horse up short. "Did you see that?"

Spade looked at where she was pointing and saw noth-ing but brown thorny branches and leaves.

"Something's in there." Ember urged her horse a little closer. Spade jumped down, then stepped toward the rus-tling brush, tossing a few pebbles into the brambles.

A hiss answered him, and a familiar one-eared tabby cat streaked out, rusty fur bristling, eyes wide and glaring.

Spade jumped as Ember laughed. "I wonder what a cat is doing all the way out here?" she said, but Spade nar-rowed his eyes.

"I dunno," he said. "But I've seen it before. It belongs to a weird old woman, an' I think it's been following me."

Ember chuckled and slid off her horse. "Maybe it likes you," she said, offering it some ham. The scraggly cat hissed but then lowered its hackles, padding across the ground. It sniffed at the ham, then plucked it from her hand, tail flick-ing in satisfaction.

Purring, it meowed softly. Then it walked toward the moor, looking back once. It meowed louder this time, insistent.

"What a strange cat," Ember mused. "It's almost like it's trying to talk to us."

"I doubt it," Spade said darkly.

The cat meowed again, a plaintive, grating sound.

Ember tapped her lip, thinking. "Maybe we should follow it."

"Follow a strange old lady's cat? An' why would we do that?"

"Well, it's determined enough to try and get your attention . . ." She sucked in a quick breath, her eyes widening. "Wait a minute! In *Wyndhail's Secrets* it said to follow the animal trails. I always thought the author meant deer and rabbit. But maybe they meant cat trails. Look!"

Dozens of feline pawprints tracked through the soft mud, some small, and some very large. Another meow came from the cat, loud and insistent.

Spade looked up to see the rusty tabby perched on the top of a rock before it disappeared over the other side and down into the mists of the valley.

He and Ember exchanged glances, then mounted their horses, trailing after the cat. Every few feet, they caught sight of a tail, or a bit of slinking orange body as it slipped between rocks and through brush. Ash circled high above, keeping a close eye as they wound downward. After a long while they reached the bottom of the valley, and the steep sides of two large hills rose before them, unease growing in Spade.

He spotted the cat as it darted off to the far left, and the horses followed, climbing along a steep path littered with rocks and holes. Pronto stumbled every few feet, and Spade's leg began to throb. He leaned against the saddle, frustration creeping in. It felt like they'd been riding for hours and he longed to stop.

Benj, he reminded himself. *Benji's sitting in the dark, an' you know how he hates that.*

Ember glanced back, worried, but he grit his teeth, straightening.

"Are you okay?" she began, and then they both spotted it: the crumbling gray tip of a tower that peeked over the next rise in the hill. The mists parted around it to reveal a sprawling manor, dark and forbidding.

At last. Relief poured through Spade as Ash circled high and caught an updraft, then landed on the highest tower at the center of the manor. As they drew close, they could make out a green blanket of ivy covering the walls and creeping over the large windows. The stale scent of abandonment had settled over the place, and yet a strange noise came from within: a soft rumbling that grew with each step they took.

A guard wall circled the place, a wrought iron gate at its center. The tabby cat squeezed through the bars, disappearing inside. Spade shot Ember a look, and they tied their horses to a tree, shouldering their packs as they approached the gate.

Spade reached out to grip the cold metal handle, then glanced up. Two statues perched on either side of the gates, casting frozen glares over the entrance. Their bodies were those of a lion, while their heads were human: sphinxes.

"Where is that noise coming from?" Ember asked, glancing around.

Tearing his gaze from the sphinxes, Spade pulled at the handles, overgrown with tangled thorns. "I'm thinking we're about to find out."

The gate creaked open easily, much to their surprise. What kind of powerful mage didn't secure the gates? They stepped inside, pushing through the tangle of rough thorns to find hundreds of roses climbing up the walls, knobbly swamp willows drooping over a garden walkway that led to the manor's massive oak doors. Gargoyles with ancient, wrinkled faces protruded from the mottled gray stone, their claws gripping the parapets, but none of this held their attention as they realized where the noise was coming from.

Draped across garden statues and lying on crooked branches, cats of every size and color watched them with unblinking eyes, a steady purring filling the air. A light brush against his leg made Spade jump. He looked down to see the rusty tabby weave between his ankles, meowing. Ember turned to Spade, her eyes wide. "Have you ever seen so many cats?"

Spade shook his head, equally awed and unnerved. Velvet bandit cats were perched beside slender white silkies, while puffed pooferans looked down at them from the towering branches. The rusty tabby meowed once, before it disappeared behind the old stone corner of the building.

"I think he wants us to follow him again," Spade said softly, meeting Ember's wary gaze. Wordless, they trailed along behind the tabby, aware of a hundred feline eyes boring into their backs. They ducked under brambles and over worn cobblestone, until the tabby stopped in front of a door that blended neatly with the side of the house, covered in creeping ivy. The cat slipped through a little flap carved at the bottom, disappearing inside.

They exchanged looks. "You have the riddle?" Ember asked.

Right. The riddle. He'd nearly forgotten. Spade reached into his pocket and drew it out, handing it to Ember.

"Here goes nothing," he said.

He raised his fist up to the wooden door and knocked.

CHAPTER 16

THE MOOR MAGE

Spade's knock echoed against the stone walls of the courtyard, loud and startling, followed by a heavy silence.

"I think we should try one last time." They'd been standing on the doorstep for several minutes, but Ember stood with arms crossed, refusing to budge.

"Well, we could try the front door—"

"No," she insisted. *"Myths of the Mages* said he never uses it. I think he's magicked it, and I don't want to be dead before I meet him."

Spade rolled his eyes and raised his fist once more to the solid wood.

It flew open, and he almost fell backward as Ember let out a startled yelp.

A short, frail-looking man stood there, dressed in long, dark-blue robes and floppy slippers, a peculiar fishing hat on his head, large bug-eyes looking up at them.

"Oh," he said. "I was sure it was tax collectors."

A white mustache drooped down either side of his wrinkled jowls, and his big, bushy eyebrows creased as he took in Spade, then Ember. He leaned heavily on a cane, a large emerald ring on his hand.

"I don't want any bear scout cookies, either," the old man continued, a few scraggly whiskers on his chin twitching. "I ate three sacks of the minty kind last week."

"We're not selling cookies, sir," said Spade. "We're looking for a famous mage that lives around here. The Moor Mage."

"The Moor Mage?" the old man repeated. "Well, he is rather famous, yes. Notorious, even." He paused. "But I'm afraid you've got the wrong house. He's my neighbor—two hills to the right."

"Oh." Spade looked at the old man, frowning. "An' can I ask who you are, sir?"

"Er . . . George." The old man said, growing more irritable. "I'm going fishing now. Please excuse me."

"You have no neighbors," Ember spoke up.

The old man turned his watery eyes on her.

"And your name is not George," she added in a firm voice.

"Uh, Ember," Spade tried to interrupt, but the old man stared at the girl.

"It is too," he said. "And why wouldn't my mother name me George? It's a perfectly reasonable name."

"Sure," said Ember, "but she didn't call you that."

The old man's eyes narrowed suspiciously. "Well, in any case, I'm awfully busy, because I have company coming.

You must leave." He glanced over their heads and licked his lips.

"No, you don't," Ember said. "You're not expecting a soul today."

The man's face reddened, and Spade cleared his throat. "Ah, Ember—"

"So, you're a truth-teller, I see," the old man interrupted Spade, hawk-like gaze on Ember's face. "Haven't met anyone with a gift like yours in a long time."

Spade stared at Ember. *Where'd she learn to do that?*

The old man squinted at them. "Well," he croaked, examining Spade. "I can see there's something a little odd about you, too, now that I come to think of it."

Spade flushed, certain the man meant his leg. But the old guy scratched his chin, squinting, and abruptly sneezed. "Bah," he said. "I knew it. One of you has got the smell of a mage on you."

Ember and Spade exchanged confused glances. "Uh, sorry, sir, but I think you may be mistaken," began Ember. "We don't know any mages."

"Of course," the old man muttered. "They're hard to come by, you know. They don't just grow on trees." He folded his arms across his chest.

Spade thought quickly. "Well, we won't be takin' yer time, then," he said, turning away. Ember shot him a sharp look, her eyes nervous. Several cats slunk down off the trees, slinking toward the base of the steps.

"Spade," Ember hissed, but he ignored her.

"It just so happens that we brought a gift for the Moor Mage," he continued. "So if you see him, let him know?

I guess we'll be going. Don't want to be caught in that downpour." He gestured to the dark clouds overhead.

"A gift, you say?" The old man peered at Spade with a shrewd eye, then at the darkening sky, tugging at the four whiskers on his chin before glancing back at them. Spade might have imagined it, but the old man's gaze seemed to pause on his pocket.

"Yes," Ember said. "A riddle. From the queen. She needs some help, you see, and we didn't want to arrive empty-handed."

The old man considered them. "A royal riddle, hmmm?" A hungry gleam crept into the mage's eyes. "How intriguing."

He shuffled to the side, gesturing down the hall. "It turns out that I am the Moor Mage, after all. Perhaps you'd like to come in?"

They wound along narrow hallways with cavernous ceilings, the old man's cloak bouncing just ahead of them.

He moved surprisingly fast for an ancient guy, Spade thought, pushing himself to keep up, though his leg had begun to ache.

They turned one corner and then another, and Spade reached into one of his many pants' pockets, drawing out a thin piece of chalk. Ember huffed for breath, pausing. "What are you doing?"

"Marking the way back," he said, and he put a small mark on each wall that they passed. It was what he did in graveyards sometimes, when all the headstones seemed the same. The mage's cloak had disappeared somewhere up ahead. "Where did he go?" Ember asked, whirling left, then right.

They chose right, passing several portraits of sour-looking people before at last reaching a large set of double doors that stood half-open, a dim, crackling light spilling into the dark hall. They peered through, but all they could see was the back of a large armchair in front of a fire and a big bookcase.

"Come in, come in," the mage's voice called from inside. "I haven't got all day."

Spade steeled himself and pushed the door open. The room had cavernous ceilings and long, black drapes that blocked out most of the sunlight. More portraits hung on the walls of this room, several of ancient, grumpy-looking men and women.

They ventured into the room, spotting the frail, old mage seated in the large armchair, his body dwarfed by its size. An enormous bandit cat perched on the back of it, its black-masked face fixed on Spade and Ember.

"Please, sit." The old man gestured to the two smaller chairs to the side of the fire.

"We must have tea," he said, and signaled with a wave of his hand. A small door in the far corner of the room opened. In rolled a tea trolley as if on its own, until they noticed a small, white munchkin cat pushing it on two legs. When it had reached the chair, the cat flicked its fluffy tail and sauntered away, eyeing Spade and Ember reproachfully.

The old man poured himself a cup of steaming tea and took a bite of biscuit before seeming to remember them.

"Forgetting my manners," he apologized, and poured two more cups. "Guests are so rare these days."

"Oh, thank you," Ember said, grateful, then paused as she lifted her cup to her mouth, and Spade spotted the brown sludge inside. The old man narrowed his eyes. "Bunbun makes a lovely cup of tea."

"Oh, yes, um, I'm sure she . . . does." She brought the cup to her lips and took a sip. Sputtering a little, she choked it down. "Num," she croaked.

Spade glanced around the room, taking in the strange portraits of what looked to be ancient relatives. His gaze landed on one of a young woman, her blonde hair cascading over her shoulders and down her back, a slight smile on her face—the only one smiling in the whole row of portraits. She was also the only one who did not seem to possess any jewelry, while the other subjects displayed broaches, canes, or rings embedded with large stones.

Her eyes shone luminous and wide, and as Spade looked closer, a funny feeling washed over him. Had he seen her somewhere before?

"My sister," the Moor Mage said, following Spade's gaze. "Extremely annoying person. Thankfully I haven't seen her in a quarter century. I've tried to remove the portrait, of course, but our mother magicked it to the wall." Frowning, he turned away, settling back into his chair and closing his eyes. He folded his hands in front of him, the emerald ring on his flinger glinting. "Now. I'm ready for my riddle."

Spade tore his gaze from the painting, his eyes settling on the mage's emerald ring. And all of a sudden, he knew:

the subjects in the portraits all wore their stones on them in order to keep them in sight. The Moor Mage was no different; this emerald must be the deepstone the queen sought.

Ember's gaze followed his, and her sharp intake of breath told him he was right.

"I'm waiting." The mage's brow furrowed, and he tapped his fingers on his armrest.

"Oh. Right," Ember said, exchanging glances with Spade. "The riddle." She reached into her pocket and withdrew the paper. Unfolding it carefully, she read aloud:

"Her Royal Highness says, 'I have just one, yet with eight to spare, I can escape most trouble and I have lots of hair.'"

The mage's eyes closed once more, brows drawn. After a moment they flew open, and he clapped his hands together, pleased. "Child's play," he hooted. "A cat, of course."

The mage stroked his beard. "You can tell her highness I am fond of that one. It's better than the riddle her last guard brought me. And you've been much more amusing than tax collectors." He paused, staring at them for a moment, then turned, raising his hand and signaling for the munchkin cat. "Bunbun! We'll have more tea!"

Spade's eyes were drawn back to the emerald ring on the old man's finger, and he shifted slightly to see it better. Up close, the stone didn't seem quite right. It didn't reflect light the way a normal emerald did; he knew this from countless lectures from Garnet and careful observation of the few they'd come across.

It was a fake, he realized, as the Moor Mage waved it about, trying to catch Bunbun's attention.

The cat didn't appear, and the mage got to his feet, stomping across the floor. "Can never hire good help, these days," he muttered, walking over to a little cat door. He rapped it with his cane. "Bunbun!"

Spade turned to Ember while the mage's back was turned. "It ain't genuine," he whispered.

"What?" her eyes darted to the mage, who was bent over, trying to peer through the cat door.

"The stone," he whispered. "It's a fake. Which means the real one's hidden somewhere, likely close by; everyone in the portraits keeps their charms on them. An' judging by the looks of them, they were a suspicious lot." His eyes lingered on the blonde-haired woman. "Except maybe her."

Ember's gaze followed his over the portraits, and her eyes widened.

"Blasted cat," the mage muttered and returned to his chair. "They're ornery, you know. But also very smart, and they love to play games." He brightened. "Which reminds me! It's your turn."

"Our turn?" Spade asked, wary. "For what?"

"To answer a riddle, of course. My riddle. It's how it goes, you see. The queen has sent you to me because she believes I know who has created the Woegan. But it's always more fun if you earn your answer, don't you think? And who doesn't like a good riddle?"

Ember started, "Wait, you know why she sent us?"

The mage frowned. "Try to keep up, girl. Of course I do. Why else would two children show up on my doorstep? Now, are you ready to play? You'll tell me something about me, and I'll tell you something about you. You go first."

"Oh," Ember said, a little surprised. "Um, let's see. I read a book once that said your manor is surrounded by guardians, which must explain all the cats. And that you enjoy bognettle tea."

The old man grunted. "Doesn't make me sound very exciting, does it? I wish they'd write a book about my exploits. Like when I tricked the hang-toothed witch in her own territory, or trekked into the Craiggarock Mountains to barter with the king of the trolls."

"Oh, the book mentions that too," Ember said. "When you were younger, of course."

"Younger!" the old mage snorted. "I'm not so very old now, girl. Only one hundred and four, if I recall."

Ember blinked. "Uh, of course," she stammered. "You seem very . . . energetic."

Spade stifled a snort. She was a terrible liar.

"My turn," the mage announced. "Here is something I know about you two: the queen sent two messengers to me because she is in need of help. Of course, I knew she would, but she must be very desperate indeed to have sent two children—though two unusual children, I'll give her that."

Ember's mouth parted a little. "You knew who we were?"

"Of course, royal niece. Your gown gives you away, as does your proud stature. Your friend, on the other hand, is, a little more difficult. Not dressed like a noble and doesn't smell like one either."

Spade frowned and glanced down at his clothes. "You can't smell like roses when you've been wadin' through bogs," he grumbled.

"I'm not talking about bog-smell. I'm speaking of Jooliesmell," the old man growled.

Stiffening, Spade glanced at Ember. The old man was wily.

Ember's eyes flashed. "It doesn't matter who we are. The fact is, we've made it further than her men."

The mage laughed, his ancient face crinkling. "Indeed. They weren't very nice to my cats. And their riddles were boring." His face changed abruptly, darkening. "Let's get to the point, children," he said, voice sharp with a rumble of power that startled them. "You want to know if I've created the Woegan."

Ember and Spade blinked.

The old man leaned in, and they could smell his stale breath. "That creature is too grotesque for my tastes. I prefer my moor cats. They're crafty, you see. They keep watch."

Bunbun purred, her strange yellow eyes narrowing, and Spade suppressed a shiver. "How can we be sure it isn't you?"

The old mage chuckled. "Just ask your friend. Her gift should tell you."

Ember cocked her head for a moment, then glanced at Spade. "He tells the truth."

"'Bout the creature? Or the cats?"

"Both." She turned to the mage. "What do you mean by 'they keep watch'? What are you on the lookout for?"

But the mage wasn't listening, his gaze turned to the window, the lines on his face deepening. He turned back to them suddenly. "I believe it's your turn for a riddle. Isn't it always more fun to earn an answer than simply have it handed to you?"

"Well," said Ember, "I—"

"Of course it is!" he crowed. "And if you can answer it, you'll discover a clue to the Woegan's master. This way, we all get to have a bit of fun."

Spade exchanged a glance with Ember, but before they could say anything, the old man got up and teetered to the double doors. "I'll just fetch us some more tea."

He swept out the door, leaving them alone.

Ember sprang to her feet. "How long do you think he'll be gone?"

"I dunno," Spade muttered, eyes darting around the room. "But here's our chance to find the real stone. Powerful folks never like to be too far from their valuables, always keeping them close. Quick—you check the bookshelf for hollow books, while I check the rest of the room."

Ember nodded and went to the bookshelf, pulling out several books. *"How to House-Train Your Cats,"* she read aloud, and snorted.

Spade moved across the room to the mantel of the fireplace. His fingers moved across a small cat skull displayed there, but all he uncovered was dust and cobwebs. A grandfather clock stood next to the fireplace and he opened up the glass door, looking behind the pendulum. The face of the clock was a cat's, its two hands whiskers. He checked inside the gears—nothing.

"How 'bout you?" he hissed.

"Nothing," Ember said, now examining the desk in the corner of the room. "Just a few hairballs and mounds of dust. Does this guy ever clean?"

Spade wracked his brains. Maybe he was wrong. Maybe it was hidden upstairs, in the bedroom? The bigger question was why the mage wasn't wearing the real stone. Was he afraid of being robbed? Or was it something else?

His gaze fell on the portraits lining the wall. An ancient, unibrowed man began the long line, followed by a prune-faced woman. The row went on, through one scowling relative after another, with the exception of the strange, wide-eyed sister of the Moor Mage. Other than her, each of them wore a large gemstone. Some carried it in a staff, some in their hat and some as a necklace. The Moor Mage stood proud in the last portrait, hands folded atop his cane, the emerald ring on his middle finger. The painter had done an excellent job, and the Moor Mage's eyes seemed to gleam, the ring on his finger twinkling.

A breeze gusted across the room, rattling the paintings. Spade whirled as the fire went out, surrounding them in pitch-black. Ember's hand found his arm, her grip like steel.

An eerie scraping sound came from the fireplace, followed by a rhythmic swishing. Spade reached into his pack and fumbled for the lantern. Ember rustled in the dark, and a match flared to life in her fingers. They lit the lantern and Spade swung it up high, light casting across the shadows of the room.

Bunbun sat by the fireplace in the middle of a pile of ashes, its tail sweeping through the charcoal dust. "What's it doing?" Ember hissed.

Spade crept forward as the cat finished a swirl, then sat back, admiring its work.

"Writing, I think."

Ember shot him an astonished look. "He's magicked them. They aren't just clever, he's put a spell on them." She inched up to the cat and peered down at the dust.

"What isn't alive, always hungry, but never satisfied?" she read aloud.

Bunbun blinked and growled, eyes flashing in its pushed-in face.

"I guess this is the riddle the mage wants us to solve." Spade tightened his grip on the lantern, and Ember took a sharp step back. "I'm thinking we solve it in another room. Away from that cat."

"Agreed."

They darted to the door and Spade reached out to grab the handle. It stuck in his hand.

"Spade." Ember's voice was sharp, high.

He looked up to see her wide gaze fixed on something behind him. He whirled—several cats had slunk into the room, creeping out from hidden nooks and crannies. They leaped atop the bookshelves, perched on chairs, sprawled across the carpet. Dozens of feline eyes fixed on them, a low hiss unfurling from one to the next. Ember stiffened, and the hair rose on the back of Spade's neck.

Bunbun crouched low by the dusty words on the floor, a deep rumble in its throat.

"Whoa, easy there, Bunbun." Spade tensed as the cats crept toward them. "I'm guessing we need to solve the riddle right here."

Ember's wide eyes found his. "What isn't alive, but always hungry . . ." She backed up another step. "I have no idea!"

Spade glanced around for a weapon, but there was nothing except the soft pillows on the armchair. He brandished the lantern high as Bunbun closed the distance between them, leading the army of cats. Maybe he could wallop at least one or two of them . . .

A familiar meow cut above the din of hissing cats. He spotted the rusty tabby in the corner of the room, flicking its tail at the bookcase.

"Got any of those ham leftovers?" Spade hissed.

Ember stared at him, hands shaking, then reached into her pack and drew out a few scraps. The cats circled them on padded paws, the fur on their necks raised.

"Here you go," Ember said in a singsong voice, throwing the meat on the floor. Dozens of furry bodies stampeded, racing for the bits of ham, slashing and snarling at each other, hissing and screeching.

Spade and Ember darted across the room to where the orange tabby had since disappeared, just as a small door began to slide closed beside the bookcase. They dove through, and a second wave of snarls rose behind them as they tumbled into a narrow stone passage. The door slid closed as cats hurtled against it, outstretched claws reaching through the crack until at last it snapped shut, sealing them in the dark.

CHAPTER 17

FELINES AS FRIENDS OR FOES

"Follow him," Spade urged, and he and Ember were on their feet, stumbling after the dim shape of the little tabby as he raced up the narrow passage. Spade's leg ached, but he didn't dare slow down. The cats knew all the secret passages in the walls of the massive manor, he was sure of it. It was only a matter of time until they were found.

The tabby veered left, and they followed, racing up a flight of steep, slippery steps, the air dank with mildew. At the top, the tabby stood and pressed against the wooden paneling. It swung open and they followed, slipping into a room that was big and lavish, a four-poster bed on the far side. Spade slammed the door shut behind them, leaning against it, gasping for breath.

"I think I'm beginning to see why none of the guards had any luck," Ember said, breathing hard.

An odd-looking birdbath stood in the center of the room, a bookshelf off to the side, filled with books. *"How* to *Avoid Magic Mishaps,*" Ember muttered, running her finger over the titles. *"Prudent Poisons, Tea with Trolls, Goulash with Goblins."* An ancient, scarred desk sat beside the shelf. The windows were drawn with thick curtains.

"We must be in the mage's bedroom." Spade turned and looked around, noting the dozens of cat doors. He raced across the room and blocked them with vases, books, anything he could find, while Ember blocked the ones closest to her with dozens of the mage's slippers, some books, and vases.

Ember groaned, glowering at the tabby. "Of all the places to bring us. Looks like he led us into a trap."

The tabby flicked its tail, indignant, and leaped atop the ledge of the birdbath, staring into the water.

"Or maybe it brought us here fer a reason?" Spade watched the tabby dip his paw in the water. He limped to the birdbath and gazed down. The ripples from the cat's paw faded, and a pool of dark, still water greeted him, with several pebbles in the bottom. "Wait a minute . . ." he muttered. There was no reflection of him or the tabby.

"Ember!" he called. "Come look."

She whirled and stared down into the black water beside him. The tabby meowed, and as they watched, the pebbles in the bottom of the bowl swirled together, then separated, spelling out a message.

"What is a place that is dark, cold and quiet, but has no walls, buildings or landscape?" Ember read aloud.

Spade glared at the cat. "Thinks he's so smart, doesn't he? But what does something that ain't alive, always hungry an' never satisfied have to do with a cold an' dark place with no walls?"

They stared at the water, thinking so hard that, at first, they barely noticed the sound. Then it grew louder, and Spade's head jolted up as Ember's face paled. A faint scratching, like chalk screeching on slate.

A cat had found them. More scratching, and the vases, books and obstacles began to inch away from their placements, dozens of furry paws reaching in, pushing at the doors.

A plaintive meow sounded behind them and they whirled. The tabby gazed at the birdbath, tail twitching.

Ember's breath came sharp and fast, her fists clenching. "I can't solve puzzles under pressure!" she cried. "I knew I should have practiced more riddles—I didn't prepare properly!"

Spade looked around. "Well, he didn't prepare fer us, either. He thought we'd be bigger, heavier, like the queen's guards. But we're not! We're small. And small thieves are better at escaping than fighting."

He grabbed her hand, pulling her across the room to a small panel in the wall. He opened it and peered downward.

"The laundry chute?" she gasped.

He nodded. They jumped in, plummeting downward, and Ember shrieked. They landed in a heap of what smelled like musty old socks in the pitch-black.

"Now what?" Ember breathed.

"Never mind his riddles," he said, thinking of the queen, of Benji. He'd been gone too long already. "We need to find the stone."

They scrambled out of what was a very large bin and made their way across the floor. Spade felt for a door, then pushed it open, and they stumbled into the dim-lit entrance hall. The dour-looking portraits lining the walls seemed to glare at them as they crept down the corridor, and Spade was reminded of the portrait of the mage in the study.

Wait. He froze, brain churning.

"What is it?" Ember whispered.

"I think I know where the stone is," he said.

They flew down the hall, Spade limp-hopping beside Ember as they kept to the shadows. Then a familiar doorway appeared on their right. They darted inside, and Spade closed the door quietly behind them, then leaned up against it.

"What are we doing here?" Ember asked, nervous. "We searched this room already."

"Sometimes people make fake decoys to hide the real object," he told her. "But what if the real object was made to look fake?"

He went to the painting and passed his fingers over the canvas. Cold hard stone met his fingers when he touched the emerald. Carefully, he plucked it out of the painting, and Ember stared down at the ring in his hand.

"You found it," she breathed. "It was right in front of us the whole time."

A plaintive meow made them turn, and the tabby slunk into the room. It darted for the window, meowing again.

Faint hisses could be heard all around them, growing louder.

"Block the cat doors," Spade said. They ran around the room, dragging objects in front of the flaps. A moment later, hissing and snarling surrounded them. Then it died as quickly as it began.

They stared at each other. "Maybe they got bored?" Ember asked, hopeful.

Silence surrounded them. Then came an eerie scraping noise.

Spade ran to the open window and peered down. At the base of the wall, dozens of cats had amassed on top of each other in a tower of fur, dragging their claws down the stone.

Ember darted a panicked look his way. Spade could never outrun them with his bad leg; he and Ember both knew it. But they couldn't let themselves be trapped now, not when they had the deepstone. Not when Benji was counting on him.

Spade peered down at the growing mountain of cats, gears in his mind spinning. Maybe . . .

He raised his head, whistled short and sharp. A moment later, Ash lit down on the windowsill with a short, nervous caw.

Spade turned to the window, ripping the curtains down. "C'mon, we need to move quick. Ash: you drop those books over there an' slow them down! Ember, we'll make the rope." He pulled a small wood knife from his pack, slitting the first curtain in two. "You tie 'em together while I cut."

Ember roped the strips together, her fingers deft, and Ash flew back and forth, clutching books in his talons

and dropping them out the window. Hisses and snarls ricocheted up the tower wall as cats fell from their perches.
The rusty tabby sat unconcerned on the windowsill,
watching the proceedings with interest and occasionally
cleaning his paws.

"Okay, that should do it." Spade hefted the long line of
curtains up, tying one end to the thick, sturdy leg of the
desk, then making a loop on the other end. He signaled to
the raven. "Ash! You know what to do."

The bird cawed once, taking the loop in his beak, and
darted out the window.

Ember ran to the window, leaning out as Ash landed on
top of the stone sphinx that crouched on the guard wall,
looping the rope around its neck, then flew back to join
them. Ember stared in horror. "That's at least fifty feet."

Spade nodded and climbed up onto the windowsill. "Yup.
Are you ready?"

The tower of cats had reached the gargoyle beneath
their window. "Quick, Ash," Spade called, "grab a heavy
book!" Ash swiped at the nearest one with his talons.

"Not *Felines as Friends or Foes*, the other one!" Ember
cried. "*Kitty Snuggles!*"

The raven plucked up the last book, a massive double
volume, and dropped it out the window. It thwacked the
highest cat, the ones below hissing in outrage.

Ember crawled up on the sill beside Spade and he took
her hand. "Move as quick as you can," he instructed. "So
yer arms an' legs don't get tired."

Ember nodded, her face white. She looked down at the
ground, then froze.

"We've got to go, Ember!" Spade urged.

She didn't move.

A hiss sounded beside them, and the tabby arched its back, snarling at Ember.

She blinked and edged forward with shaking legs. Took hold of the rope.

And swung her legs out.

CHAPTER 18

A DARING ESCAPE

S pade had always disliked cats.

Especially in this moment, as the tabby sprang up onto the windowsill, fixing him with a smug look before it slipped down onto the curtain-rope after Ember.

Spade glowered at the cat, then lowered himself down onto the rope. He gripped it tight as his legs dangled in midair. The rope sagged for an instant, stretching, and farther along, Ember shrieked as they swayed. Spade froze, afraid that she'd let go, but after a moment, she flung her hand out again, inching forward.

A snarl sounded below Spade and he glanced down. The tower of cats had reached him. He kicked at one as it lunged, but it moved faster, latching onto his foot. He yelled as the cat dug its claws in and inched its way up his leg, another cat latching on to his other leg. Ash crowed above him and dove at the first, tearing it off as Spade kicked hard, trying to dislodge the second, but it held on tenaciously. Releasing one hand, he reached down to swipe at it, and its teeth sunk into his hand. He yelled, and his other hand began to slip. His stomach plummeted as he glanced down at the distant ground.

"Spade!" he heard Ember scream. Something landed hard on his back, and a streak of orange fur whisked over his shoulder. The tabby. It raced down his body and launched itself at the cat on his leg. Fur and claws flashed, and then his attacker fell, plummeting downward. The tabby climbed up his body and back onto the rope, balancing along it like a tightrope walker.

"Thanks," Spade croaked in relief. He grabbed hold of the rope with both hands, swinging along as fast as he could. Ember had reached the stone sphinx and was now cheering him on. His arms began to burn, palms slipping with sweat while Ash dipped and soared above him, cawing.

His feet hit the stone sphinx and Ember hauled him over the statue and onto the guard walkway as Ash swooped toward him. The tabby jumped down beside him, licking its paws, and Ember darted forward, unlooping the rope from the sphinx's head. The tower of cats crashed to the ground.

"We did it," Spade croaked. He climbed to unsteady feet, heart pounding. "Quick! Let's get to the gate an' grab the horses."

But Ember wasn't looking at him.

He followed her gaze to the orange tabby, back arched, fur raised.

The mage stood below them, blocking the gate. His mustache twitched in a dark grin, Bunbun crouched beside him.

Ice slid down Spade's spine.

The mage snapped his fingers and a whirl of power and wind surrounded Spade. The ring flew out of Spade's pocket, controlled by an unseen force, and spun through the air, coming to rest in the old man's hand.

"It belongs to me," the mage said. "And, therefore, it listens to me until the day I die. Though I have to admit, you were far closer to succeeding than any of the queen's guards! Normally, I'd kill you immediately for being so impertinent. However, I've really enjoyed our game. Now. Are you ready for your last clue?"

"Do we have a choice?" Spade spat out.

"Come now, it's been exciting, hasn't it?" The mage pressed his hands together in anticipation. "You have one minute!" he announced, folding his hands together. He cleared his throat:

"What has no face and no name, seeks companionship, but is never given a friend?"

Spade's breath left him, and Ember's face turned white.

His brain tore through the clues: something that isn't alive, but always hungry, and never satisfied. Something that lives in a cold, dark place, with no walls or landscape.

It wasn't a creature; it wasn't alive. A dead body? But a dead body didn't crave food.

A ghost? But it had no face and no name, and ghosts were people once.

"Tick-tock." The mage's finger hovered in the air, and his grin grew. "Tick-tock goes the clock . . ."

Spade swallowed, trying to think.

What had no face or name and wasn't allowed any friends?

"Tick-tock! Tick-tock, tick, tock!" The mage chuckled, the sound breathless and giddy. The pillar of fallen cats had recovered, their hisses sharp on the air. They crept across the courtyard, amassing along the wall below Ember and Spade. Ash croaked high overhead, though Spade knew the bird was helpless to combat so many cats.

Think, Spade commanded his petrified brain. *Think. Think.*

Little flashes of memory crept over him. Long nights spent digging graves. Traveling through the cities, watching children play, but never allowed to make friends. The glares the villagers would give them when their Joolie carriage passed through a town.

"Loneliness."

He heard the word spoken out loud as he opened his lips, only it wasn't him that said it.

The mage's finger wavered, surprise etched on his face.

"It's loneliness," Ember repeated, her voice a hoarse whisper, her face shadowed.

The mage stared at her for a long moment, then chuckled again. "And such is the creature you seek. It is twisted and lonely, just like its master, for it takes the shape of its master's greatest fears."

His eyes turned cold. "It's a pity you won't be able to use your new knowledge." His hand darted into the air and his emerald ring flared bright.

Spade froze. "But the riddle," he sputtered, "we solved it!"

The mage tapped his chin. "True." He considered this, then shrugged. "But you can't possibly leave. You'd share your secrets with the world, and I wouldn't be a mystery anymore. People would show up on my doorstep all the time, and we can't have that." He shuddered.

A loud hiss interrupted him, and the old man's bushy brows darkened as the munchkin cat arched its back. "Not now, Bunbun," he growled. "I'm busy being nefarious."

The cat's hiss became a yowl. In every direction, fur rose on the backs of the felines, and they bolted toward Spade and Ember, clawing up the wall. Ember shrieked and they hunkered down and covered their heads. To their amazement, the cats flowed around them in a sea of fur as they streamed up over the wall and along the parapet, bolting in the opposite direction.

Ash crowed, black eyes fastened on something through the manor gate.

And then they saw it: a strange mist, crawling across the hills toward the manor, seeping through the wrought iron. A musty odor hung in the air, the stench of rotten meat.

Cold fear filled Spade's veins.

"The Woegan," Ember breathed.

CHAPTER 19

THE WOEGAN

Being a gravedigger, Spade had smelled a lot of awful things.

But nothing was quite like this: the putrid stench of rot, combined with something else he couldn't quite name . . . something strange and melancholic.

A soft moan sounded below them. He and Ember looked down to see the mage standing alone in the courtyard, Bunbun hissing in his arms, the mist circling his feet. "It's come," the old man whispered.

A sharp twinge shot up Spade's leg, heat searing through the fabric, and he jumped. A faint glow seeped from his pocket.

Ember stared at him, then his pocket. "The moon-gem?" she whispered.

Spade reached into his pocket and drew it out. The little rock flared to life, the glow brightening with each second.

"What is that in your hand, boy?" Spade looked down to see the mage staring up at them, eyes fixed on the stone. "It looks like a moon-gem, doesn't it?" he muttered to his cat. "And yet . . . that is no ordinary moon-gem, is it, Bunbun?" The mist circled his waist now, and he darted a look at the gate, his face shadowed with fear.

The mage trembled and clutched at his chest, eyes lit with a crazed light. "Quickly, pull me up, boy. I know another way out!"

Spade stared down at the mage for a moment, and Ember leaned down next to him. "Don't even think about it," she said. "He's deranged. And he tried to kill us."

The mist curled higher, and through it, Spade saw a huge shadow appear outside the gates, heard the scrape of its claws on the iron.

"Please," the old man begged. "Lift me up before it's too late!"

"We can't just leave him," Spade muttered.

Ember sighed, then nodded. They dropped to their knees, and Spade ripped off his belt, lowering it down. He and Ember leaned back, hauling the old man up to them.

The mage climbed over the wall, bent-backed and wincing. "My thanks to you," he said, as Spade helped him to his feet. They stood, and then the mage drew a short dagger from his cloak, an inch from Spade's chest. "The moon-gem, boy. Now."

Ember hissed in outrage and Spade froze. Ash released a panicked caw overhead, circling.

A crooked grin spread across the mage's face as he

raised the dagger, then a flash of orange vaulted off the sphinx's head and landed on the mage's tufted hair.

"Traitor cat!" the Moor Mage roared, flailing. "I should have known you weren't one of my darlings."

Spade stumbled backward while Ash dove, furious.

And then the mage took one step too far. He tripped, toppling over the edge of the parapet. Spade reached out, grasping one of his hands as he went over.

Below them, a massive creature appeared in the mist, wisps of smoke writhing around it.

The mage's sweaty hands began to slip from Spade's grip.

Wraithlike tentacles crept across the courtyard, spreading through the mist and up the wall, curling around the mage's legs. He screamed, and Spade and Ember leaned back, gripping tight.

The black wisps curled higher, enveloping the mage. His fingers yanked out of Spade's, something cool and metal slipping off them and remaining in Spade's hand.

The emerald deepstone ring.

The mage fell, disappearing into the dark mist below.

A flash of gnarled, dark hair, and long, scythe-like claws slid between the swirls of fog, and the creature reared up. The mage screamed.

Ember and Spade stared down at the mist, sickened, and then a deafening crack filled the air. They whirled in time to see the stone walls of the great manor house split, massive chunks of rock falling from the tower.

Ember gasped. "The Moor Mage's magic must have been the only thing holding it together."

Spade shoved the ring in his pocket as Ash swept down to his shoulder.

A plaintive meow pierced the fog, and they spotted the tabby across the parapet. It meowed again, urgently, and they jumped to their feet, running and stumbling after it. The orange blur ducked down a narrow set of stairs, and then out a small hole in the wall. Ember squeezed through the hole, Spade following, and in another minute, they spotted the horses in the trees. The cat swished its tail once, then disappeared into the brush.

"Quick!" Ember sat astride her horse, the tendrils of mist creeping over the heather, circling the horses' hooves. The deafening roar of stone cascading over stone thundered over the manor walls, and the gates themselves began to fold inwards, the stone sphinxes crumbling.

Spade grabbed Pronto and heaved himself up into the saddle. He swallowed and dug his heels in hard as they rode across the moor, galloping without looking back.

The sun sank low, its muted rays disappearing beneath the darkened horizon. Wind whipped at Spade's face as they crested a hill and spotted Wyndhail's towers jutting up in the distance. Ash circled high in the air, scouting the land.

"Whoa, boy." Spade slid off his horse, leg aching, and the raven flew down to perch on his shoulder. He reached up to stroke the bird's neck. "Brave Ash," he said. "Thanks for all yer help back there."

Ember slid off her horse, exhausted and dirty, and dropped to the ground beside him.

"So, about your 'moon-gem.'"

He glanced up at her. She stood with arms crossed, wild red hair tangled about her face. "I think it's about time you told me where you got it."

Crud, Spade thought. This was what he'd been avoiding. He didn't need the queen's niece knowing any more of his secrets than she already did. But could she tell if someone was lying even if they were just thinking of lying? Maybe he could distract her instead. He narrowed his gaze in return. "I'm not the only one hiding things. You coulda told me 'bout yer weird truth-telling ability."

Ember sighed and shoved her hands in her pockets, glancing to the side. "Yes, um. Sorry about that. It's just something I kind of learned to do, I guess. I've grown up in a castle where no one ever tells me anything." She shrugged. "It's a useful sort of skill to have. But if anyone knew, people would think I'm, well . . ."

"A freak?" Spade raised an eyebrow. "You don't think I understand what that's like?"

She looked him over, observing his ragged pants with a dozen pockets sewn on the outsides, lumpy with his Joolie tools. Her gaze moved over his muddied, scuffed boots and came to rest at the raven on his shoulder. A small, sheepish smile turned up the corners of her mouth. "I guess you would."

She glanced back at his pocket once more, frowning. "You changed the subject. Are you going to tell me where you found it or what?"

"Um . . . in a graveyard." There, that was enough.

Ember pursed her lips. It was the truth, but not all of it, and Spade knew Ember wasn't fooled. To his surprise, she didn't pry. "Well, what would the mage want with it?" she asked after a moment.

Spade wondered that himself. "I dunno . . . but it seems to light up whenever the Woegan's nearby."

Her brow crinkled. "Hmm. Maybe there's something about the creature it senses. Sort of like a Woegan-compass."

Spade liked the sound of that. "Something that can sense the Woegan could be a valuable thing," he agreed. "No wonder the mage wanted it. Speaking of which . . ."

He rifled in his pocket, pulling out the mage's emerald ring. He held it up in the fading daylight. "Now we definitely know it ain't the mage that was controlling the Woegan. I'm pretty sure the creature wouldn't hunt its own master."

"I know," she sighed. "But at least we have something to bring to the queen. She can't doubt you made it there when she sees the ring. We're the first of her emissaries to come back alive—well, alive and sane."

"What?" Spade stared at her. "You said they all *failed*. You didn't make no mention they all *died*!"

Ember shrugged. "I wanted you to feel optimistic. But we did do great, didn't we? And if we know the master isn't the Moor Mage, then we've narrowed down the possibilities . . ."

Her eyes were lit with excitement, and he could almost see the gears in her mind turning. Spade frowned, realizing who he was talking to.

He shoved the ring back in his pocket. "Oh no you don't! I know what yer thinking. An' I appreciate yer help, but you can't be seen with me. My chance to save my brother's already hanging by a thread. You need to get back home before Her Majesty discovers yer missing."

"Wait!" she exclaimed. "Are you forgetting what a fantastic team we made back there? Think about it: I know everything about the castle and everyone in it. And you have your instincts and thievery abilities, not to mention Ash. I already have an idea for our next—"

"Listen!" he cut in, exasperated. "Yer the one doing the forgetting. I'm a Joolie. A *Joolie*, remember? Spinniker and Henchcliff will have my head if I'm caught anywhere near you. And if I step a toe out of line . . ." He sucked in a breath and clamped his mouth shut. He didn't want to think of what would happen to Benji, sitting alone in that cold cell.

Ember stared at him, her shoulders dropping. She frowned, then shook her head. "Fine," she said. "You try and find the Woegan's master on your own and see how far you get. I'll do it my way."

Mounting her horse, she kicked it hard and rode up ahead, not looking back.

A prickle of guilt plucked at Spade's stomach, but he couldn't afford guilt right now.

He hefted himself onto Pronto and focused on the horizon, ignoring the stink-eye look that Ash gave him.

CHAPTER 20

TO SNEAK INTO A CASTLE

Wyndhail castle loomed gray and massive at the top of the hill as Spade and Ember crept along the ditch in the dusk. One guard stood at attention on the left side of the gate while another stood to the right, munching a snack.

Ember pulled her hood over her head, her face grim as she crouched lower behind the bushes that grew along the castle road. Spade glanced at her, then the guards. They hadn't spoken the rest of the way home, but now he supposed they'd have to.

"I hope you have a good plan to sneak back in," he muttered.

She stiffened. "Of course I do." Her face faltered a little. "Or I did. I hoped we'd make the guard change— that's how I snuck out the first time. But now they've gone and done it early." She glanced down at her dress, ripped and stained, covered in mud, her arms scratched from the bog. "Listen, the faster we can figure something out, the faster you can be rid of me, right?" She scowled and turned away.

Spade sighed, a heavy knot settling in his stomach, but she was right. As much as he didn't like this, he needed to get her back into her rooms, safe and sound. And he needed to do it fast.

"How about you distract the guards while I slip in the kitchen doors?" she proposed.

The knot in Spade's stomach tightened, but he nodded.

"First we have to do something about yer horse. We'll say he was my packhorse, and we'll stash the saddle here in the tall grass. We'd better hope the night guards are different from the ones that saw me leave yesterday morning with just one horse."

Ember grinned. "Good idea."

He scowled. "Maybe. Let's find out."

They dragged the saddle off and carried it into the trees, covering it with leaves. Spade rode the horses up the path while Ember ducked down into the ditch along the road, following him. Spade called Ash to him, tucking the raven into his jacket. When he neared the guardhouse he glanced down, glimpsing Ember hiding in the shadows of the tall brush beside the gate.

"State your person," one of the guards called out, spotting Spade. A sliver of relief darted through him: it was a new guard, just as he'd hoped. "You—you're that boy," the man said in surprise. He adjusted his hat, peering up at Spade. "Well, I can't believe it. You're alive!"

"Yup. Lucky me," Spade said.

The second guard eyed Ember's horse, tied to his own horse's saddle. "Isn't that the Royal Miss's horse?" he asked.

"I took it to pack supplies on." Spade shrugged. "The queen let me borrow 'im."

The guard narrowed his eyes, suspicious. "Little Miss rarely lets anyone touch that horse."

"Yes, well, the queen insisted I have the best. Speaking of which, I have some important news for Her Majesty," Spade hurried, before the guards could ask another question. "But first, would you like to see a magic trick? I've been practicing all day—it was a long ride back."

The guards looked at him dubiously. "What kind of magic trick?"

"You'll need to give me something shiny."

One of the guards rolled his eyes and tossed Spade a coin. Spade caught it and flipped it between his fingers, then pretended to put it into his ear, feeding it down his jacket collar instead.

"That wasn't for you to keep, Joolie," the guard grumbled, and Spade grinned.

"I wouldn't dream of it." He opened his jacket, and Ash exploded out in a show of feathers, soaring overhead and dropping the coin at the guard's feet.

"Bloody creature!" cried the guard, making a symbol over his heart, eyes raised to the heavens. The second guard ducked and covered his head.

Ember slipped around the guard's turned back as he batted at the raven, dipping and wheeling above him. She raced through the gate and bolted around the corner just as the guards turned on Spade.

"Keep that demon bird out of my sight!" the guard on the left bellowed. Ember darted behind a statue of the queen, then a monument of a horse, as she made her way across the courtyard, slipping out of sight.

"Apologies," Spade said, and opened his jacket. "He's such a rascal." Ash dove down and nestled inside as Spade let the flap fall. "Won't happen again."

The guard on the right glared at him. "You're to go straight to your rooms and wait for the queen to send for you," he said. "You think of doing anything other than that, this will be your last night as royal spy."

Royal spy? Spade had to admit it had a certain ring to it.

He saluted, guard-style, plastering a smile on his face as he urged Pronto through the gate, leading Ember's horse behind him. He could feel the guards' gaze following him as he headed for the stable. The stable boy came and unsaddled Pronto, and Spade headed for the kitchen door.

He slipped inside, and the aroma of mouth-watering stew and steak washed over him. The cook, a rosy-cheeked woman, bustled around humming. When she spotted him, she clucked her tongue. "Well, I'll be! If it ain't the royal spy, back safe 'n' sound!" She came up and pinched his cheeks, inspecting him thoroughly.

"Is everyone calling me that now?" he mumbled, trying to sidestep her reach.

"'Course," she said, and gave him a conspiratorial wink. "It's not every day a common boy-thief is employed by the queen. All the servants are talking about it. Spinniker's about fit to be tied." The cook grinned and ducked behind the cupboards, bustling around.

Spade stared at the woman's ample back. The queen herself had given him the title?

"Skinny as a beanpole, you are," the cook continued, her voice muffled. She reappeared with a large scone, its heavenly smell drifting sweetly to his nose. "We need to fatten you up," she chided.

Spade mumbled his thanks, cheeks still smarting from her pinches, and escaped with his scone along the narrow kitchen aisle.

A shadow of movement caught his eye, and Ember slipped out of the darkened pantry and walked beside him. "Cook likes you," she said, a hint of a grin on her face, glancing up at him from under her hood. "And thanks— that magic trick was brilliant. How did you and Ash get so good at that?"

"Uh, practice." He and Ash often spent hours in cemeteries, waiting for mourners to leave or night watchmen to pass by. He had learned to be creative to avoid the boredom.

Spade glanced down the hall to the left. "You'd better go act like a princess." He turned to duck down the opposite hall.

"Wait," she whispered. He turned. "You're headed the wrong way."

He paused, then sighed.

"Just so happens I'm headed the right way," she added.

He grit his teeth and she grinned. "You'd think you'd have the whole place mapped out, being a Joolie and all."

"Castles are different than graveyards."

A shadow crossed her face. "Not that different, actually."

They hurried down the kitchen corridor and Ember led them up a servant staircase, through a narrow door and down a wide corridor. Spade recognized the balcony where he'd first spoken to Ember, then they heard the heavy walk of a guard approaching.

Ember froze.

"Quick," she hissed, dragging him to a large door at the end of the hall. "It's Henchcliff. I'd recognize his walk anywhere."

The bootsteps rang out loudly now, turning into the main corridor.

Ember grasped at her doorknob, eyes wide. "It's locked— it's never locked! I can't believe it."

Spade reached his hand into a small pocket on the flap of his jacket, pulling out a thin wire. He threaded it into the keyhole, jiggled it once, then twice, and a small click sounded.

"How did you—" Ember whispered, then stopped. "Let me guess. More 'practice.'"

They darted inside, and Ember raced to the bed, grabbing the mannequin from under her covers and shoving it beneath the bed. Then she jumped under the covers as a hard knock sounded at the door.

Spade tucked Ash into his jacket and dodged behind a pair of frilly purple drapes on the far wall. The door creaked open, light streaming into the dark room.

Henchcliff's silhouette stood framed in the doorway, just visible through the thin curtain as Spade pressed himself up against the wall, holding his breath.

"Miss Ember?" he said. "Your maid has informed me that you haven't come out of your room since yesterday."

"I've been unwell," came Ember's muffled voice. "I took a nap."

"A nap," Henchcliff repeated, and even though he couldn't see him, Spade could sense him looking around the room.

"Yes," Ember mumbled. "Very tired. Go away, please."

"As you say, Miss Ember. But I noticed there were muddy footprints in the queen's hallways."

"Muddy footprints?"

"About the size of a young woman's, Miss Ember," Henchcliff said, his voice a growl. "They lead to your door."

A sharp beak jabbed Spade in the ribs, and to his horror, a wheezy puff sounded from inside his jacket—Ash, sneezing.

"Ah," Henchcliff said, whirling to the curtain. "So we have a visitor."

Spade thought fast, unzipping his jacket. The raven flew out from behind the curtains and into the room, flapping and squawking, coming to rest on Ember's bedpost.

"Well, ah, yes," Ember said, her voice raised a slight notch. "I forgot to mention that I went out to the garden to get Ash. I wanted some company."

"How interesting."

Spade inched as far back into the curtains as he could, and his fingers brushed something soft covering the wall behind him—a tapestry. Cool air drifted over his fingers as he touched it. A breeze? Could there be an opening behind it?

Henchcliff's hard gaze moved back to the curtain. "I forgot to mention something, myself: there were two sets of muddy footprints. And one of them seems to lead to your curtains."

The breath froze in Spade's chest. With fumbling fingers, he shifted the tapestry aside, searching for the source of the breeze, and discovered a small, oval-shaped wooden door. Spade pressed the latch on the door and it swung silently inwards. Heart pounding, he squeezed through and tugged it shut behind him just as bootsteps approached the curtain.

Darkness enveloped him, and he slid into the dark, feeling his way along a narrow corridor. Up ahead, a small shaft of light shone into the corridor, which ran parallel to the room.

He pressed his eye up to a small hole in the wall. A peephole! He could just make out the shape of Ember's bed and the shadowy form of the guard approaching. Henchcliff paused in front of the frilly curtain, then drew it aside. The guard looked closely at the tapestry, his mouth curving downward. His cold eyes flashed as they shifted over the peephole.

Spade took a quick step backward.

Could Henchcliff . . . could he already know about this tunnel?

He held his breath in the dark, muscles tensed for flight. After a long moment, he heard the guard shift and his bootsteps walk away.

Spade drew in a shaking breath, then risked a glimpse through the peephole.

"Must have been the maid's muddy shoes," Ember's muffled voice sounded from her bed. She sat up and shrugged. "I asked her to get Ash a few berries from the garden."

Henchcliff grunted, his shoulders stiff. His gaze darted to the tapestry once more, his expression dark. "I will wait outside until you are ready, my lady," he said at last. "And I will escort you to a late dinner in the tearoom." After a quiet pause, he added, "We must make sure you get there."

"In the tearoom?" Surprise flashed across Ember's face. "But I'm to have dinner with my aunt tonight."

"Not tonight, my lady. The queen has a headache."

A long sigh echoed from the bed. "As usual."

"My lady." The granite-faced guard bowed and strode to the door. As soon as it had closed behind him, Ember threw her covers off and leaped to the floor. "Spade?" she whispered, frantic.

Spade crept back to the crawlspace door and tugged at the hidden latch. He slipped out, and Ember's mouth fell open in surprise.

"Where did you go?" she hissed. "Was that another magic trick?"

"Nope. There's a passage behind the wall."

Eyes wide, Ember stared at the wall. "What?"

She raced to the tapestry and disappeared behind it, returning a moment later. "There's a spyhole!"

"Yup." Spade glanced at the door to her chamber, careful to keep his voice low. "And I'm pretty sure Henchcliff knows about it."

Ember paled. "That must be how he discovered I'd left my room. He's been sending someone to spy on me."

"I'm thinkin' he knows about most of the secret tunnels in this castle. But he couldn't follow me without revealing he knew about the passage." A chill crept up Spade's neck. He'd have to be more careful than he thought.

A sharp knock sounded. "Ready, Miss Ember?" Henchcliff called through the door, his voice a low growl.

Her gaze shot to the door. "I need another minute!" she called. She turned to Spade with a deep sigh, glancing longingly at the tapestry. "You'd better get going."

Spade nodded and Ash flew to his shoulder. The raven gripped tight with his talons as Spade slipped behind the tapestry and through the hidden door, moving quietly into the dark.

CHAPTER 21

THINGS THAT GO BUMP IN THE NIGHT

The tunnel curved left, then right, branching off to smaller rooms, and Spade remembered rumors he'd heard once that Wyndhail castle was built hundreds of years before, during a war with creatures from the north. Spade's father had always claimed that escape tunnels wove throughout the castle, though he'd never been able to find an entrance.

Ash clung to his shoulder as Spade walked along the narrow stone corridor, and they began to descend. An idea lit in his mind: the dungeons! Of course, there must be a branch of tunnels that lead there.

He'd only have a few minutes before Henchcliff and his guards would come looking for him. Spade picked up his pace and raced along the narrow corridor, feeling the walls in the dark. He had a match or two in his pocket, but he wouldn't waste those—not yet, at least.

He'd have to use his senses. He kept to the cold, steep

paths, running his hand along the same wall so that he wouldn't turn in circles, Ash muttering at every turn; the raven hated enclosed spaces. "Don't worry, Ash," he panted. "We must be gettin' close."

The echo of a stone skittering across the ground sounded just ahead. Spade paused. Had he kicked it?

Then another, and the patter of footsteps, the scrape of claws on stone. A low grunt.

Wait. Did rats . . . grunt?

He froze, listening. Ash croaked, shifting nervously.

Nothing.

As if *it* were listening for him too.

Another long moment passed, and then a few more pebbles bounced across the ground, followed by a *squelch, squelch* sound. Faint orange pinpricks of light bloomed in the darkness at the far end of the tunnel, and Spade pressed himself up against the wall. Several smallish, misshapen objects sat outlined by the dim glow, though he couldn't see them clearly.

He crept closer to get a better view, and his foot crunched down on a rock.

The lights went out.

Skittering and shuffling noises echoed through the tunnel, the scrape of claws heading toward him.

The hairs on Spade's neck stood on end, Ash's nervous croaks growing louder.

A grunt sounded right in front of him. Another to his left.

Spade held his breath.

Squelch, squelch, grunt.

A long, sharp claw brushed against his arm.

His shaking hand darted for the match in his pocket.

They surrounded him now. Ash croaked with fear and dug his talons into Spade's shoulder.

Spade struck the match on the wall. It flared bright, illuminating a wide face with mottled gray skin the texture of a rock, tiny, pale eyes staring back at him from beneath a fold of wrinkles.

These weren't rats.

It drew its lips back, revealing rows of delicate sharp teeth, and blew.

The flame sputtered and died.

A terrified caw sprang from Ash as Spade stumbled backward, ramming into the wall. "What do you want from me?" he croaked, fumbling for his slingshot.

They surrounded him, sniffing, their sharp claws dragging along his coat. One of the creatures knocked the slingshot out of his hand, sending it clattering across the ground. They rummaged in his pockets, his backpack, closing in on the pocket with the moon-gem and the Moor Mage's ring. The one nearest his pocket sniffed, then jerked away as if it had been scalded.

The creature grunted and whined, a noise of surprise rippling through the horde as they scattered in the dark.

Spade stood stock-still in a cold sweat, waiting for them to return. A moment passed, then two. Silence steeped the darkness.

His breath returned, painful and slow. He limped forward, one step, two, and stepped on something in the dark: his slingshot. He bent to retrieve it, peering into the black tunnel. What were those creatures? And how did they sense the ring without looking in his pocket?

Edging around a corner, his fingers passed over a smooth section of wall different from the craggy stone. He felt along it, daring to light his one remaining match. A narrow wooden door appeared in the sudden flare, and a small lever. He pulled down, and the wall slid open on a silent mechanism.

He blinked. An odd green glow lit a stone corridor that stretched before him, several dungeon cells lining the wall across from him. He ducked out of the tunnel and inspected the row of cells, searching for the source of light.

The third cell in, he realized.

His brother's cell.

He edged closer. The glowing spots seemed to be creeping along the wall. Something shifted at the back of the cell, and a very bedraggled boy stood to his feet, eyes wide in his face.

"Spade?"

CHAPTER 22

A DUSTY ROOM

"Benji," Spade cried, relieved. He hurried forward, pressing up against the bars as his brother ran to greet him. Benji reached his arms through to grasp him, his hair matted and dirty, his skin pale.

"Spade! Ash!" The boy stroked the raven under his chin. "I knew you'd come! But where'd they take you?"

"I'll tell you in a sec. But first . . . what are those?" Spade nodded at the green blobs creeping along the walls behind his brother.

"I call them glow-slugs," said Benji, looking proud of himself. "They keep lighting my cell as long as I remember to feed them."

Ash leaned forward, cocking his beady eye at them.

"They're not tasty, Ash," Benji warned the raven. "I tried them."

Spade stared at Benji. "Are you crazy?"

"I only licked it, an' my tongue went numb an' glowed fer hours."

"An' where'd they come from?"

Benji shrugged. "Dunno. Was the strangest thing. I woke up one day, an' spotted a little sack outside my cell, a greenish glow coming from inside it. They light my cell at night, when the sunlight leaves that crack in the wall."

Spade stared at the one closest to him, then shook his head. "You can tell me more once we get you outta here." He glanced up, locating the thick padlock, then followed it to a thick steel bar that crossed the cell door. His heart sank. This was no ordinary lock, and his flimsy tool wouldn't work here.

"I already checked, Spade." Benji's voice was quiet in the dark. "It ain't so easy. Now tell me where you've been, while we still got time. The guards will be coming soon."

Spade took a deep breath, shoving his disappointment down. He couldn't let Benji see it. Instead, he offered his brother a grin. "Have I got a story for you."

Leaning up against the bars next to Benji, he told him about Ember, then the misty moors and the old mage, their run-in with the Woegan, and finally, the emerald deepstone ring.

"Wow," Benji breathed. "Can I see it?"

Spade reached into his pocket and drew it out.

Benji's eyes widened. "Dad'd faint for a ring like that."

"Yeah." Spade shoved it back in his pocket. "But I gotta give it to the queen, show her I finished her task."

"Hey—what's that?"

Spade glanced down, following Benji's gaze to his pocket. It shimmered with a faint light, and he pulled out the moon-gem pebble. "Oh yeah," he said, passing it to Benji. "I found this in the tax collector's grave we dug that night. It's been real helpful—it lights up whenever the Woegan comes, like some kinda Woegan-sensor."

Benji turned it over in his hand, but the glow abruptly died. "Huh," he said. "Seems a bit broken." He frowned at it, thinking. "Or maybe it only works fer you, Spade."

"Fer me?" Spade studied it for a moment, then shrugged. "Seems strange that it would do that."

Benji handed the pebble back. "Well, it's not as reliable as glow-slugs, that's fer sure." Then his face brightened. "I can't believe it, Spade—yer a real-life spy!"

Spade swallowed. "Listen, Benj . . . there's more."

Benji quieted, looking at his brother's face.

A familiar heavy feeling dug down in Spade's stomach. "I'm not sure the queen will let you go just yet."

"Why not?" Benji's face tightened. "You got the ring back, didn't you?"

Spade's chest seized. "I made a bargain with the queen that I'd find the deepstone that controls the Woegan. But after what happened to the mage . . . I'm thinkin' his stone wasn't the one that masters the creature after all." Spade's stomach twisted. "I let Queen Carmelia fool me. I shoulda guessed the bargain wasn't straightforward."

Silence filled the cell for a moment. Spade forced confidence into his voice. "Don't worry, Benj, I'm working on it. And the royal niece, Ember, she knows a lot 'bout stuff here that no one else does. I'll find the master."

Benji nodded slowly. "I know you will, Spade."

Spade's chest tightened. Turning away so his brother didn't see the doubt in his eyes, he pulled off his pack, rummaging inside. "Here. It's a nice riding cloak from the queen; it should keep you warm down here. I wish I had some food, but now that I know 'bout these tunnels, I'll bring some the first chance I get."

Benji smiled and pointed to a little stone bowl in the corner of the slug-lit room. "That's okay. I've got enough pudding to last me a lifetime."

Spade frowned. "How'd you get that?"

"Same way I got the slugs. The first night you were gone I was dreaming of being Benjini, an' when I woke up, I found this bowl." He grinned, remembering. "So I sniffed it, and would you know it—it was sticky toffee pudding! Just like in yer story!"

"You sure it was pudding?" Spade glanced uneasily down the dungeon tunnel.

Benji nodded. "Yup. I ate the whole thing—except fer some I saved fer the slugs, they love it too—an' the next time I woke, the bowl was full again. Just like magic."

"Benji," he said, wary. "Never sleep too close to the bars, okay? I just don't want whoever's leaving you presents to get any ideas 'bout trying to hurt you."

The boy shook his head. "Whoever it is, they ain't trying to be mean, Spade."

But Spade wasn't taking chances. "Even so. You need to be careful. Don't trust anything you don't know." He clamped his mouth shut about the creatures he'd seen in the tunnels. He didn't want to scare Benji.

The creaking hinges of the dungeon door sounded as it slammed open in the far corner of the dank space, and the sound of grown men groaning for their dinner reached their ears, then the shout of a guard, telling them all to be quiet.

"I'd better go," Spade whispered.

Benji nodded, then turned to grab a couple slugs off the wall, plopping them into a little sack. "Here," he said, reaching through the bars and shoving the sack into Spade's hand. "You got no lantern; take some of these so's you can light yer way back."

Spade shook his head and grinned. "Thanks, Benj. That's quick thinking."

The bootsteps grew closer now, and Spade could hear the jangle of the guard's keys swinging at his belt. Spade slipped back along the corridor and through the sliding wall, Ash nestled in on his shoulder. He stood a moment in the dark, guilt ripping through him at having to leave Benji again. Ash croaked softly, reminding him they had work to do.

He slid his hand into the sack, grasped at the sticky green blobs, and held them up high.

The corridor grew warmer as Spade passed through silent tunnels, and he breathed out in relief. No sign of the tunnel creatures in sight. At last, the corridor widened, and he held the glow-slugs up to cast their light.

Three stone doorways stood at the end, the one closest to him carved with beautiful inscriptions. Maybe this was Ember's room. Spade pressed his ear against it and listened.

Silence. He pushed the small door open, stepping into a fabric wall that he guessed was the tapestry behind Ember's curtains. Cautious, he slid it aside and peered around it. A massive room extended before him, the ceilings high and arched, the dim embers of a fire still aglow in the hearth of the stone fireplace. A huge bed rose in one corner, covers untouched and pristine, cathedral windows spanning the length of the wall.

Not Ember's room.

If he'd thought the royal niece's room was magnificent, it was nothing compared to this. *Never let a golden opportunity go by, son,* he could hear his dad say in his head. He noticed a vanity in the corner, sparkling jewelry laid across it. Ash chattered in his ear—the raven loved glittery objects.

Drapes obscured a portrait above the vanity, and he slipped across the room and drew them aside. His stomach dropped.

A painting of Queen Carmelia and Weston looking young and radiant hung there, cloaked in a fine layer of dust. He froze, gazing around the room with new eyes.

The opulence, the bed, the portrait.

Spade had stumbled upon the queen's quarters.

Nerves taut, he backed into the shadows. Henchcliff had said the queen had a headache. He held his breath, scanning every nook and cranny, but the room remained still. Where was she?

Then he remembered something Ember had said: the queen loved to spend time in the graveyard when she was upset. He breathed out in relief and turned back to the portrait.

She wore very little jewelry—no charms or amulets, her neck bare of the sapphire pendant, with only a small circlet of silver around her head to indicate who she was. The queen stood beside her lost husband who looked every bit how the stories described him, with a strong jaw and laughing eyes that crinkled in the corners. Spade gazed at them for a moment, drawn to the life and vibrance in the queen's face. How different she looked now, so thin and drawn, fragile.

He glanced down at the vanity, taking in the rainbow of jewelry and gems, rings that must have cost a fortune. Funny—like the painting, these were covered in dust as well. He picked one up and shone it on his jacket. If his dad were here, Garnet's eyes would have danced with the same light as the diamonds. Ash leaped off Spade's shoulder and perched on the edge of the vanity, dipping and bobbing his head as he examined the dozens of necklaces and bracelets arranged there.

A small carved bird placed atop a jewelry box caught Spade's eye, almost lost amongst the necklaces. It was so small he'd almost missed it, and then its small sapphire eye caught the dim light. It was fine craftsmanship, so realistic that Spade thought the little wren might burst into song. Benji would love it—he'd adored birds since they were little. He remembered Benji's lucky frog carving, lost somewhere in the grass.

Picking the small figurine up, he ran his finger over its sparkling blue eye, and went to the long, arched window.

The queen's rooms had the best view in the castle, overlooking the main gate and courtyard. In the farmlands beyond, several specks of light flickered amongst the hills—the Joolie tents. What he wouldn't give for him and Benji to be back at camp with the others. As he stood there, a carriage trundled up the steep road to the castle.

It bounced and jolted unsteadily, its horse straining. Spade pushed open the glass pane a crack, watching as the driver reached the castle gate, waving his hat at the guards.

He exchanged hurried words, and then the guards allowed him in and drew the gates closed with a bang. One of the guards went running as more guards appeared in the courtyard below. "The creature's been sighted near the castle," the gate guard said, his terse voice carrying to the queen's window. "Secure the gates—all of them. Be on your highest alert."

The guards moved at once to all the gates, and then Spade noticed it—the dim glow from his pocket. The pebble. Ash croaked a warning. The queen would be back any moment in order to be kept secure in her room. He slid the wren into his jacket and darted across the room, ducking back into the tunnel once more.

He and Ash slipped through the second door this time and Spade ducked out from behind the curtain to find himself back in Ember's room, which stood empty. Crossing the polished floor, he cracked open her door, peering around. The hall was quiet.

He'd almost made it back to his room when he heard the heavy bootsteps.

"I see you've returned from the moors," Henchcliff barked, eyeing Spade suspiciously. "My guard mentioned he'd seen you at the gate over an hour ago."

"Had to go to the bathroom," said Spade. "An' I got a bit lost in the corridors."

Henchcliff's hard face flickered. He stepped past Spade, key in hand, and unlocked his door. "You'll remain in your room tonight," he growled. "The queen will not see you until tomorrow." He leaned in close, black eyes flashing. "And do not even think of trying to wander the halls, Joolie, or of letting that demon bird loose. The creature hunts tonight and would enjoy you as a snack." He chuckled, low. "Though I'd relish such an accident."

He whirled, the door slamming behind him, and the key turned in the lock.

CHAPTER 23

A FEAST FIT FOR A SPY

The late morning sun's rays streamed through Spade's window. Ash perched on the sill, staring out into the courtyard, but still, no one had come to bring them to the queen.

Spade stood and paced around the room for the forty-sixth time. Had the queen somehow found out about Ember's escape? About how he'd visited Benji? His hands grew clammy, his stomach taut as the sun rose even higher in the sky.

He'd have picked the lock long ago, but Henchcliff was no fool; he'd stationed a guard outside the door. Spade could hear the man humming to himself.

At last, evening gathered, and a key rattled in the lock. The guard stood to the side as a thin, frazzled maid hurried in, some fancy clothing folded over her arm. She frowned, looked him up and down, then clucked her tongue. "You stink," she informed him. "Most unfitting for a meeting with the queen. And only half an hour to prepare you!"

An embarrassing twenty minutes later, he'd been scalded in a hot bath before dressing himself in the clothes he'd been given: nice new pants and jacket, though the cuffs were a bit frilly. The maid bustled back into the room, glowering, and tried to comb his unruly hair while she muttered something about filthy Joolies. She didn't notice Ash, eyeing her from the rafters. The bird swooped down, entranced by her shiny hairpins, and plucked one out. She screamed and ran, and that was the end of Spade's beautifying.

A knock on the door sounded.

Two guards stood there, and Spade followed them down the long corridor, then and down a marble staircase to the elaborate doors he'd seen before. He drew a deep breath and steeled himself, waiting, Ash puffed up on his shoulder as if he knew they were important guests.

The doors swung open, and Spade stepped inside. He jolted in surprise; Ember sat at the far side of the long dining table in a green satin dress, while Queen Carmelia sat at its head, clad in a black gown and black gloves, blue pendant twinkling at her neck. She tilted her chin, nodding at him to come forward.

Spade limped slowly to the table, where a server pulled his chair out, nose wrinkling at the sight of Ash. He sat several seats from Ember so as not to draw attention to her, though he saw her eyes spark before she looked back at her plate.

"Well, Royal Spy." Queen Carmelia sat back in her chair and fixed her gaze upon him. Her face was pale and haggard, but her eyes were curious. "What have you discovered?"

Spade cleared his throat, his hands clammy. Ember's gaze flicked toward him and she leaned in slightly.

He took a deep breath. "The Moor Mage didn't create the creature, Majesty."

The queen tensed, hands gripping her chair. "And how can you be certain of this, boy-thief?" she breathed.

"I think it got him."

Her eyes widened slightly. "'Got' him?"

And so Spade told her the whole story, leaving Ember out. He started with the vanishing house and the creepy cats, and ended with the Woegan devouring the Moor Mage, for dramatic flair. When he'd finished, the queen sat staring at him, lips parted in wonder. "The Moor Mage, dead! Who would have believed it?" She paused. "And the ring?"

Spade reached into his pocket and pulled out the emerald ring. He stepped forward and bowed, placing it in her hands. As he straightened, he briefly caught Ember's eyes.

The queen nodded in approval. "We owe you our thanks, Royal Spy. At least we can be certain that the ring doesn't fall prey to the Woegan's master if it is here in our sight. In fact, I will keep it on me, as my royal guard ensures that I, myself, am the safest place in the castle." She glanced at Henchcliff with amusement. "I am rarely let out of sight."

"It is my job to protect Your Majesty's safety," said Henchcliff, narrowing his gaze at Spade.

A sharp knock on the door sounded, and Spinniker slipped into the room. "My lady," he murmured.

"Have you news to report?" she asked.

He cast a wary glance at Spade, then approached the queen. His voice was low, but even so, Spade heard him utter, "It remains untouched, My Queen."

She nodded, relief visible on her face.

What remained untouched? Spade wondered, but Spinniker turned, glowering.

"And does this vagrant bring any news, my lady? Or has he been bothering you?"

"On the contrary." The queen's lips curved upward, and Spade blinked. He'd never seen the queen smile. "You can be rid of that dour look, Spinniker, and give the kitchens an order to prepare a celebration meal."

Spinniker gaped at her, then closed his mouth, mustache twitching. "Of course, my lady."

"We will celebrate the return of our royal spy," she announced. "For his bravery and wisdom. He is the only one to have both passed the mage's tests and obtained the mage's ring. He will eat like a king tonight!"

Out of the corner of his eye, Spade noticed a faint flush creep over Ember's cheeks, the clench of her hands at her side. She stared at her fruit plate, focusing hard on the grapes.

"Well, Joolie? What would make you very happy tonight?"

"Can it be anything, Majesty?"

She furrowed her brow. "What do you desire?"

"That my brother could have some of the feast sent to him."

The queen frowned, then nodded slowly. "A plate for the prisoner it is." She snapped her finger at the guards. "See that it is done. This is a day to remember: the day a Joolie single-handedly defeated the great Moor Mage and escaped the Woegan. Something none of my men could do!"

He forced a smile. "Thank you, Yer Majesty."

Ember stabbed a grape with her fork.

They ate until bursting, the queen, Spade, and Ash, though Ember mostly picked at her food. When they were done, Spade and Ash performed a few magic tricks. The queen laughed, the sound surprising and light, as Spade pulled a coin from Ash's beak and then later from behind the queen's ear. Even Ember smiled once or twice, before looking away.

Servants bustled in and out of the room more slowly than usual, their curious gazes riveted on Spade and Ash, then on the queen, whose face was bright. They muttered, prodding each other, and even the guards standing at the door chuckled a bit. Spinniker spoke to Ember at the far end of the table, instructing her on something that must have been boring, because she stifled a yawn. Spade glanced at the older man, remembering his earlier, mysterious whisper in the queen's ear—*it remains untouched.*

What had he meant, he wondered. He was eating his third bread bun, still thinking about it, when a prickle crept over his neck. Spade turned and caught himself under Henchcliff's steady scrutiny. Then the kitchen doors opened, diverting Henchcliff's gaze, and Spade sighed in relief. A rounded cook pushed a trolley into the room, burdened with a chocolate pie the size of three dinner plates.

Spade's mouth opened at the sight of whipped cream piled high at its center, decadent chocolate glaze dripping over its sides.

He'd never seen anything like it—Benji would have fainted at the sight.

A sharp pang hit him in the chest as he thought of his brother. Servants scurried across the room, delivering slices. A giant slice arrived in front of Spade, but all he could do was stare at it.

"What's wrong?"

He looked up to find Ember standing beside him. The queen was busy laughing at Ash's charms as he snuck a crumb from a saucer she held, while Spinniker watched the bird's antics with disapproval.

"Nothing," Spade said, forcing himself to take a bite.

Ember pursed her lips. "You were thinking of your brother, weren't you?"

Spade hesitated, then nodded.

She leaned in, lowering her voice. "I wish we could get him out somehow, but Henchcliff . . ." She glanced over at the guard, whose steel gaze was fixed on them. "He's always watching," she whispered, frustrated. "Like a shadow."

Her voice held a tone of despair, and Spade was reminded that he wasn't the only one with troubles.

"Listen, Ember," he said. "I'm sorry about tonight."

"You've got nothing to be sorry about," she said stubbornly. "You kept my secret. That's all I can ask for." She glanced down at her own untouched pie.

Spade tried to think of something that would cheer

her up. "One day you'll get yer chance, Ember. They'll see that yer clever, an' brave. They'll see the truth."

She looked surprised. Spade was a little surprised too—he'd actually meant all that.

"Thanks," she said, flushing. "But I'm not so sure."

He shrugged. "I am. Truth is yer middle name. An' besides, adventure seems to find you, like fleas to a dog."

A crooked grin pulled at her mouth. "Promise?"

"On my best shovel."

"A Joolie's promise. But I'll take it."

Before he could reply, Henchcliff started moving toward them with a glower. Just as he reached them, the queen stood and clapped her hands together.

"I am tired now," she said, "but I don't believe I've enjoyed myself so well in a while." She nodded at Spade and gestured for him to move closer to her. Spinniker stood nearby, a disgruntled look on his weathered face. Ember shot them a curious look, then busied herself with stabbing at her pie, trying not to look too interested in what the queen had to say.

"Our bargain still stands, Joolie. We have not yet found the Woegan's master." The queen's face dimmed, falling serious. "There is more you must know. The Moor Mage's stone is not the only one to have such power. You see, there is yet another." She regarded him for a moment. "When the deepstones were first found deep within the Quaren mines, they were given to my father, King Alistair, to help him govern. But the king had not even had them a year when one was stolen. The Moor Mage broke into the castle vault, demolishing the king's guards.

"My father was devastated and swore that he would protect the second deepstone better, and he placed it under lock and key in Wyndhail Tower. It was during his illness that the second stone, too, was stolen—directly from Wyndhail Tower."

Spade's mind churned. "Stolen by whom, Yer Majesty?"

Queen Carmelia's eyes flashed with a cold gleam. "Only someone cunning and brave could wield one of the deepstones and take it from under the nose of Wyndhail. I thought it was the Moor Mage yet again. But now I realize that the enemy was not from outside, but from within the castle itself."

Spinniker took a halting step forward. "My lady, are you certain we should tell this thief of the royal family history?"

"And why not, Spinniker? He cannot help us if he has no clues." The queen turned her gaze on Spade. "My father had a half brother and half sister, my aunt and uncle. Being eldest and the only full-blooded royal heir, my father, Alistair, inherited the kingship. Uncle Murdoch trained in the dark arts and magic and Lyrica, my aunt, became the royal castle healer.

"When my father received the deepstones, Murdoch became jealous, as he craved magic. He managed to steal the first and escape. He was banished afterward, earning himself the nickname Moor Mage."

The Moor Mage was King Alistair's brother? That would explain a lot of the old man's determined hate for all things royal. Spade glanced at Ember, whose eyes were wide. "I . . . I thought his brother died," she said.

"Yes, well, we decided to let people think so," the queen murmured. "It was easier that way.

"Years passed, and the king thought the second stone safe, but he thought wrong." The queen gestured to a guard who stood quiet in the corner, humming to himself, his eyes far away. "Come here, Balfry," she said. "And tell this thief your story about the night the second stone was stolen."

The man flushed slightly. "I . . . was guarding the tower 'round midnight when I saw someone in a green dress approach me. She moved with a weird shuffle-walk, like an old lady would, so I thought nothing of it. She wore a hood, frizzy white hair sticking out, though I couldn't see her face. And then, it was like I blinked—and she was right there beside me. At least . . . I think she was. I can't always remember clearly.

"I reached for my weapon, for something didn't seem right, and that's when I felt it: the ground upheaving beneath my feet. Something wrapped around my legs and hit me in the back of the head."

His blush deepened. "When I woke up, I was lying on the ground. The little old lady had vanished, and the thing that clobbered me too. I thought I'd imagined the whole thing, but then I noticed something in the dirt. A pair of full-moon spectacles."

The words flooded Spade's mind, and with them, the image of a pair of riveting green eyes and snow-white hair. And all of a sudden, he realized who the painting in the Moor Mage's house looked like: a very young version of the old lady from the cemetery. He could have kicked himself. How had he missed the resemblance?

"A fitting description of my Aunt Lyrica," the queen said, folding her arms. "You see, no one suspected her. Uncle Murdoch had been banished, and my father had taken ill. It was said that while no one was paying attention to her, their sister had begun training in magic. Many said she was a witch. But the king had become too weak from illness to maintain a close watch on the deepstones."

The queen's eyes flashed. "The day the second stone was stolen was the day Aunt Lyrica disappeared from Wyndhail, the deepstone along with her. It is presumed she is dead."

Spade swallowed, glancing between the queen and Spinniker.

"Actually, Yer Majesty. She's not."

CHAPTER 24

A LONG-LOST RELATIVE

If Spade had thrown a bucket of mud at the queen and danced around the room in his underclothes, he couldn't have caused a bigger ruckus than with the words he'd just uttered.

Spinniker drew in a wheezing breath and leaned forward to clutch the table. Ember leaped from her chair, knocking her forgotten pie to the floor.

The queen herself fixed her ice-blue gaze on Spade, her cheeks a ghastly white. "No one has seen Lyrica for years. What do you mean by this, Joolie?"

Spade looked between their shocked expressions.

"I've met her," he said slowly, and the memory of that day in the Wyndhail cemetery swept over him. The strange old woman, her unnerving smile, the enormous bench. The ugliest cat he'd ever laid eyes on.

"I am in no mood for tales, thief." The queen's words cut through the air, dangerous and low. The room stilled.

Spade could feel the eyes of the attendants turn to them, Ember hovering close by.

"I'm not lying, Yer Majesty. I swear it on a golden grave."

"And where, tell me, would you have met her?"

Spade hesitated. His father's voice rang in his ears: *A Joolie's secrets are to keep, while a wandering mouth brings tears to weep.*

"Majesty," he said, lowering his voice. "I'd rather not say in front of all these folks, in case I were to offend them by the, uh, dirtier parts of my family's trade. But I can tell you this: I've seen her in this very castle, as well as outside."

"Impossible," the queen breathed.

"Pardon, Majesty, but she's got magic, right? An' ways of disguising herself. I'm certain of that." He shuddered at the memory of the old woman drifting across the great room between dozens of guards, unnoticed.

Slowly, the queen nodded. "Yes, she always had an uncanny way about her with plants and animals. When I was little, I was certain it was magic when I'd watch her in the garden." She paused, considering Spade. "And do you think you can find her?"

Uncertainty pricked at Spade, but he ignored it. He'd find the old woman for Benji's sake, no matter what it took. "I'm thinkin' I can, Majesty," he said, drawing himself tall to appear the picture of confidence.

The queen considered. "You did retrieve Murdoch's deepstone, it's true. But Lyrica is a far different creature. She's cunning in ways that Murdoch was not."

Spinniker's worried gaze went to the queen. "Surely then, Majesty, that's reason enough for why we cannot send this . . . this boy-thief—" he sputtered, but the queen raised her hand, silencing him.

"Foolish as it may be, we have no choice. The Woegan grows bolder."

She turned her piercing eyes on Spade.

"You have two days," she murmured. "And that is all, Royal Spy."

Spade pushed the churn of misgiving down in his stomach, and grinned. "Thank you, Majesty. You won't be disappointed."

Spade's footsteps moved soft over the dirt and grass, a smattering of rain making him pull his coat tighter. He held the glow-slugs that Benji had given him up high, casting faint green light into the misty night.

Ash flew overhead, landing on the familiar crooked elm in the center of Wyndhail cemetery. Spade had left Pronto tied to the gate behind him, instructing the horse to be quiet.

His gaze raced over the tombstones, the mist casting them in a sea of gray. Part of him wondered what he'd been thinking, telling the queen he'd find the old lady. But he'd had to come up with something if he was going to get Benji released from the dungeons.

Weaving between the graves, he kept his eyes glued to the ground. There had to be a clue somewhere.

He spied the drag marks where he'd hauled the bench up the hill and followed them up to where it sat lonely at the top. The ground was bare of footprints, no trace of her.

Ash hopped from tombstone to tombstone behind him as Spade limped to the other side of the hill. It was as if she'd appeared out of thin air. The mist grew thicker here, and he tripped over a tree root, cursing his crooked leg, then paused.

The root protruded from the soil in an area seemingly void of trees. He bent, noticing another knobby root a few feet away. Crouching with his face almost level with the ground, he spotted another, the soil soft and fresh around it. He frowned. Where had these roots come from?

"I'm not sure sniffing mud is going to help you find Lyrica."

He whirled at the familiar sound. Ember stood with her arms crossed, wearing pants and a stableboy's vest, a dirty cap on her head.

"You've gotta stop doing that," he demanded. "You could give someone a heart attack or make them pee their trousers."

Her gaze darted to his pants, eyebrows raised.

"'Course I didn't." He scowled. "I'm just saying."

He turned and peered through the mist, spotting the big, beautiful stallion that waited at the bottom of the hill outside the gate. "I don't even wanna know how you escaped this time," he muttered, then paused. "An' I wasn't sniffing dirt. I was tracking."

Ember's gaze lit up. "I'm good at looking for clues, you know."

"Nope. No way." He stood and crossed his arms. "You can't be here, Ember. You can only make up so many stomach flus."

"I didn't have to come up with anything." She shrugged. "It's the week of the Harvest Moon festival."

Spade looked at her. "So?"

"This time of year, the queen often spends whole days locked in her rooms. The feast tonight . . . that was something she hasn't done in years." She shook her head and sighed. "Most of the time, she doesn't even notice I'm gone."

"Why does she lock herself up?"

Ember glanced out across the town to the shadowed castle that rose above it. "It's the anniversary of her daughter's death."

He would likely hide in his room, too, on a week like that. "An' what about Henchcliff?"

"Prowling the markets." She shook her head. "Every year he goes out looking for a gift to buy for my aunt, something to distract her from this week. They both think I'm reading in my rooms." She shrugged. "It'll be a full day before anyone comes to check on me. I left a note with the serving maids saying I'd like to take my meals in my room, and to leave them just inside the door."

"They'll notice no one's eating the food."

She grinned. "I left the old castle hound in my room. When he's not busy napping, he'll devour it. Besides, Balfry's guarding the hallway tonight while Henchcliff's away, and the maids are all a little afraid of him."

Spade frowned. "Do you mind tellin' me what happened to that guard? Do you think it was getting hit on the head that made him . . . like that? Not all there?"

Ember thought about that. "Balfry was different even before his encounter with Lyrica. He used to guard the deepstone tower day and night before the theft. Sometimes I wonder if the stone itself did something to him. Just being close to it, you know?"

A shudder traveled up Spade's back, and a droplet of rain hit his forehead. He looked up, and several more droplets splattered across his coat.

A friendly croak sounded and Ash swooped low and landed on Ember's shoulder. He nuzzled her for treats.

Spade sighed. "I think it's time you told me why yer always so determined to get in trouble."

Ember crossed her arms and glared at him, as if deciding something. "My parents were on the expedition," she said at last. "The one that never returned. They were adventurers, courageous and bold. Some of the guards used to tell me stories about them, though the queen never speaks of them herself."

Understanding began to creep over Spade. She was lonely and missing her parents. And she wanted to prove herself—a feeling he knew well.

"I won't end up like my aunt," she whispered, her voice wobbly. "Locked inside my rooms."

Spade met her gaze and nodded. "I get it now." He glanced at Ash, who took to the air again, flying free. He'd hate to be pent up in the castle all day. "I'm sorry. For misjudging you."

"Well. Um, I'm sorry too. For earlier. On the moors. And, you know . . . looking down on you."

A small grin tweaked his lips.

"So . . ." She looked away, obviously not used to making apologies. "Are you going to tell me what you saw in the mud?"

Spade hesitated. But if he was going to find this old lady, he could use some help.

He gestured at the ground. "Tree roots. But there's no tree 'round this part of the hill. An' it's almost as if they're growing in a funny pattern."

Ember's eyes widened a fraction as she bent to stare at the ground. She swiveled, looking over the hillside. "I . . . I didn't think the stories were true."

"What stories?"

"About my great-aunt." She stared at the roots, face pale. "And her powers."

CHAPTER 25

TRACKING A GHOST

Thunder rumbled overhead and the rain thickened, darkness surrounding them as the clouds blocked out the moon. Ash swept down and landed on Spade's shoulder as he and Ember ran down for the crooked elm, sheltering under its leaves.

"What kind of powers do they say yer great-aunt had?" Spade asked Ember when they'd escaped the rain.

"Well." She thought for a moment. "She could grow plants better than anyone—they say the castle gardens were incredible once. Some people even said that she could talk to them, and they grew according to her will."

Thoughts whirled in Spade's mind. "You mean to say she can control trees?" He stared out into the night, thinking. "The roots are moving in the same direction," he muttered, "heading uphill." His eyes widened. "That's how she did it."

"Did what?"

"Moved the bench all the way here! She commanded the tree roots to push it."

Ember's eyes lit up. "Wait a minute—didn't the guard say that something wrapped around his ankle when he met her? And he didn't see what it was?"

"Must've been roots," Spade agreed. "It's how she broke in and stole the deepstone."

Excitement tugged at him. "Maybe, if we follow them . . ." Reaching into his pocket, he drew out the glow-slugs Benji had given him.

"Ugh." Ember's eyes locked on the slugs. "What are those?"

"Oh, uh. Glow-slugs. I . . . found them."

Ember frowned, and he knew her truth-sensor thing was going off. But instead of saying anything, she drew closer and poked at one. "Weird."

"Yup. But they make a better light than a lantern because they don't go out if it's wet." He ducked out from under the tree, limp-hopping up the hill.

"Wait," she called. "I'm coming with you."

Glow-slugs held high, they followed the protruding roots along the ground using the eerie green light, until at last they came to the far side of the cemetery and a high stone wall.

"She must've come from here," Spade said, eyeing the wall. "But I didn't think there was a gate on this side . . ." He walked along it, feeling along the wall, until they reached a patch of ivy.

Pushing it aside, he grinned. A small wooden door sat nestled in the stone wall, its handle worn and rusted.

Ember's eyes sparkled with curiosity in the glow-slug light.

"Here goes nothing."

He reached out, fingers wrapping around the handle, and pulled.

A grassy hillside stretched before them in the dark, boulders strewn throughout, casting strange shadows in the moonlight. A steep slope rose beyond it, meandering into the foothills of the mountains. Spade stepped out into the wind and rain, holding up the glow-slugs.

"I can't make anything out," said Ember, her voice muffled under her hood.

They needed something brighter than the glow-slugs to see what was out there. Spade slipped off his pack and dug through it, pulling out the lantern. He rummaged in his soaked pants, searching for matches.

"Crud," he muttered, and then felt something cold and smooth—the moon-gem. Of course!

He pulled it out, and the pebble reflected the moonlight with an iridescent glow, illuminating the darkness. They followed the tree roots up the hill and into the rock, where they disappeared beneath the ground.

"Now where?" Ember asked, raising her voice against the wind and spattering rain.

Spade shook his head, frustrated, and held the stone up high. He searched the craggy nooks, trying to find something, anything to give them a clue to the old lady. Ash cawed suddenly and swooped down to his shoulder, peck-ing his ear sharply.

"What's wrong, Ash?" Spade shifted around, casting the pebble's light out across the rocks.

A glimmer of something winked in the night, followed by a scuffling noise.

Spade froze, Ember beside him.

"What was that?" she hissed.

They stared into the rain, and then a snort sounded. Spade swung around, and the pebble's dim light reflected off a pair of pale, luminescent eyes.

Eyes he'd seen before, deep within the castle walls.

Another pair of eyes joined the first, followed by another. Several misshapen shadows scuttled around in the dark, surrounding them.

"What—what are they?" whispered Ember, her voice scratchy. "What do they want?"

The eyes blinked, creeping between the rocks, edging closer.

Spade and Ember took a step back.

The nearest one approached the edge of the pebble's circle of light, remaining just out of view, then halted.

The moon-gem pebble seared with heat in Spade's hand, and he nearly dropped it. It flared brighter, and he froze, staring at it.

"Ember," he hissed.

But her gaze was already fixed on the pebble, her mouth open.

A high-pitched grunt made them jerk their gazes to the nearest of the strange creatures as it backed up, ramming into the others. A cacophony of their shrill warbles filled the air.

On the wind came a sour, stale scent.

The creatures' eyes disappeared as quickly as they'd arrived, and a billowing mass of black seeped through the wooden gate in the cemetery, across the rocky hillside.

Spade and Ember backed against a boulder as the mist surrounded them. Something writhed in the center of black smoke, taking shape and gathering into a gnarled, bent creature right in front of them.

Spade gripped the pebble, its light washing over the Woegan.

Its onyx eyes burned with fury, rimmed with raw, red flesh set deep in its face. Folds of scarred skin drooped down its cheeks and over four protruding fangs. Dark, tangled black hair covered its body, its mammoth feet lined with six hooked claws each. Dozens of thin, glistening spikes blanketed its shoulders, a grotesque sort of armor. It was like nothing Spade had ever seen. Not even digging up corpses could prepare him for the sight.

A scream ripped from Ember's throat as the creature lunged for Spade. Slammed backward, Spade sprawled on the ground, the breath knocked out of him. The Woegan lumbered forward and bent its great hulk over him, gaze fixed on the pebble. One by one, its claws extended and it reached for the moon-gem in Spade's hand.

The stone seared Spade's palm with a sudden, painful surge, flaring bright. The Woegan jolted, stumbling backward, as a wave of light surged toward it. It snarled and lashed out, wrapping its claws around Spade's neck.

Spade choked, fighting for breath as the creature forced

him to look into the endless black pits of its eyes. Humming buzzed in his brain, and his thoughts melded together, confused and jumbled.

Why not just give the pebble over? he found himself wondering. *What was all the fuss 'bout? This creature needed it. But Spade didn't, did he?*

He couldn't quite remember.

His grip loosened on the pebble. He felt himself hold it up, extending it to the creature before him.

"Spade!" Ember screamed, her voice far away.

He glimpsed Ash, tearing down toward the Woegan like an avenging dark angel. Ember lifted a heavy stick, and with a bloodcurdling scream, she jabbed it at the creature's back. The Woegan snarled and turned its gaze from Spade, whirling on the girl and the raven.

Spade blinked, his mind released from the sudden fog. He scrambled backward and hauled himself to his feet, leg aching. The creature descended on Ember, entwining her in its tendrils. Ash shrieked and dove at its head, and Spade yanked his slingshot from his pocket.

Scooping a stone from the ground, the moon-gem still clutched in his palm, he aimed, hitting the monster square in the back of its head.

It roared and released her, turning and lashing out in a movement faster than Spade thought possible. He lunged to the side, his bad leg collapsing beneath him.

Sprawling backward into a deep puddle, he looked up at the creature, the moon-gem glowing in his palm. The creature lowered its shadowed head to his, the meaty stench of its breath roiling Spade's stomach.

He closed his eyes and awaited the feel of its razor-edged claws. He felt it pause, its warped face only a foot from his own.

Cracking open an eye, he saw that the creature wasn't looking at him. It stared at the puddle surrounding them, its onyx gaze fastened on the moon-gem's light reflected on the water.

An unearthly howl ripped from its lungs, the ear-piercing sound tearing through Spade. Ember dropped to her knees and Ash cawed shrilly, blasted backward by an unseen force.

Spade rolled to the side as the creature brought its fist down in the water and rose to its full height, another scream shattering the night.

Hands covering his ears, Spade grit his teeth against the white-hot pain in his leg and scrambled for cover as Ember dove behind a rock nearby.

An abrupt silence settled over the dark.

Trembling, Spade peered out from behind his rock. Ember's ashen face popped up from behind her own rock a few feet away.

The hillside lay empty, the Woegan having disappeared into the gloom.

Darkness surrounded them, all signs of pale-eyed creatures gone.

The rain pattered to a stop, and Spade and Ember stood in front of the secret gate to the cemetery once more. Ember's hair stuck out in a frizzled mess beneath her cap; Spade was so water-logged that his shoes squished when he walked.

"So," said Ember. "That was pretty exciting." She said it nonchalantly, but her wild eyes betrayed her, her voice high-pitched with fear.

Spade's heart was still pounding in his chest. "I'm not sure I'd call it exciting. Maybe a vomit-like kinda thrilling."

Ember glanced up at the stone wall of the cemetery. "At least we learned a few things, like the fact that the creature is interested in your moon-gem."

They edged back through the door, cautious, and their voices sank to a whisper. "Looks like it," he agreed.

"If the pebble is something the creature wants, it's proof that it's no ordinary moon-gem, right?" she continued. "But why didn't it just take it?"

"It tried." The memory of the creature's eyes boring into his made Spade shudder. It wanted it badly, of that Spade was certain. The pebble had seared hot and nearly burned his fingers off when the creature had reached for the stone. And the creature had tried to get into his thoughts, to force him to give in to it. "I get the feeling it can't take it," he murmured, "unless I offer it. Like it's attached to me, somehow."

"That makes sense. But what scared it away?"

"Something 'bout the puddle, I think." He shook his head. "But I got no idea what." He glanced back at the water and mud-soaked hill. "C'mon. I don't wanna run into the creature again out here, or those green-eyed things."

"What were those?" Ember asked, curious, as they walked through the cemetery.

"Dunno," he whispered. They moved quietly now.

"Do you think the Woegan's gone?"

Spade glanced at Ash, riding on his shoulder. "He'd let us know if it was coming," Spade said, nodding. "I'm pretty sure it's back in whatever dark hole it came from. Not to mention the stone would be glowing in my pocket, burning a hole in my leg."

He ducked through the bushes and slipped through the gate to where the horses were tied. "We'd better get you back to the castle before they find you're missing," Spade said. He pulled himself up onto Pronto, who shifted nervously.

Ash stilled on his shoulder and uttered a sharp caw.

"It's a little late for that," a rough voice rang through the dark.

A tall, familiar figure detached itself from the shadows that surrounded them. Henchcliff jerked his chin, and three other guards stepped out of the shadows on either side of the path behind Spade.

Spade uttered a curse. He should have known there was something wrong from Pronto's edginess.

"Escort the royal niece back to her rooms," Henchcliff growled at the guards. His eyes drifted over Ember, coming to rest on Spade and Ash.

"I will deal with the Joolie."

CHAPTER 26
THE KIDNAPPER

His feet dragged along the ground as two guards hauled Spade into Wyndhail castle's gatehouse, following the sharp snap of Henchcliff's cloak as he strode up ahead.

"Toss him in there," Henchcliff barked, and the guards obediently hauled Spade into a shadowed corner of the gatehouse, then dumped him into a hole as wide and tall as a man. A barred door slammed shut over his head and they retreated quickly, leaving him alone with the queen's captain of the guard.

Henchcliff peered down at Spade, his eyes flashing with malice. "It's called the grave-pit," the captain spat. "An appropriate place for the likes of you. You'll sit here in silence and wait."

A dark shadow swept overhead, and Ash landed on a narrow ledge above the hole. He uttered an angry caw, and Henchcliff jerked his chin at the bird. "That goes for the demon bird as well."

The captain whirled and strode away. "Horace, watch him," Spade heard him snarl. Footsteps sounded and another guard's shadow loomed across the hole as he took his position nearby.

Spade sighed and huddled against the far corner of the cell. He thought of Benji somewhere below him in the dungeons. He wished he'd been thrown back in the cell with his brother—at least then he'd have had the chance to say goodbye.

He lay back against the cold dirt and squeezed his eyes shut.

The sound of sharp voices jolted Spade awake sometime later, and two guardsmen peered down into his hole.

The barred cover flew open and the guards hauled him out, then dragged him across the courtyard.

"Where are we going—" he tried to ask, but his teeth knocked together as they jostled him up the castle steps and through the great doors.

Ash swept in through the grand entrance before the guards could stop him, following closely behind.

They reached a heavy oak doorway. Henchcliff stood at attention beside it, his stance rigid, mouth pressed in a thin line. The guards dropped Spade on the floor and Henchcliff reached down and hauled him up by his collar. "There's no easy way out of this one, boy," he snarled in his ear.

With a sharp push, the captain of the guard shoved Spade into the room. Spade stumbled and sprawled across the floor, bruised and panting. Ash darted in after him, perching in the shadowed rafters like a watchful specter.

Dim-lit with a few sconces, the room stretched long and narrow, the far wall lined with arched windows. The Craiggarock Mountains rose in the distance through the glass panes, the morning sun beginning to peek across the sky. Queen Carmelia sat on a raised dais at the far end of the room in a blue silken dress, her skin almost translucent. Her sapphire necklace matched the dress and the cold blue of her eyes, though dark circles hung beneath them. Her pale hands gripped the armrests of her throne, the Moor Mage's emerald ring glittering on her finger. Spinniker stood beside her, mustache drooping, a severe look on his lined face.

"And what made you think that kidnapping the royal niece would be helpful in keeping your head in its place?" The queen enunciated each word, her voice brimming with anger. "I trusted you to find Lady Lyrica, and instead my captain finds you holding my niece hostage in a cemetery, likely robbing graves."

Spade swallowed hard. If he gave up Ember's secret, she'd be punished. But if he didn't, he'd never see Benji again. And he would not lose Benji—he couldn't. He just needed to buy a bit of time to think. He cleared his throat, mind churning frantically.

Before he could speak, a commotion sounded in the hallway, and Ember burst through the door, her face flushed and angry. A guard followed close on her heels, limping and rubbing his knee as he frowned at the back of her head.

The queen's scowl deepened. "Ember, I asked you to stay in your rooms. You need rest after your ordeal with this Joolie thief."

"He didn't kidnap me," Ember shouted. The queen turned her head sharply. "I followed him. I snuck out when Henchcliff went to the market."

Lips drawn in a thin, white line, the queen's face darkened.

Spinniker shuffled closer to the throne, his voice low. "Majesty, perhaps we should discuss this tomorrow. You do not want to tax yourself . . ."

"Why," the queen interrupted her advisor, her glare fastened on Ember. "Why would you do such a foolish thing?"

"Because I am never allowed to do foolish things, or even to decide on my own if they are foolish or not, that's why!" Ember's voice shook, her fists clenched. "You may like this sort of life, holed up in castles, but I don't—I want adventure! I know I can help find the Woegan's master. Your guards have failed you, so why not give me a chance?"

"Those were grown, trained men," the queen snarled. "You are not! Reading storybooks teaches you nothing of the real world and its dangers."

"And do you expect me to learn about the world sitting in a stone cage?" spat Ember. "I know as much as any of your guards. I've encountered the Woegan and survived, haven't I?"

"The Woegan?" Carmelia's face turned a sickly shade, and she rose to her feet.

Spinniker gave a hoarse croak.

"Please, Majesty," Spade stepped forward. "I wasn't robbing graves. I was looking for yer aunt, I swear it. An' I didn't kidnap yer niece. But if it weren't for her, I might not have found a clue regarding yer aunt an' wouldn't have lived long enough to figure out the Woegan's weakness."

Ember glanced at him, and he thought he saw a glitter of appreciation in her eye.

The queen's trembling fingers quieted, and she drew in a long breath. Slowly, she lowered herself back into her throne. After a long moment in which Spade was pretty sure she was contemplating which way he'd die, she leaned back. "Take her to her rooms," she instructed the guard at the door in a cold, clipped tone. "And see she does not leave them."

Ember's hands balled into fists at her sides. The guard bowed, then marched to the girl, but she whirled, eyes spitting fire. "You may lock me up the way you do this castle, Aunt, but it will not stop your nightmares. And it won't stop the Woegan from coming." Her voice shook with anger, and the queen stared at her for a moment, then turned her head away, flicking her hand at the guard.

Ember was escorted out of the room. Henchcliff watched her leave, eyes narrowed.

The queen turned her gaze on Spade. "You have one minute to hold my attention, grave thief."

Spade took a deep breath and said a prayer. Plunging in, he told the queen about the tree roots and their link to the old woman's power. He told her of the Woegan's attack, and how something about the water had scared it. "There was something about its reaction," he finished. "Something that scared it deeply."

"And how do you know that?" Her blue eyes fixed upon him, riveted.

He searched for the right words. The creature's black eyes rose before him, the memory of the hot pulse of the pebble in his hand. That weird sensation . . . like he could feel the creature's thoughts.

Somehow the pebble had allowed him to see into the Woegan's mind.

He paused, warring with himself. He should tell the queen about the pebble, shouldn't he? And yet . . . there was something in him that wanted to keep it a secret. Joolie instinct, maybe. But why shouldn't he? It was his, after all. He'd found it.

"Uh, just a feeling, I guess," he said, careful. "It had a sort of look in its eyes when I saw it up close."

"The boy lies." Henchcliff stepped forward. "He's hiding something. No one's ever looked into its eyes and lived. It mesmerizes its prey."

Spade tensed. "Well, I have. Whether yer wanting to believe me or not."

Henchcliff's lip curled, and Spinniker frowned. "Majesty," Henchcliff growled. "All Joolies are trained in the art of deception—"

But the queen raised a hand, cutting him off. Silence fell over the room.

The guard swept Spade with a venomous look, and Spade knew his instincts had been right about Henchcliff:

the man hated him, he was sure of it. And there was something about him that wasn't right, a haunted sort of look in his eye that spoke of a man with secrets. *Listen to yer gut,* his dad always said. *It knows more than yer brain.*

When Spade did decide to show the queen the pebble, it couldn't be in front of the guardsman.

Queen Carmelia turned to Spade, her eyes lit with a rare spark of emotion, and Spade could swear it looked a bit like hope. "If what you say is true, Joolie, then there's a chance that the creature has a weakness . . ." Her voice trailed off, and the spark in her eyes faded.

"Even so, we are no further ahead. My great-aunt has hidden herself well for decades now. She has become a ghost, impossible to trace."

Spade's stomach tightened, desperate. "Yer Majesty, please. Give me another chance. I can find her, I know it."

But the queen shook her head. "Not even a Joolie can find someone that leaves no trace." A deep sigh rattled her chest and she brought her thin fingers to her forehead, massaging her temple. "Perhaps you are of no use to me anymore, grave thief."

Spade's breath caught. No. He couldn't give up, not with Benji in that forsaken place.

Spinniker stepped forward, concerned. "My lady," he said. "Your headache returns; I must insist you rest."

"Please, Majesty." Spade found his voice, even as it cracked. "Your promise. My brother—"

The queen pinned her pale gaze on Spade. "An impertinent wish, after abetting the escape of the royal niece."

Iron curled in Spade's stomach.

"And yet. I cannot deny that you have brought me useful information, despite everything." She gestured to Henchcliff. "Escort him to the dungeons for one last visit with his brother."

Her gaze turned back to the window. "I will decide both of their fates tomorrow."

CHAPTER 27

INVISIBLE FRIENDS

Benji leaped to his feet in the corner of the cell as Spade approached, Ash flying close behind. Henchcliff ground to a halt in front of the cell.

"You've got an hour," the guardsman rasped, dark eyes scrutinizing the skinny, dirty boy. He unlocked the cell and let Spade inside, shoving a lantern at him, then slammed it shut. Ash slipped through the bars and landed on Spade's shoulder as Henchcliff whirled away, bootsteps fading down the corridor.

"Spade! Ash!" Benji gripped his brother in a fierce hug, his eyes sunken and huge as he blinked, unaccustomed to the bright light of the lantern. "Did you find the Woegan's master?"

Spade swallowed the knot in his throat, noting his brother's pale skin. "Not yet, Benj," he said, his voice almost cracking as he fought to keep it steady. "I'm still working on it."

Disappointment flashed across Benji's face, but he hid it well, forcing a tremulous smile. "'Course," he said. "So . . . why'd they let you down here, then?"

Spade forced confidence to his face. The last thing he needed was for his brother to see his fear. "Well, 'cause the queen promised I could come see you." He reached into his pocket and pulled out some of the bread and nuts he'd been saving, then drew out the little stone wren from the other pocket. "An' I wanted to give you this."

A faint smile cracked Benji's face. "Reminds me of the bird I had when I was small."

"Thought it might."

His brother held the little bird, almost reverent for a moment. He stood and walked to the back of the cell, placing it on a stone shelf beside a little tin box and a thin blanket, things that Spade hadn't noticed before.

"Where'd you get all this stuff, Benj?" he asked. "The guards?"

Benji shook his head. "My friends. They call themselves lumpskins. They bring me little bits of things, an' I tell them stories."

"Lumpskins?" Spade asked, incredulous. "They're real, after all? You've seen them?"

Benji grinned. "One night, I waited up for them. An' sure enough, once the cells were quiet and the guard was snoring, they came sneaking out of the dark, almost like they'd crept right outta the walls. Now they come every night. I tell them stories an' such."

A faint yelp interrupted them, and they whirled. Ash croaked, squinting into the dark, and then a glimpse of blue fabric and a whirling cape, and a small figure appeared in the shadows, seeming to emerge directly from the corridor wall. The person stepped into the light and withdrew their hood.

"Ember," Spade hissed. "What are you doing here?"

She whirled, a basket in her hands, her mouth in a small *o*. "Thank goodness," she breathed. "Those tunnels are confusing, I thought I'd gotten lost."

She must have slipped out of the secret door in her room, Spade realized, and guessed her way to the dungeons.

"You shouldn't be here," he huffed, exasperated. "I can't afford any more trouble."

Guilt flashed across her face. "I . . . I came to bring your brother some food," she said, holding up the basket. "And books. I . . . well, I know you can't read, but maybe you can look at the pictures."

"Benj, meet Ember," Spade said.

Benji's eyes grew wide. "Wow, thanks," he said. "Didn't think I'd ever meet a royal person, let alone be accepting gifts from one."

A wistful look crept across Ember's face. "I'd rather not be a royal anything, actually. Just call me Ember, please."

She reached through the bars, handing Benji the basket. He glanced down and his eyes lit up. "The lumpskins'll love these."

"What are lumpskins?"

"Benji's invisible critter friends," Spade grunted, "which are none of yer business."

"They're not invisible," Benji muttered. "You just can't see them all the time."

"Invisible?" Ember's eyes lit up with curiosity.

"Oh, no you don't." Spade scowled, turning his gaze on Ember. "This don't concern you. You've given him yer gift, an' now you've gotta leave before any of us get caught."

"Wait," Ember pleaded. "I also came to find you. I knew you'd be down here because I overheard Spinniker talking." She twisted her hands together and met Spade's gaze. "I wanted to say I'm sorry for the trouble I've caused. Spinniker told me that my aunt is deciding your fate tomorrow."

Benji stiffened, and Spade felt his brother's gaze on him. "You didn't say nothing 'bout that, Spade," he said, his voice hoarse.

Spade swallowed. "I didn't want to worry you none."

"Worry me none? What happened to telling each other everything?"

Ember looked between them, face pale. "Well, I, for one, haven't given up. I've been poring over my books." She reached into the bottom of her basket and held up a thick volume, *Wyndhail's Witches and Mages*. "There's got to be a clue in here about her, one that we've missed. Witches aren't usually very inconspicuous—it goes with the territory of poisoning apples and eating princesses and summoning thornbushes . . ."

Benji nodded. "Hmm. Maybe not all witches are the same. That doesn't sound like the witch the lumpskins serve."

They all turned to stare at Benji, even Ash.

"Or at least," he amended, "I've never heard of her eating any princesses. 'Course, maybe she does in her spare time—"

"Benj!" Spade interrupted, his chest seizing. "Who are you talking about?!"

Benji shrugged. "The lumpskins mention her sometimes, in their funny kinda talk. I saw them gathering moss from the walls, an' glow-slugs an' stuff. They told me they're bringing it to her."

Ember frowned. "What is this woman called?"

Benji shrugged. "Dunno. The lumpskins call her the Lady. They say she's got magic, an' she uses the herbs an' slugs an' things for her concoctions."

"It's her!" Spade breathed. "I know it!"

"What d'you mean?"

"The witch that the queen wants Spade to find," Ember explained, excited. "She's believed to have stolen one of the deepstones from the Tower of Wyndhail."

"Did they say where she lives, Benj?" Spade asked, excited.

"Nope. They're pretty secretive. But it can't be far. Every night 'round midnight, after visiting her, they show up at my cell ready for stories. If there's no guards, 'course."

Ash nuzzled against Benji, and the boy's face brightened. "I almost forgot, Ash. The lumpskins snitched a tin of cookies last night, an' I saved one fer you." He stood with the lantern and walked to the small stone shelf, rummaging around in the tin box. He pulled out a biscuit for Ash, who gobbled it down while eyeing the little wren on the shelf next to him, as if it might come to life and steal his biscuit. Benji laughed.

Ember's gaze fell on the bird figurine, and she straightened from where she leaned against the bars. "Where did you get that?" she asked, her voice tense.

"Spade gave it to me," Benji said, shooting Spade a glance.

Crud. Spade cringed.

"You stole it," she murmured. "Didn't you?"

"I, well, I found it. Um, in the queen's rooms . . ." He glanced away.

Her lips pursed, eyes flashing. "Once a thief, always a thief, I guess."

He sighed. "Listen, Ember . . . it wasn't like that. It's the only thing I took, I swear on my honor."

"The honor of a Joolie." She shook her head. "I should have known. I thought you actually wanted to help. That you were more than just a thief."

Spade stared at her, trying to think of something to say. Ash flew to her shoulder, nuzzling at her ear, but she glared at them both, shaking the raven off.

"You didn't stop to think, did you?" Her voice was cold, quiet. "That bird isn't just any bird."

Benji went to the shelf and took the wren down. "The queen can have it back, Ember," he pleaded. "Spade didn't mean no harm . . ."

Bootsteps rang out in the hall, interrupting them. Ember jolted away from the bars of the cell, into the shadows of the corridor. She cast them one last silent look, then slipped through the hidden entrance and back into the tunnels.

Spade stared after her a moment, and he felt Benji press the stone wren into his pocket. "Give it back to her, okay?" he whispered.

"Time's up," Henchcliff called, bootsteps drawing near.

The guard's frame filled the doorway, hand resting on his belt, ruby buckle flashing in the lanternlight.

"Say your goodbyes."

CHAPTER 28

A MEETING
IN THE DARK

The big hand on the clocktower inched toward the twelve, and Spade crept out of his bed. Thirty minutes to midnight. He hoped it would be enough time. The guard stationed outside his door yawned and stretched, humming an off-key tune.

Spade crept to the window and peered into the dark.

Ash perched on a stone gargoyle beneath a window on the castle wall opposite Spade. A pair of telltale purple frilly curtains could be seen through the glass, lit by a dim lamp in the room.

Ember's room.

The big hand on the clock moved: twenty-five minutes to midnight.

Ash croaked once, low and short, the signal that the coast was clear.

And then Spade was teetering barefoot on his windowsill, his pack strapped to his back. He inched forward slowly, his bare toes gripping the stone and mortar, fingers digging deep into the narrow crevices that ran between the stones of the wall. One foot in front of the other, ignoring the ache in his crooked leg. Ash circled above him, uttering a soft croak.

The first gargoyle loomed beneath him, and his toes found a hold: one foot in the gargoyle's mouth, between his two lower fangs, the other in his angry stone eye sockets. He risked a glance at the clock. Fifteen minutes.

More inching. His back began to sweat, and his palms trembled. He didn't dare look the seventy or so feet down to the ground.

Whistling drifted toward him as he reached the second gargoyle. Grabbing onto its wings, he clambered up onto its body and crouched down on its back, trying to resemble a hump. Ash landed beside him, beady eyes focused on the ground.

A guard ambled past. All of a sudden, he stopped directly beneath him.

Crud, Spade thought.

He peered between the gargoyle's wings, recognizing the humming guard from the banquet room—the one Ember said had gone a bit loopy after his time spent guarding the deepstone.

The man raised his head slowly and his eyes found Spade.

Spade's breath stuck in his chest.

The guard smiled, tipping his hat at Spade.

Spade froze. The man turned and ambled away, humming once more.

A whoosh of breath escaped Spade, too relieved to question what had just happened. Either the guard really had lost it, or he was Spade's guardian angel. Spade shook his head, then climbed onto the tip of the gargoyle's wing.

Latching onto Ember's windowsill, he pulled himself up, then pushed the pane open a crack and slipped down into the room. Ash dipped in beside him, landing on his shoulder.

The lone lantern still flickered in the window, Ember a lump asleep in her bed.

A pang of guilt crept over Spade. Ember would want to come with him, but he couldn't risk Benji's life again. If he somehow succeeded, he'd apologize later.

Slipping his hand in his pocket, he pulled out the little stone wren.

With practiced skill, he slunk silently across the room and peered into her bed. Her mess of red hair splayed across the pillow. He reached out to place the figurine on the pillow, then paused. There was something peculiar about her hair—he leaned in closer, then narrowed his eyes. A wooden knob jutted out from the center of the tangled red strands.

The hair wasn't hair at all. It was a mop.

He shoved the wren back into his pocket.

Bong! Bong!

The first chimes of midnight rang in the clocktower outside, and a faint breeze tickled Spade's arm. His gaze caught on the slight flutter of the tapestry that hung on the far wall.

Spade was pretty sure he knew where Ember had gone.

Cold air blasted Spade, Ash's talons gripping his shoulder as he limped through the tunnels, his glow-slugs casting a dim light before them.

They descended deeper and another sharp breeze tore around the corner. He pulled his jacket tight and rounded a bend, holding the slugs high, when Ash croaked a sharp warning.

Squelch, squelch, squish.

The odd, familiar sound carried on the breeze, reverberating along the tunnel walls. He'd heard that sound before.

The creatures.

Squish, squish, squelch.

It grew louder, joined by a cacophony of grunts and warbling. He froze, pressing his back up against the wall. He shoved the slugs into his pocket, hiding the light.

The wind rushed by in the pitch-black, dozens of warbling voices carried with it, and the sound of flapping, squelching feet, a whirlwind of noise. Dozens of somethings rumbled by, and then there was silence.

He waited a long moment, then crept out of hiding, rounding a bend in the tunnel. He stepped forward, and his foot landed on something soft.

Something alive.

Something that wrapped its bony fingers around his arm.

"Argghh!"

The yell-scream blasted Spade backward, and he knocked his head against the wall, Ash croaking as he leaped off Spade's shoulder.

A small voice sounded in the dark. "Spade?"

"You," he muttered. "I knew it."

He heard some shuffling, then a swish, and a lantern flared to life, revealing Ember's startled expression, eyes wide in fright. Her gaze narrowed as he rubbed his head, scowling.

"Well, it was you who stepped on my foot," she grumped. "I suppose you're busy escaping. After you steal a few more things, of course."

"You know I'd never leave Benj. I'm here to find the creatures an' ask them 'bout the witch."

"Sounds like we had the same idea." She glanced down the tunnel. "And it looks like we found them. At least I think it was them. Were those the same creatures outside Wyndhail cemetery?"

Spade bent down to the ground, squinting at the small imprints of strange, flat-footed feet in the dirt. "Pretty sure. An' I'm thinking they're Benji's friends."

Ember bit her lip. "I was kind of hoping they'd be cute. Or at least furry. Like little bunny-monsters or something."

Spade snorted. "Believe me, they ain't furry forest critters."

Ember gulped. "Well, I guess it's time we found out."

CHAPTER 29

LUMPSKINS

"An' that's when the evil ogre Drucinda jumped out of the cave an' gobbled up her wart-covered ogre-prince Borgol! She got a terrible stomachache afterwards, of course." Benji's voice drifted down the corridor to the small tunnel entrance where Spade and Ember crouched.

Sounds of squeaky laughter echoed off the walls. "We likes it, Benjini!" several voices cried. "We wants more!"

Spade and Ember crept forward, listening.

"Okay," Benji's voice came. "But this time, I wanna read my favorite. The dragon that burned down the bakery an' ate all the muffins."

"Oooooh, we loves muffins, Benjini! We sneaks seventeen of them today from the castle bakery! Cook was red and squishy in her face, and she yells and yells!"

"It's not smart to steal from the cook," said Benji, in his best scolding voice. "You might get caught." He paused. "Did you bring me any?"

Rustling, and then, "Hmmmm, shoclite ship, my fravrite . . ." came Benji's muffled voice, full of muffin.

Spade peered around the corner, Ember beside him. Benji sat on his hard bunk, surrounded by several large gray lumps. Some sat on the floor as well, while still others perched on his table, his toilet bucket and the bars of his cell.

"Benji?" Spade took a hesitant step forward, and Ember raised the lantern, the fingers of light spreading across the floor.

Benji looked up. In an instant, the lumps vanished.

"Spade!" he cried, then lowered his voice. "Ember!"

He glanced around his cell. "It's okay, these are my friends: my brother and Miss Ember, the royal niece."

Silence.

Then one gray shape flickered into view, seated beside Benji.

Spade took another cautious step, peering into the cell.

A small, lumpy creature the color of mottled stone stared back at him, tiny, pale eyes blinking in its wide, wrinkled face, two button-sized ears on its oversized head. Spade couldn't tell where its belly ended and its neck began; its body was rounded, with folds upon folds of warty skin, and it was about the size of a chicken. It rose to its feet, which resembled flat flippers, and then a *pffft* sound filled the room along with the smell of rotten eggs.

"Excuses me," the creature said. "I gets gassy when I's is nervous."

Spade forced a smile, holding his breath. "It's okay," he choked.

The creature extended a long-fingered hand in an attempted handshake, and Spade stared at its sharp claws. With a sudden jolt, he realized that these were the creatures that he and Ash had stumbled upon in the tunnels.

The creature followed his gaze to its claws and frowned. "We's is sorry abouts our first meeting," it offered. "We's was scared."

"Same here," Spade said. He shot a wry look at Ember. "Cute enough for you?" he whispered.

Ember's eyes watered at the smell. "B-big-headed can be beautiful," she stammered in a low voice.

The lumpskin's tiny eyes examined Spade, then it turned its head around the cell, making a sharp signal with one long finger.

One by one, other lumpskins appeared, melting into their gray color, and Spade blinked.

"Goodness," Ember murmured, "I think they're rock goblins. I saw them in a very old book once, a long time ago . . ."

"Whatever they are, they're real good at camouflaging," Benji agreed. "The guards have no idea 'bout their night-time visits."

Spade and Ember watched as a lumpy shape that blended perfectly with the thin blue blanket shifted back into its natural mottled gray, transforming before their eyes. Another lumpskin appeared on top of the toilet-bucket, while several others materialized from the walls around them. At last, nineteen stone-colored creatures were revealed. They stood silent, small eyes squinted and cautious.

The first one to appear wiggled its ears slightly and stuck out its long-fingered hand. Spade stepped forward to shake it.

In one quick movement, the creature pulled Spade toward it. It opened its wide mouth and stuck a long, black tongue out, then licked his hand.

"Ugh!" Spade jerked back, but the creature's grip was like steel.

"He tastes . . . good!" the lumpskin announced, and the other lumpskins muttered in approval, nodding their heads. Spade darted a look at his brother, and Ember's eyes widened in fear.

Benji, for his part, grinned from ear to ear. "He means that you taste *good*, like in yer heart. Not the delicious kinda good."

Spade stared down at the creature, who shook his hand with enthusiasm. "Nice to meets you, brother-of-Benjini and Royal Miss. They calls me Grubble. Please excuses my licking. Lumpskins can never be too careful."

Spade frowned. "How does evil taste, then?"

Grubble's eyes narrowed. "Like mouldy cheese."

"How come you didn't taste her?" Spade demanded, jerking his chin at Ember.

Ember glared at him.

"Cause Grubbles smells her." The lumpskin's wobbly mouth stretched in a smile. "She is a truth-teller, and truth-tellers is always good."

Spade snorted and Ember grinned. Grubble turned his gaze on Ash, perched on Spade's shoulder. The raven squawked, beady eyes flashing.

"Maybe Grubbles don't licks that one," he decided. The lumpskin settled back, crossing his spindly arms over his fat belly. "What is Benjini's brother Spade doing down here, deep in dungeons? Are you freeings our friend?"

"We're tryin' to," Spade said. "I—I have an agreement with the queen. If I can stop the Woegan, she'll set Benji free."

The lumpskin raised its eyebrows, even as several of the lumpskins hissed at the name. "The dark creature is our fearsomest enemy," Grubble said. "It eats us when it catches us."

Spade took a deep breath. "Well, that's kinda why we're here, actually. We thought maybe you could help us, an' we could help you in return. We need something powerful to kill the Woegan with, something that we think the Lady Lyrica might have—the one they call a witch. D'you know her?"

The lumpskins stirred, and Grubble's face rippled in an expression Spade couldn't read.

A smaller lumpskin jumped up on the bunk next to Grubble. "We's can't tells them, Grubble," he warbled in a whisper-yell. "Lady's secrets aren't for humanishes."

Grubble peered over the top of the lumpskin's head at them. "True, true," he agreed. "They's is humanishes, even if they tastes good." He cocked his wrinkled head and looked at his friend. "But what ifs they gives us their word, Fidget? And closes their eyes?"

Fidget frowned, or at least Spade thought it was a frown, as his folds of skin drooped under his chin. "Fidgets don't thinks theys will fits through the secret spot."

"We's can tries, though?" He glanced at Benji, who sat solemn, observing their conversation.

Fidget looked at Benji. His eyes welled with tears. "But Fidgets likes his stories. If Benjini don't lives here, Fidgets gets no stories. And then the queen will fills his cell with another humanish. A *bad* humanish, that don't likes tellings stories and don't likes sticky toffee puddings."

"I can still tell you stories," Benji said, his voice firm. "We're friends no matter what, ain't we? An' you can find me wherever I am. I know it, 'cause you can smell so good."

Fidget twiddled his fingers together, considering. He heaved a sigh and kicked at the blanket. "Okay, let's votes. All in favor of bringing the humanishes to the Lady, raises their ears."

One by one, nineteen pairs of ears flickered upward.

"It's decided," Grubble said. "We takes you to her. It's our best hopes to stop the Woegan."

He paused suddenly, his small ears twitching. Lifting his wide nose into the air, his nostrils flared, and his hands started to shake.

The warbling lumpskins quieted, all their nostrils flaring at once. At the same moment, Spade felt a familiar heat warm his pocket.

"The creature comes down the far passages." Grubble turned to Ember and Spade. "We's must moves quick."

CHAPTER 30
THE BATTLE

Cold air blasted them in the face, shuddering down their bones as Spade and Ember raced through the dark, following the sound of flapping feet.

"This ways," Grubble grunted. "To the left."

They veered sharply, Spade feeling the walls, trying not to trip on his own feet. The lumpskins had insisted on leaving the lantern behind, the glow-slugs hidden in Spade's pocket. "No lights," Grubble warned. "We uses noses and earses instead."

A faint, familiar stench whirled through the tunnels behind them, carried on the chill breeze. Spade paused, thinking of Benji sitting scared and alone in his cell.

But safe, he reminded himself.

"Mustn't slows down," Grubble warned them, somewhere to their right. They followed his voice, and the stench grew stronger.

The *squelch, squelch* of lumpskin feet stopped ahead of them, and a blast of rank air greeted them.

"Creature's turned," Grubble warbled. "Fidget! Take some of us and stalls it! We goes another way!"

Squelching feet echoed in the dark as lumpskins rushed around them like a tidal wave.

Then Grubble was beside them, gripping Spade's hand in one clawed fist, Ember's in the other. He pulled them along now, guiding them through tunnels that didn't feel like the dungeon's smooth stone anymore, but rougher and narrower.

"Waits!" Grubble ordered, and a pinprick of light flared to life ahead of them.

Spade stared at the tip of the lumpskin's pinky, glowing orange in the dark, and he jolted in surprise, while Ember squeaked in alarm.

"We each has a pinky light," the lumpskin explained. "A sorts of magic that our kind has."

"Amazing," Spade breathed.

"We can't use it long, the creature mights see it," Grubble said, "buts you humanishes need lights for this part." The soft glow spread through the rough-hewn tunnel and its downward-sloped ceiling, illuminating a small opening at its end.

"We has to squishy you through that hole," he explained, the orange light washing over his determined, wrinkly face. "Yous is small humanishes, not full-grown yet, and Grubbles thinks yous is still able."

Ember's eyes widened, but she nodded.

Spade swallowed. "Like a grave," he muttered to Ash,

who clacked his beak nervously. "It'll be just like crawling into a grave. Nothing we haven't done, right, Ash?" He clutched the raven to his chest and he and Ember hurried toward the hole, following the herd of lumpskins, Grubble's glowing finger like a beacon in the dark.

The first lumpskins dove in, Ember crouched on the lip of the hole, when a tornado of wind rushed through the tunnel behind them, knocking her into Spade and the lumpskins. They sprawled on the cavern floor, black smoke rising thick in the air around them as Grubble teetered to his feet, pale eyes wide with fear.

"Creature's come," he whispered, and his finger-light vanished, leaving them in darkness.

"Where is it?" Ember croaked, as they pressed up against the tunnel wall.

The air grew thick with its stench, and the *clack, scrape* of claws on rock reached them.

The pebble in Spade's pocket seared to life, its light spilling out across the tunnel.

The Woegan crouched on all fours less than thirty feet away, its hulking, hairy body pressed against the walls. A blast of foul wet-dog smell wafted over them, and its red-rimmed gaze locked onto his.

Spade slammed his eyelids shut. "Don't meet its eyes, Ember," he hissed. "Just make a run fer it."

They whirled and lunged at the hole carved in the wall. Ember was halfway through when a dark tentacle wormed across the ground and wrapped around her leg, hauling her back out of the hole.

Spade whipped his head around to see the Woegan's wraithlike tendrils curl toward him, and he stumbled to the side.

The beast flicked a finger and the smoke tentacles tightened, dragging Ember toward it.

Spade lunged for her and grabbed her wrist. He clung to her, digging his heels into the ground, ignoring the pain in his leg. "Let her go!" he yelled, panic erupting in his chest. The Woegan's magic crept up, encircling both her legs.

"Spade!" Ember screamed. Black mist crept over her face, obscuring her as it dragged them both across the jagged floor.

Gray bodies swarmed over them, warbling and hissing. Before their eyes, the little lumpskins linked arms and moved as one, spreading across the tunnel floor. They piled into a tower and surged up and over the creature, biting down with their razor-sharp teeth.

The Woegan growled and ripped several off, its black coils bashing dozens of others against the cavern walls. And yet those remaining kept up the attack, Grubble leading the charge.

"We's is here!" A high-pitched warble rang out, and Fidget's group rounded the corner, leaping onto the Woegan from behind. The beast stumbled and thrashed, its jaws opening in a roar. Dozens of lumpskins hit the ground, gashed by claws, bleeding and stumbling, and still they fought. Buoyed by their courage, Spade clung to Ember's arm with every ounce of strength he had left, tears burning the backs of his eyes.

The creature's curling tendrils of smoke released Ember and Spade and flung them backward. Gasping and coughing, they scrambled to safety, where they watched in horror as the Woegan shrieked, flinging the brave lumpskins off its back.

"I've gotta do something," Spade yelled to Ember. Desperation and fear hit him, and as if in answer, the pebble seared into his leg, and he remembered when the Woegan reached for it on that cold, wet night, how it had burned the creature.

He shoved his fingers into his pocket and closed his hand around the pebble's warmth. A strange, sharp feeling curled up his arm and coursed through him, and he stumbled in shock.

Gold tendrils rippled out of the pebble as Ash shrieked at his shoulder, claws digging into him in fear. Ember gasped, but he barely noticed.

His body shook, the tendrils cutting a path straight for the Woegan.

The monster stilled. Lumpskins hobbled to their feet, eyes wide.

The pebble's golden stream whirled around the Woegan, then converged on its massive body, swarming it. The creature snarled and hunched over, its tendrils retreating. As power surged through him, Spade felt a strange sense of excitement. For perhaps the first time in his life, he wasn't weak. He clung to the stone, took a step forward.

And stumbled. His foot caught on a rock, and he lost focus.

The Woegan's head snapped up, narrowing in on Spade. It roared, sending a black maelstrom of magic surging toward him, writhing and twisting like a thousand snakes.

"Spade!" screamed Ember.

He crashed against the tunnel wall, his bones shuddering at the impact. The pebble flew out of his hand as his aching leg buckled beneath him, white-hot pain slicing through it.

The pebble bounced across the ground and rolled to a stop several feet from the Woegan.

The Woegan's eyes flickered in triumph and a twisted grin carved itself across its face.

And then something strong lifted Spade, and he was being carried on a sea of lumpskins, Ember carried along behind him.

"No!" he screamed. "The stone!"

"Can't go back!" Grubble grunted beneath him. "Creature will gobbles you up."

The pebble flared as they whisked him toward the hole in the tunnel wall. He struggled against them. "It's mine," he panted, and a terrible desperation raged through him. "I won't let that creature have it!"

Then Ash tore from his shoulder, shooting over the heads of the horde of lumpskins. The raven dove for the pebble as its light began to dim, reaching it in the same instant that the Woegan reared up.

The pebble flickered out, leaving them in darkness.

A quiet swish carried through the tunnel, and a soft thud.

Then a weak, gurgling croak.

"Ash!" Spade roared into the pitch-black. Panic ripped through him, cutting through the fog of his brain.

"No—not Ash—" he wheezed, struggling against the lumpskins' small, wiry hands. "I need to go back for him!"

But the lumpskins moved like an army of rolling boulders, tumbling through the small dirt opening, and Spade and Ember were hurled into the earth.

CHAPTER 31

A SACRIFICE

Bits of dirt and wriggling worms rained down on Spade's head as the lumpskins tugged and carried him along the narrow dirt tunnel, so shallow he couldn't stand up. Ember whimpered somewhere up ahead. Little creatures groaned and grunted all around them.

"They's is so heavy," Spade heard one say, somewhere in the dark. "I knows it," Grubble agreed. "But we keeps going!"

The walls narrowed and the lumpskins surged around them like a raft, buoying them forward. Spade's shoulders were the width of the passage now, and right when he thought he'd get stuck between the walls, they reached another hole, tumbling through it onto a ledge of rock.

Grubble and the other lumpskins held their pinkies up, the glow washing across a mammoth cavern. Stalactites the length of three men jutted down through the dark like jagged teeth, stalagmites protruding from the floor around them. Twinkling green lights shone somewhere high above them, hundreds of glow-slugs crawling along the ceiling.

But the incredible sight was lost on Spade; he could only think of Ash, lying alone somewhere in the dark of the tunnels behind him. An ache burned in his chest.

A blast of wind carried through the tunnel behind them, the stench of the Woegan thick in the air as the lumpskins half-carried, half-dragged them down a steep path.

"Creature's gathering strength," Grubble warbled urgently. "He creeps into the hole, whirls hisselfs into a dark wind. Takes them, quick!" he grunted to the others, then turned and hurried back through the hole.

"Where is he going?" Ember hissed, even as they could hear a lumpskin shriek from somewhere behind them, "The smoke tendrils! They's is coming!"

Dozens of lumpskins fell into a silent line as they wove a path through the dripping stalactites, Spade and Ember at the center. They held their pinkies high like fireflies hovering in the dark, nothing but the sound of their squelching feet echoing through the vast cave.

They began to climb, following a trail the lumpskins seemed to know by heart, until at last, another cold blast of air hit him. But this time it smelled of trees. The tunnel widened, and Spade glimpsed stars above him as the lump-skins flew out of the dark earth into the open.

Rocky foothills spread before them, the sharp peaks of the Craiggarock Mountains jutting up in the distance, lit by the dim creep of dawn. The castle lay just below, silhou-etted against the town of Wyndhail.

The lumpskins cleared a space around Spade and Ember, warbling and whispering as someone hurried through their midst. Spade recognized Fidget as he drew close and lay something soft and feathered in Spade's arms.

"Your Ashes," the small lumpskin said, his voice soft.

Spade swallowed, his throat thick. "Thank you," he whispered.

Spade looked down at the still raven, Fidget's pinky finger casting a soft glow over the long, jagged wound scrawled along Ash's side. Lead settled in Spade's stomach, and he lay his head against the raven's feathered chest as it rose slightly, the flutter of a faint heartbeat under his ear.

He's still alive, Spade realized, his breath stilling. His fingers trembled at the slight movement beneath them. His muscles strung tight, Spade felt a desperate hope sliding through him. *Maybe, just maybe . . .*

"The Lady," Ember murmured, her eyes on Ash. She whirled to Fidget. "Are we close to her home?"

"Close," Fidget said. "Gettings closer."

A roar echoed in the cavern entrance behind them, and they sprang to their feet once more. Fidget stood by the entrance, peering into the dark. After a moment he turned to the others. "We's can waits no longer for Grubbles," he said, in a mournful voice. "Creature's found us."

Lumpskins grabbed on to them, pulling them forward as Spade clutched Ash to his chest. A skinny lumpskin paused, gaze raised to the sky. "The stars are almost sleepings, Fidget."

Fidget looked up. "We goes anyways," he said, voice soft, a flicker of something heavy in his luminous eyes. "We'll never be rids of the creature unless we's do our best. We gets them to the Lady, like we promises."

The thin lumpskin nodded and swallowed, and then Spade and Ember were scrambling upward, buoyed by the lumpskins.

"Hurries, lumpskins!" Fidget warbled. "We must hides them!"

Black tendrils poured out the cavern entrance behind them, gathering shape, and the lumpskins dragged Spade and Ember toward a craggy outcrop of boulders, then pushed them down to the ground. Spade felt something roll out of his pocket, saw the stone wren carving fall to the ground and tumble out of sight.

But there was no time to get it. One by one, five lumpskins crawled on top of them, Fidget at the front of the mound.

"What are they doing?" Spade whispered, but Fidget put a finger to his lips.

"They're camouflaging us," Ember murmured, "to look like boulders."

Through the heap of stock-still lumpskins, Spade glimpsed the black mass of magic as it converged at the cave entrance, unfurling into the Woegan's form. Tendrils of black shot out at several lumpskins running in the opposite direction— a diversion tactic. His chest tightened as the magic tentacles swept them up, hurtling them against the rocks.

The Woegan twisted around, wrinkled snout raised in the air.

It was searching for them. But Spade no longer had the pebble. Surely it couldn't smell them?

The lumpskins, he realized. The little creatures carried magic in their pinkies.

Prowling toward them, the Woegan stopped and inhaled, its nostrils flared. Spade could feel Fidget's chest pressed above him, the little lumpskin's heart thumping.

And then the monster stood over them.

Three more lumpskins rose from the rocks behind the Woegan and hurtled their bodies at it, sharp teeth displayed. The beast roared and its black tentacles shot out, dashing them to the side. The lumpskins lay crumpled, unmoving.

The Woegan turned, red-rimmed gaze narrowing on the mound, and Spade knew they'd been found. Their lumpskin shields leaped up, claws unsheathed. Fidget stood at their head, eyes blazing.

A rumbling groan sounded in the creature's throat. It stood to its full height, two long canines protruding from its lower jaw.

Spade closed his eyes, praying for a quick death.

And then the rumbling groan died and became a scream.

He cracked one eye open.

The Woegan reared back, covering its eyes with its gnarled hands as the first rays of sunlight glinted off its bedraggled hair. It hunched forward, shrieking.

Dirt and wind churned around it, and the creature burst into a cloud of black, writhing magic that tore down the hill and into the cavern as the sun broke over the mountains, bathing the valley and trees in golden morning light.

Spade looked up and stilled.

The four lumpskins remained resolute in front of them, unmoving.

Spade's breath died in his chest as he reached out and touched Fidget's arm. It was hard, cold.

"No. No—it can't be," Spade whispered.

They'd turned to stone.

A crushing wave of sadness wrenched through him. Throat swelling, he sank to his knees in front of Fidget. The little lumpskin stood frozen, one hand shielding Spade and Ember, the other raised, a resolved look on his face.

"They died protecting us," Ember said, her voice breaking. "I—I'd forgotten what the book said about rock goblins . . . that they cannot survive the sunlight." Tears traced paths of dirt down Ember's face, and she reached out to touch Fidget's wrinkled stone cheek. "I'm sorry," she whispered to them. "You were all so brave."

She curled her knees up and wept, Spade sitting beside her.

A hollow place echoed in Spade's chest, and guilt clung to him. He was alive because of these creatures . . . the lumpskins had barely known them, but they had sacrificed their lives for him and Ember.

What had he done? If he hadn't been so desperate for the pebble, Ash wouldn't have risked his life. The lumpskins might have escaped.

But not now.

Now they sat on a mountainside, their friends turned to statues. Spade clutched Ash to his chest as the warmth slowly began to seep out of his raven. He gazed around the grassy slope, no sign of the witch's house in view, despair curling at him. He leaned his head on his knees, closed his eyes.

Swish, scuffle.

Spade's ears perked up. A flicker of movement caught his eye, and something darted behind the Fidget statue and into the tall grass that surrounded them.

"Ember," he whispered.

Ember raised her head, snuffling. "What?"

He glimpsed a streak of orange, the whisk of something furry. Spade peered into the grass, and between the tall, golden blades, he spotted a familiar, mashed-up face, with one tattered ear.

Ember stood slowly, and they exchanged a glance.

"The rusty tabby," she said. "But what's it doing out here?"

The cat purred, its tail gliding above the grass, and they watched as it disappeared up the mountainside.

Wordless, they climbed to their aching feet and followed.

CHAPTER 32

THE WITCH OF WYNDHAIL

The tail moved fast, hovering above the grass, darting between boulders, and Spade and Ember scrambled to keep up, Ash bundled under Spade's jacket. His leg seared with pain but he stumbled forward, determined to keep the cat in his sight.

"He's got to be taking us somewhere," Ember said, breathing hard. "Why else would he be out here in the middle of the mountainside?"

"Maybe he's lurin' us to a gruesome death," Spade muttered, thinking of the Moor Mage's cats.

"I don't think so. He would have done it earlier," she reasoned.

She had a point.

The cat's tail whisked over the tall grass and between a few lone, massive evergreens, and Spade and Ember followed. They reached the edge of the trees, then halted.

The cat had disappeared.

"Where is it?" Ember groaned. "It was right here!"

Spade took a step forward, scanning the hill. Nothing.

That dirty, stinking cat.

He glanced down at Ash, the raven's warmth nearly gone. Desperation crept up into his chest.

"Spade!"

He whirled to see Ember standing just past the pines, a look of wonder on her face. "Come closer," she whispered.

He hobbled over to her, and as he did so, he felt something wash over him. He blinked.

A small cottage sat in the middle of the evergreens, surrounded by a beautiful mountain garden of wildflowers and vegetables, a twisting brook weaving between them. Foxgloves and tiger lilies grew along a white fence, a small orchard of apple trees in the clearing beyond.

Spade shook his head, baffled by the sudden appearance of the beautiful scene. Wisps of smoke puffed out the cottage's chimney, a rocking chair on its porch.

And the cat sat on the chair cushion, watching them with his uncanny eyes.

The cottage stood silent, smoke puffing lazily from the chimney as they approached.

Humming drifted to them on the breeze, and then a small, bent-over woman rounded the corner, muddied boots on her feet, a wide-brimmed sunhat covering wispy white hair. She looked up at them with her familiar bug-eyed spectacles and smiled, gaze drifting to Spade.

Ember sucked in a breath. "Lady Lyrica," she whispered.

Spade simply stared at the old woman from the cemetery.

"Well." She nodded at them. "It looks like you've arrived just in the nick of time, though I'd expected you to arrive sooner . . . I was sure it was yesterday, but oh well. I often get dates mixed up."

"Expected us?" Spade found his voice and shook his head, confused. "But how could you be expecting us? Wait—has he been following us?" He gestured at the cat. "Did he . . . tell you?"

The woman gave them a scraggle-toothed grin. "Of course," she said. "Oliver needs to make himself useful, or he'll get lazy." She lowered her voice, turning away so the cat couldn't hear. "He's not so bad, really, once you get to know him."

Spade and Ember exchanged looks.

"Anyhow, it's thanks to Oliver that you found me; no one can see my home unless they're in the company of one who's been here before."

She paused. "What else was I saying? Oh, yes. As to your other question, I'm a seer. They call me Lyrica, as you know, or Lady of the Mountain, though that's a bit of a mouthful, wouldn't you say? Of course, some simply call me witch."

Spade cleared his throat. "An', uh, which one d'you . . . prefer?"

"Oh, different ones for different days. But today, my great-niece is here! And so you shall call me Great-Auntie Lyrica." She winked, and Ember forced a smile, nervous eyes darting to Spade.

"Now hurry." The woman gestured to the cottage. "If we're to save your bird, we'd better hope one of the things they call me is true."

Spade and Ember exchanged wary looks as the woman went inside. They crept up to the doorway and stepped over the threshold, peering into the small cottage. Scents of sage, cinnamon and lemon filled the air, a curious mix but nice. Herbs dangled from every rafter in sight and a fire crackled at the hearth, something simmering in a pot.

The woman lay Ash on a table and began to mix and pound different herbs that she plucked from jars, turning them into a paste. With gentle hands, she spread the mixture across Ash's wing and chest while Spade watched, nervous. Then she scooped up the bird and hobbled across the room, placing him on a blanket spread over the windowsill. She poured a few drops of something into his beak and looked down at the raven for a long moment, brow creased.

"Is he going to be okay?" Spade heard the tremor in his voice.

"Only time will tell," she replied, thoughtful, and Spade clamped down on the fear rising in his heart.

"How much time?" he croaked.

Instead of answering, the old woman wandered toward the kitchen, bending over the fire. "You look hungry, my dears," she called over her shoulder. "How about you tell me your story over a bowl of soup?" She lifted the lid off the simmering pot, and a heavenly, robust smell wafted across the room.

Spade's stomach rumbled despite himself.

Could they trust her? He looked at Ember, whose ravenous eyes were fixed on the soup pot. But they were here to find the deepstone, he reminded himself. They didn't have a choice.

And he could never leave without Ash.

"Of course not," the woman muttered, while filling three bowls of soup. "That would be silly."

Spade frowned. Had he spoken out loud?

They sat down, and Ember sniffed the soup. "It doesn't smell poisoned," she whispered. And it didn't have eyeballs or frog's feet in it, Spade reasoned. And he remembered the delicious biscuits she'd given him in the graveyard.

Within a moment, they'd each polished off two bowls.

Lyrica chuckled. "How about another?"

Bit by bit, their story came out, and the woman listened without interrupting. When at last they got to the lumpskins and their courage, her big green eyes sparkled with tears.

"Oliver told me of our little friends and their sacrifice." She nodded. "They are very loyal creatures, indeed."

Spade's chest felt leaden, but Lyrica turned her gaze on him. "You should also know, dear, that once a lumpskin has decided something, you can never convince them otherwise. They are equally as stubborn as they are loyal."

He nodded, but he still couldn't help but feel a heaviness in his heart.

The kettle's boil filled the room, and Lyrica stood stoutly. "And now, it is high time for tea."

A moment later, she passed around the teapot and some cookies, and the warmth of the firelight filled the room, softening the shadows.

"Great-Aunt," Ember said. "You said that Oliver told you what happened. Does he . . . speak to you often?"

"He's quite sassy, actually," she mumbled, wiping crumbs from her face. "Be glad you can't hear him." She cocked her head thoughtfully. "Though he can be quite useful, sometimes. He's got an uncanny sense for when someone's in trouble."

Spade blinked and looked over at the orange tabby curled on the porch chair, one eye cracked open, watching them. That cat did always manage to show up in the strangest moments.

Lyrica chuckled and went to her kitchen, then began mashing some more herbs together.

Whoo-hoo, whoo-hoo.

A rush of wings and feathers startled them, and Spade jumped up as a great horned owl swooped through the shutters and landed on the lady's shoulder. A low hoot rose in the owl's throat and it uttered several soft clicks with its beak.

"I see," she murmured. "Thank you, Wendall."

The owl clicked its beak softly, then lifted off her shoulder and flew out through the window once more.

Lyrica went to the window, gazing out to the trees. "Excuse me, dears. I need to go do something, before I forget. I do have a terrible memory." She sighed. "I'll be back soon. Have another cookie."

She crossed the room and took her cloak. They watched as she crossed down the path, wispy white hair blowing in a slight breeze.

Spade snuck a look at the cat on the porch. "I'm pretty sure that cat's been following me since the day in the cemetery. But I still can't figure out what she was doing in the graveyard."

"Well, she's a witch. Maybe it's where witches like to, um, spend their time," Ember suggested. "You know. Since it's creepy and everything."

He shook his head, thinking. "But why the bench?"

"What bench?"

"When I first met her, she asked me to drag this huge bench up the hill—the one we passed that night."

"Maybe to sit on, and watch over things?"

Spade stood and stared around the room. Nothing seemed that unusual: ivy crawled along the rafters, and yes, there were owl nests in the ceiling. But no preserved hearts in jars or eyeballs or the kind of stuff he'd expect of a witch. "I've got no idea. But something just doesn't feel right."

Spade turned to stare at the cat seated on the porch chair, one eye cracked open again. "An' it's something to do with that deranged cat."

Her face paled. "You don't think . . . did it lure us here after all?"

Spade's gaze went to the garden. "Ember," he whispered. "Look."

She turned to the window and her eyes widened.

The lady had reached the flowers, and as she passed, the violets seemed to dip their heads, while the tiger lilies turned their orange faces toward her. When she reached the trees, the massive evergreens bent, their branches bowing in her direction. She said something to them, and their needles swished, as if in reply.

They looked at each other. "There's only one way that she could have that kind of power," Spade said. "She must be wearing the stone."

CHAPTER 33

A GOODBYE

The grass whisked soft beneath their feet as they followed the old woman's bent shadow, careful to make no noise. They held their breath as they passed beneath the pines, but the trees stayed silent, to their relief.

Ember stilled when they reached the last tree. Several yards ahead the lady made her way toward the steep mountain slope, hobbling in the direction they'd come from.

"I don't know if this is a good idea," she whispered. "I didn't see any jewelry on her, no pendants or rings. How can we be sure?"

"By following her," Spade said, putting a finger to his lips.

The tall grass parted before the lady as she walked through it, and they crept after her at a distance as she crested the hill.

They peered over the top, spotting her standing in the middle of the slope. Before her stood the four lumpskin statues of their fallen friends. She lifted her face to the sky and the wind carried her words to them.

"Blessed be your lives in the ever-after, my friends," she said, her voice tremulous. "I have no doubt you'll like it there." She reached out, and Spade's breath stilled as she touched each one on the nose.

Fidget vanished into dust, and one by one, the others disappeared as well.

They watched the lady in stillness. Spade blinked back a burning behind his eyes, and tears streamed freely down Ember's face as the dust whirled over the meadow and upward, upward into the deep-blue sky.

Lyrica turned, her eyes red, and met their gazes. "Well, you might as well join me on my walk," she said.

They shook their heads as if coming out of a dream, remembering with sudden shame why they were there. Spade flushed, embarrassed. "I'm sorry," he said. "We didn't mean—"

But she shrugged. "No matter. Grief is better shared together." She walked past them, her dress billowing in the wind, and a single tear rolled down her cheek. "There," she exclaimed, catching it on the tip of her finger. "Woegan masters surely don't cry, do they, Joolie?"

He flushed. "I—well—didn't . . ." He trailed off.

"We, we thought—" Ember stammered.

Lyrica sighed, glancing up at the sky. "I know what you thought. Come. Walk with me and I will show you the garden."

They fell into step beside her as she walked back toward the shelter of the pines, following a small footpath.

"I have no stone," she told them, as they moved past wildflowers. "If I did, you'd have known it by now."

The apple trees rustled their branches at them as they drew near, and Ember looked up into their leaves. "But the plants and trees bow to you, and wild animals serve you. Isn't that stone magic?"

The woman chuckled. "They are free to do as they wish. I do not force them or control them. Nor do I control the lumpskins. They followed you from a sense of duty, you see. It was the lumpskins who've been trying to reunite the deepstones, ever since the miners stole them from their tunnels."

"The lumpskin tunnels?" The queen's story came back to Spade in a rush. "You mean . . . the cavern that the miner stumbled into, it was a lumpskin cavern?"

She nodded. "Yes, many years ago. The lumpskins discovered them first but knew their power was strange. Fearful of the deepstones, they took it upon themselves to keep them hidden, and filled the entrance to the cavern. But they could not anticipate men digging so deep in their search for magic gems."

"But wouldn't the lumpskins have wanted the deepstones' power for themselves?" Ember asked.

The old woman beckoned for them to follow her. "The lumpskins are wise creatures," she said, passing a hand over the tree trunks they passed as they walked. "Because you see, they possess a magic that is much older than even the deepstones. It's known as old magic or spirit magic, a natural magic that comes from the soul of the creator of our world, and a seed of it resides in each living creature."

Spade was reminded of his great-uncle Malachi's stories. He glanced at Lyrica, glimpsing something old and sad in the depths of her eyes. "There was a time when the world was ripe with it," she murmured, "but not anymore."

Her gaze drifted over Spade. "Even so, there's a little left, hiding here and there. Enough that I can sense when a different sort of magic is near." The lady gave him a long, piercing look. "Be careful, young gravedigger," she whispered, and her eyes grew cloudy. "Some things hold a power not easily broken."

A strange feeling echoed along Spade's bones. Then the old woman blinked, and her expression returned to normal. "What was I saying? Oh, yes . . ."

She reached into her pocket and withdrew something. "I found this tucked inside your raven's beak. An unusual thing to find in a raven's mouth."

Spade stilled, and Ember caught her breath.

The moon-gem lay in her hand, the barest glimmer passing over its surface.

CHAPTER 34

TO BE A WOEGAN

Relief rushed through him, and Spade stared at the stone in Lyrica's hand. "I—I thought I'd lost it," he stammered.

A small smile curled the old woman's lips. "Perhaps it was meant to be found once more." She stepped forward, laying it carefully in his palm. "Ravens are more insightful than we think, you know. And he seems very determined that you have it."

Spade's throat swelled as he tucked it back into his pocket. *Ash. That crazy, brave bird.* "He loves sparkly things," Spade admitted, heart heavy. "Just can't get enough of them."

"Hmmm," Lyrica mused. "Perhaps. What was it, now, that they say about ravens?" She paused, thinking, then sighed. "Ah well, my old forgetful mind, you know. I'm sure it'll come to me when I need it. But speaking of cheeky birds . . ."

She turned, craning her neck upward. "Wendall! I believe you have something to return." She gave a stern look to the owl, who blinked down at them from a nest tucked into the tree and clacked his beak peevishly.

But at another look from Lyrica, he hooted and bobbed his head. "He'd like you to look in his nest," she said.

Ember and Spade exchanged glances and Spade climbed the tree, meeting the owl eye to golden eye. Wendall ruffled his neck and shuffled aside, allowing Spade to reach his hand into the nest and pull out a small gray item.

He held up the little wren, its sapphire eye twinkling.

"Wendall tells me he found it in the tall grass, near the entrance to the lumpskin tunnels," Lyrica commented. "Is it yours?"

"I—well, you see . . ."

"It belongs to the queen," Ember interrupted, eyes flashing. "He stole it." She brushed off her torn dress. "Like he does a lot of things." She turned and marched down the path, leaving them behind.

"Ember, wait," Spade called, but she didn't turn. He shoved his hands in his pockets, frustrated. He couldn't figure out why someone would get so hung up over a little sculpture.

Lyrica's sharp gaze followed the girl, a curious look on her face. "Perhaps it's time for some more tea," she murmured, and trailed after.

Spade drew in a heavy breath and walked over to the cottage windowsill. He peered in at Ash, lying so still he could barely see the rise and fall of his chest. A lead pit formed in Spade's stomach. Nothing had turned out as he'd thought.

His brother was imprisoned, and his best friend lay weak and dying. The lumpskins had turned to stone. And Ember distrusted him, maybe even hated him, because of the stupid figurine in his hand—another one of his mistakes.

He looked down at the wren with its twinkling eye, and he had the sudden urge to be far away from it. He placed it on the sill next to Ash and laid a hand over the raven's chest for a moment. He whispered a prayer, or maybe a plea, though he didn't know who would hear it.

Spade turned and walked into the trees, letting the forest swallow him.

The brook lay eerily silent as Spade approached. He'd expected the sound of trickling water or the croak of frogs, but he'd nearly stumbled into it before he noticed it, the water a whisper at his feet.

He glanced back at the cottage nestled in the trees, his chest heavy. Picking up a flat rock, he skipped it across the surface of the brook and watched it sink without a sound. He walked to the edge of the bank and peered down into the silky, clear waters. It couldn't be more than three feet deep, but he couldn't see the bottom.

The water looked cool. Inviting. Without thinking, he crouched, touching his palm to the surface. A ripple spread from the tips of his fingers, and something shuddered in the dark depths.

He jerked his hand back, but it was too late. His vision blurred and he felt himself falling, then jolting to a stop.

A memory appeared in his mind, so vivid his heart raced.

He sat on the rooftop of their family's carriage while it teetered down a dusty road, his brother running alongside it, skipping rocks at its wheels. Benji laughed out loud, throwing his golden head back as the wind caught his hair. Spade watched Benji, a mixture of admiration and sorrow on his face—longing for a feeling that would never be his. The feeling of flying feet, his body moving effortlessly, easily.

Another image arose. It was the first moment Spade had ever seen a coffin. He was only five. Benji was a baby at the time, so Malachi was lookout, while Spade and Garnet stood over the dug grave.

"Like this, Spade," his father instructed, showing him how to use the shovel. "You got to dig in deep, use yer backbone." Within a few minutes, Spade's thin arms tired.

He stood up and caught a glimpse of worry on his father's face. "Can I go try lookout now, Dad?" he asked. But Garnet shook his head. "This is what you need to be best at, Spade. This is what you were made fer, son." He noticed his dad glance at his leg, before pulling his gaze away. "Back to work, my boy."

One last image, this one sharper still.

Spade sat alone on a hill. Benji ran down the far path into town to spy on their next heist. Spade could never go, of course. People remembered a boy with a crooked leg, and he couldn't make a quick escape. Benji returned a few hours later with stories of what town life was like, voice brimming with excitement. Spade listened, envy in his chest, and a familiar ache washed over him.

"Wake up, Spade."

A hand with an iron grip tugged his shoulder, and he

jolted, almost tumbling forward into the brook. He fell onto his back and looked up into Lyrica's curious face.

"What happened?" He struggled to sit up, then spotted the stream. "The water," he mumbled. "It did something to me . . ."

Lyrica tilted her head. "I should hope so, it called to you. Still, not everyone's prepared for it." She glanced down, a faraway look in her eye.

"What does it do?" Spade asked, his head feeling fuzzy. "Why did it show me pictures of my past?"

She sighed. "It's different for each person. It's a strange stream, this one. But they aren't just any pictures, though, are they?"

The memories tugged at him, sitting heavy on his chest. "No."

She nodded. "Its waters show us our darkest, hardest things. It's a rare person who can face those things."

He looked up at her then and saw that she wasn't looking at him but at the trees, and there was something reflexive in her look.

"Look again," she whispered.

It was the last thing he wanted to do, but he gritted his teeth and peered down once more.

A dark shape lumbered through a mountain pass, alone, all creatures silent as it passed. The Woegan.

Fear lanced up Spade's neck. He could smell the creature's rank odor, hear the grit and snap of twigs beneath its feet. The creature moved between trees, searching, smelling, and a terrible need spread through his veins like a fire. With a sickening dread, Spade realized he was inside the Woegan's head.

He looked down at the grotesque body, the long, curled claws. A gnawing hunger roiled inside him, boundless and consuming. Hunger for magic. But there was something else. Spade stilled, waiting, sifting. He became aware of something lurking in the back of his Woegan-mind, a shadowy figure, its presence hooked into his being, pulling him. Fighting against him.

The Woegan's master, Spade realized.

The Woegan reached a pond and bent down, bringing its mangled snout close to the surface. It drew in a deep breath, and for a moment, Spade caught a glimpse of its face. The creature reared back, howling, and stumbled into the forest.

Spade felt the trees rush by, the twigs snagging at his long fur, and his thoughts collided together like pieces of a puzzle falling into place.

He woke with a start, breathing hard, and he felt a slight tingle in his pocket: the stone.

"Well!" Lyrica said. "I believe you learned something useful!"

The rainy night came back in a flash, and the puddle of water. He knew what the Woegan was afraid of. What its master was afraid of.

"It . . . it's afraid of itself," he murmured.

CHAPTER 35

ASH

The evening curled in, spreading its fingers through the trees as Spade sat on a small stone bench next to Lyrica.

The old woman tilted her head up, and her eyes had that faraway look again. "The Woegan is not so different from you and me, is it?"

He thought about this. The creature and its master hunted people for power, all because it didn't like what it was, what it had become. "It's tryin' to forget, ain't it?"

She nodded. "The creature's master is a lonely sort of person, I imagine. Of course, we all get a little lonely, but some of us get stuck there. And when you've lived there a while, the darkness starts to creep up, like soot in the lungs. Everyone needs a good chimney sweep."

And suddenly Spade knew why he'd recognized the look in the Woegan's eyes: he'd felt the same. The longing when he saw kids running, climbing. That aching, desperate wish that he was anyone else.

She sighed. "The deepstones are a way to make you forget what's real. They make you depend on them, and they steal the things that are true. But friendship and love—that's a whole different kind of magic, isn't it?" She patted his knee, gazing into the trees. "They help you remember who you are."

He thought about that while Lyrica gazed at the pond. "You know, it's never very easy," she mused, "to face your truths. It wasn't for me."

He glanced up, surprised. "But you're a seer, my lady."

She laughed, a crooked sort of laugh. "Doesn't matter," she said simply. "I came here long ago because I was running from myself. The past is a tricky thing for me. I can get lost in it sometimes." She chuckled. "Lucky for you, you have good friends and an inner compass to help you find your way."

Spade shook his head, his chest hollow, the familiar ache shooting up his leg. "My compass is likely broke by now, my lady." *Like the rest of me*, he thought, glancing down at his leg. "I'm a thief, after all."

Lyrica bent her frail frame and met his gaze with her wide eyes. "Then maybe you need to dig a little deeper, gravedigger. Sometimes strength comes from our weakest parts."

Spade almost snorted out loud. His leg was no help that he knew of. His limp had slowed them down, forcing the lumpskins to carry him. He wasn't quick enough to save Ash, hadn't been quick enough to escape the Woegan on the mountainside, and it had cost the lumpskins their lives.

He tore his gaze from Lyrica. For all her knowledge as a seer, she'd missed the truth about him. He gazed down at the pond, a heavy weight settling hard in his stomach.

"Time to go," she murmured, her voice soft. "It grows dark outside, and we shouldn't linger in this place."

Ember burst out of the door when they reached the cottage, her face lit with urgency. "Where were you?" she demanded. "Come inside, quick."

Spade's heart stalled.

Ash.

He broke into a limping gallop and brushed past Ember, running for the windowsill.

It was empty.

Ember rushed in behind him as he whirled.

"Where is he?" he croaked, scouring the empty room.

"But he was right there, on the windowsill. . . ." Ember's voice trailed off as she spotted the empty blanket.

The sounds of skittering claws made them both jerk around. Ash scuttled across the stone floor, a cookie in his beak.

When he saw Spade, the raven hop-skipped over and the boy knelt, amazed. Ash gave a wobbly flap and sprang up onto his shoulder, croaking and nibbling at his ear. Spade blinked back tears as he checked the raven over, disbelief growing. The deep wound in Ash's chest had healed, leaving only a scar, his broken wing straightened. Spade had never seen anything like it.

Ash croaked and tilted his head. He dropped the cookie into Spade's hand, then hopped over to his perch. He returned again, this time with a second cookie for Ember.

She laughed as he dropped it into her hand.

"Clever bird," she said, planting a kiss on his feathered head.

He flew up to his perch on the windowsill, croaking. Spade walked over and saw that he'd pilfered a whole pile of cookies from the cupboard, plus a few glittery baubles, as well as a lumpy object he'd hidden under the blanket. The raven retrieved the object with his beak and dropped it into Spade's hand, head bobbing up and down in excitement. He crooned deep in his throat.

Spade curled his fingers around the small stone wren. Guilt, as well as amazement at the raven's courage, swept over him. "Thanks, Ash," he said at last.

The bird ruffled his feathers, pleased with himself, and settled down on his perch. He kept one beady eye focused on Spade, as if afraid to lose sight of him.

"He's quite a friend." Spade turned to see Ember standing behind him.

Spade nodded, his throat dry. "Listen. I shouldn't have stolen your aunt's bird carving. I just . . . I wasn't thinking."

She shrugged and looked away, her mouth pursed.

Spade stared down at the stone bird. "I took it for Benji. He lost his lucky frog carving, and I wanted to give him something to cheer him in the dungeons. But it was wrong." He held out the wren. "Here. Take it back to the queen—please. I'm sorry."

Ember stared down at the little sculpture in his outstretched hand. With a sigh, she took it. "I know you are," she said after a moment, then looked down at the ground. "It's only . . . I'm used to everyone hiding things from me and telling me half-truths. Like Spinniker and my aunt, because they think I'm too young to help." She paused. "And I guess I have a hard time forgiving people."

She met his gaze now. "What I'm trying to say is, I'm sorry too. For not giving you a chance to explain."

"That's okay," Spade said. "You had a pretty good reason to be fuming mad."

She shook her head. "The thing is, it's not just any old bauble. It was made by my uncle Weston for my aunt before he left for the mountain expedition, the one he didn't return from. Wren was going to be the name of their baby daughter." She turned the bird over, her eyes sad. "It was his parting gift to her."

Spade swallowed, and guilt hit him with a sharp pang. "Crud. I didn't know."

She handed it back to him. "Maybe it's better off with Benji. It reminds us all of sad things, anyhow."

He looked at it for a long moment. Maybe he could return it to the queen's room. If she decided not to hang him, that is.

Ash cawed, finishing his final cookie, and flew up to the mantel to preen himself, looking in a small bronze plate. Spade squinted. He'd seen dozens of those plates before, usually on coffins. He went over, reading the words scratched into the nameplate.

Bagman Grute.

The tax collector.

He froze as the door blew open and Lyrica came in, her gaze landing on Spade and Ember.

"Ah," she said. "The raven is awake."

Spade looked between her and the plate, and the cemetery flooded back to him. "Do you . . . do you know this man?"

Lyrica smiled. "Not really, but I keep his coffin plate to help me remember where I kept it." She tapped her head. "My forgetful brain, you know. It would be a terrible thing to forget where I hid the deepstone, wouldn't it?"

CHAPTER 36

SEEKING AND STALKING

The old woman crossed the hearth and bustled over to the teakettle, as if she hadn't just said something completely shocking.

"Wait," said Spade. His heart began to thud in his chest. "You don't mean the pebble?"

"It's not just any pebble, my boy."

He stared at her. "The *pebble* is the lost deepstone of Wyndhail?"

The old lady nodded, producing a pot of tea.

"But," he sputtered. "But it was in a tax collector's shoe!"

The old woman grinned. "Isn't that funny?" She poured three cups. "Well, not too funny, when you consider what it can do. After all, that was the reason I stole it from my brother in the first place."

Spade's thoughts whirred, scrambling together. "Yer—yer saying I've had a deepstone the whole time."

She nodded, humming and stirring a little sugar into her cup.

They stared at her. "I don't understand," Ember said.

The old woman sank down into her chair, joints creaking. "When we were children, Murdoch—you know him as the Moor Mage—Alistair, and I, well, we did everything together. We were inseparable, the closest brothers and sister there ever were, despite Murdoch and I being half brother and half sister to Alistair. Alistair was the king's only full-blooded son, you see, his mother being the queen of Wyndhail. But the queen died in childbirth with Alistair, and the king was devastated for a time, until he met an unusual woman: the village healer. He fell in love with her, though many said she was a witch. She had two children with the king, myself and Murdoch, though no one of royal lineage ever really accepted her, and she refused to marry the king.

"Despite this, she allowed us to stay and be raised at the castle with Alistair. Of course, we knew that Alistair would one day become king, but the three of us promised each other that our bond would never change." She smiled, sad. "How foolish we were.

"When they began grooming Alistair to be king, Alistair had less time for us, and we were left behind. Jealous and lonely, Murdoch threw himself into learning dark magic from the castle mage and began avoiding me and Alistair.

"On our brother's coronation day, Alistair was given a gift of strange magic stones, given to the royal family after their discovery in the Wyndhail mines. But our brother

Murdoch burned with jealousy; *he* had devoted himself to the magical arts, after all." A shadow passed over the older woman's brow. "And he adored dark magic the most, the kind that came with tremendous power. Murdoch devised a plan and stole one of the deepstones from the vault under our brother's very nose. Furious, King Alistair banished Murdoch, but Murdoch had already fled. Alistair guarded the other deepstone carefully, and for a while, he ruled justly, using its power to build, its knowledge to discover secrets. But over time, as much as the deepstone's magic gave, it took." She sighed and blinked, shaking her head. "He became different. I recognized it, of course. I had seen it in Murdoch, as he'd begun to learn dark magic. And it wasn't long before my brother the king grew sick."

She met their gazes. "One day, I decided I'd had enough. I stole the deepstone hidden in Wyndhail Tower and left the castle. I made my home here, hidden away in this cottage. I became an outlaw, but at least I'd saved the King of Wyndhail—or I thought I had." She shook her head. "Alistair succumbed a few months later to a strange illness—a slow wasting away that I now know came from the power that the deepstone held over him.

"The moment Alistair died, I knew Murdoch would come looking for me and for the deepstone. So I hid it in different places through the years. Just days ago, I hid it once more, in the last place Murdoch would ever look. The grave of a tax collector." She chuckled. "Murdoch hated royal tax collectors."

Ember snorted and Spade remembered the Moor Mage, his gaze suspicious as he opened the door to the manor.

Lyrica's eyes flashed behind her spectacles. "Of course, seers can't see everything. I could not anticipate a grave thief coming across it mere moments later."

"Wait," Ember frowned, thinking. "Does this mean that King Alistair created the Woegan?"

Lyrica shook her head. "If the Woegan's master dies, so does the Woegan, as they are tied together through a magic bond. I learned a thing or two about magic as well, during my time at the castle." Her eyes grew faint, remembering. "Murdoch did not create it, nor Alistair."

Spade stared at the old woman. "Are . . . are you saying . . . I'm its master?"

The old woman chuckled. "A master has to be aware they're a master in order to create an evil servant. And you, my boy, have always known the deepstone, or 'pebble,' as you call it, to be only a moon-gem."

It was true. But somewhere deep inside, Spade had known there was something more to the pebble too. It had spoken to him.

Lyrica watched him, and a shadow passed over the woman's eyes. "But perhaps you have also felt its power, hmm, grave thief? Tell me—have you noticed that whenever you use it, the Woegan appears?"

Sharp pieces of memory swirled in Spade's mind, and he felt a lump form in his stomach. "An' why's that?"

"Both the deepstone and the creature are made from the same magic. The Woegan can sense whenever a deepstone is used."

The lump in Spade's stomach grew.

"You mean to say I've been calling the creature all along?"

Shadows lengthened in the room, the trees' branches swaying outside.

Spade's mind raced.

"That's how the Woegan found us," he murmured. "First, on the moor, then at the mage's house . . ."

"And again in the cemetery, and the lumpskin tunnels," Ember finished. They stared down at the pebble, and he quickly placed it in his pocket.

Lyrica nodded. "Indeed. It's been tracking you. You see, its master wants sole control of the deepstones. The power would be tremendous."

"But if Spade didn't create the Woegan—and if Murdoch and King Alistair didn't—then who did?" Ember asked.

Lady Lyrica paused. "There is something the queen hasn't told you, I'm afraid. You see, there are, in fact, three deepstones."

Ember's jaw dropped. "Three?"

The old woman nodded. "Very few knew of the third, only the king and a handful of his closest advisors. But upon the king's death, Spinniker would have told the new queen about it, of course."

Spade remembered Spinniker coming into the room, whispering something in the queen's ear. *It remains untouched*, he'd said. Finally, Spade understood: Spinniker had been referring to the third deepstone.

A shadow crossed the old woman's huge eyes. "This is one of the reasons I asked Oliver to bring you here. I was hoping someone could find it. I have reason to believe that someone has been using it without the queen's knowledge for a few years now. The very person that I am certain has created the Woegan."

"But how?" Spade asked. "I heard Spinniker talking to the queen—I didn't realize till now, but he was talking about the stone. He said it's safe."

"Then perhaps his eyes deceive him, my dears." The old lady shook her head. "Can you not think of how he might be fooled?"

Spade's mind churned. "The Woegan almost always appears at night. Which means that someone could be using it every night and returning it in the morning. It'd have to be someone close to the queen, though. Someone she trusts."

The old woman nodded, pleased. "A clever lad, you are. But she will never believe this from me, the Witch of Wyndhail." She smiled, a little sadly. "And time is wearing thin. The trees and lumpskins have whispered to me about its growing power, and I can feel it in my very bones."

"An' what happens then?" Spade asked, wary.

"King Alistair believed that when all three deepstones were together in the hands of someone with great magic, they would be almost unstoppable. But he also said something else." She paused, and for the first time, Spade glimpsed a hint of fear in the old woman's eyes. "The Woegan knows that if the deepstones are united, it will be freed, no longer bound to its master. Its master may not know this."

Ice trickled into Spade's veins. "You mean that it could wander around day or night and do whatever it pleases?"

The woman nodded. "But there's a silver lining, of course. As is often the rule with magic, whatever released the deepstones can also destroy them, if all three are brought together once more. I do not know if the queen told you, but when Alistair received the stones, he also received the miner's pickaxe alongside them—the tool was passed down along with the stones, in case it should ever be needed."

Spade's mind went to the painting in the castle hall, the portrait of a miner coming out of a tunnel, something glowing in his hand, a pickaxe in his other hand.

And then the portrait of King Alistair on his coronation day, accepting a small chest, and a long tool laid upon a pillow. The pickaxe, he realized.

"Wait," Ember murmured. "Where would he keep the miner's tool?"

"In the same place the third deepstone rests," the old lady said. "My brother never left anything to chance."

"And there is not a single clue as to where the stone or tool are kept?" Ember asked, incredulous.

"There are always clues, my dear." Her eyes fastened on them. "Luckily, I can think of no better children to find them."

Ash flew over to Spade's shoulder cawing, and Lyrica's face suddenly brightened.

"Now I remember that thought about ravens!" she said, clapping her hands together. "They love magic. They're attracted to it like candy, cheeky things. Some say they can even sense those who have the gift of magic in their blood."

Spade stared at Lyrica, then snorted. "Well, Ash got bad luck when he chose me. I'm good at magician's tricks an' that's about it."

A strange smile curled Lyrica's lips. "Perhaps. But I find that animals are good at noticing things we don't."

A rustle of feathers filled the room, startling them, and Wendall dove through the window with a loud hoot. Lyrica listened for a moment, then sobered.

"Just our luck," she said. "It appears you have more than one stalker." She crossed the room, lowering the lamplight, then gestured to the window. Spade peered into the dark and spotted a tall silhouette on the mountainside above the cottage, seated astride a familiar stallion.

Henchcliff.

Lyrica drew the curtains. "You're safe for now," she said. "I've spoken cloaking wards into the trees, whispered protections over them. They will hold, but I do not know for how long. You'd best leave tomorrow, for that man's appearance means one thing: Her Majesty has lost her patience."

CHAPTER 37

A DESPERATE PLAN

The narrow road lay deserted at this time of morning as Spade and Ember crept along the edge of town, darting between houses, their packs stuffed with food from Lyrica.

Urgency clawed at Spade. Was Benji all right? Had the Woegan attacked anyone at the castle? They needed to get to the queen, and the sooner, the better. She needed to know that the Woegan had found a hidden way into the castle and she wasn't safe.

You can't return through the same tunnels that brought you here; the Woegan will expect it, Lyrica had warned. *You must find another way into the castle.*

And so they ducked behind shops, sneaking through alleys. The castle's main gates loomed at the top of the road, guards stationed at the towers. As they watched from behind a shop, a contingent of guards on horses swept out of the gates, marching down the hill toward them.

"What's our plan?" Ember whispered. "There's no way in through the main gate now; they'll be watching it like hawks."

Spade's thoughts returned to Benji. They needed to get to the queen's chambers without being seen, and they couldn't waste time being detained by guards, or in Spade's case, rotting in dungeons.

Ash croaked from inside Spade's jacket. The raven didn't like being cooped up, but Spade couldn't risk him being seen; every guard in the castle would be on the lookout for the black bird.

The creak of a door sounded, and Ember darted a panicked look at Spade. Before they could find a place to hide, a boy came around the corner, carrying a bucket of dirty water. He dumped it down the sewer lane, then glanced up. His gaze met Spade's and Ember's, and his eyes widened.

Spade and Ember froze.

The little boy turned and raced back down the alley, bucket jangling.

"He's gone to tell the guards," Ember hissed. "My aunt must have sent a messenger to the town, warning everyone to keep a lookout."

They ran, ducking into another alley, and then through the back door of a clothing shop. They huddled in the dark, listening to the shopkeeper bustle around upstairs. "Quick," Spade hissed. "Disguises."

A pair of big, floppy ladies' hats hung on coat hooks, as well as several long fur coats. Spade grabbed a wispy blonde wig and pulled it on, followed by a flowered headscarf.

Ember stared at him.

"What?" he demanded. "I'm playing the part. A frou-frou lady noble."

Ember snorted. "You do remind me of my cousin Gertrude," she admitted, tugging a wide-brimmed hat over her red curls.

They slipped in between the stalls as the vendors set up their stands. The guards had reached the town and were riding through the streets.

"Duck," Spade whispered as two guards rode by. They crawled behind a zucchini stand, and one of the guards stopped his horse in front of it.

"What's wrong?" the one asked.

"Dunno," he replied. "Thought I saw something."

Spade held his breath, Ember white and still beside him.

"Hello, sir," a familiar voice said. "I was wondering if I could have yer help. See, I saw a thief stealing from the jewelry stand over there, and then he ducked into the alley. He looked to be a young lad."

"A boy?" The crunch of gravel sounded as the guards spun away from the zucchinis, footsteps retreating.

Spade stood up slowly and came face-to-face with an old man dressed in fine clothes, though a bit faded and tattered.

"Uncle Malachi," he breathed.

His great-uncle grinned, and the same small boy they'd seen earlier popped out from behind the corner of a shop. Malachi slipped him a few coins, and the boy nodded. "Thanks, mister," he said, and skipped away.

Malachi shot Spade a sly look. "Yer not the only spy 'round here, my boy."

The shadows of the narrow alleyway engulfed them as they ducked down the lane, following the swirl of Malachi's tattered cloak.

"How'd you find us, Uncle?" Spade asked when they'd stopped to catch their breath and discard their costumes.

"Townspeople were talking, saying the guards were looking for you an' the Royal Miss," Malachi explained, his gray eyes watching the bustling marketplace at the other end of the alleyway. "I knew you'd show up sooner or later, so I sent my little messengers to look fer you."

"We're trying to get into the castle without being seen, Uncle." Spade peered out at the street, the clopping of the guards' horses drawing near. "We need to find the queen an' warn her that the Woegan's in the lumpskin tunnels."

"Lumpskin tunnels?" Malachi's brow creased.

"Rock goblins," Ember explained.

"Well, I'll be. I'd heard tales 'bout creatures living under Wyndhail, a long time ago . . ."

"Yes, Uncle." Spade nodded. "But there's more. The tunnels connect to the castle dungeons."

His great-uncle's eyes darkened. "That's where Benji's being held, ain't it?"

"Yeah." Spade's chest tightened.

Malachi pulled his hat down lower. "Then we best hurry. I've an idea."

The entrance loomed dark and narrow, just wide enough for one person to fit through at a time. Spade glanced up the hill to the shadow of the Wyndhail cemetery perched at its crest.

Ember's eyes widened, her gaze fixed on the half-hidden opening in the side of the hill. "How'd you know about this?" she asked his great-uncle. "*Historical Wyndhail* makes no mention of it—"

"It ain't in any books." Malachi raised his lantern and stepped inside, illuminating a rough-hewn rock corridor. He glanced back at Spade. "Yer dad an' I stumbled across it when we were kids. It ends up in a cavern, and once, I thought I heard creatures talking in the dark, though I never saw 'em with own two eyes."

"A cavern!" exclaimed Spade. "The lumpskins took us through a cavern . . . an' if it's the very same, we could likely get into the dungeons . . . but we'd have to be careful." He glanced down at the pocket where he kept the deepstone. "We don't know where the Woegan is hiding itself."

Ember swallowed hard. "At least we have the dee—I mean, moon-gem, to warn us." Spade met Ember's glance. He wanted to tell Malachi about the deepstone, of course, but something stopped him. "Later," he whispered, and Ember nodded.

Malachi looked between them, then down at Spade's pocket, his eyebrows raised. "Sounds like a handy moon-gem to have. In we go."

The light spread its dim fingers ahead of them as they wound through the narrow tunnel, racing downward. At last, a cool blast of air hit them, and they stumbled into a massive cavern.

Malachi's lanternlight shone deep into the darkness, illuminating the familiar stalactites and the hundreds of glow-slugs that speckled the ceiling, like stars in the night sky. Ash cawed, looking up at them with a beady eye. "They're not to eat," Spade reminded him. "Remember Benji's tongue?"

At the thought of Benji he turned, hurriedly retracing their steps. Where were the stairs? Malachi shuffled behind him, eyes sparkling as he gazed around. "I'd forgotten 'bout all this," he said, but Spade urged them on.

"Hurry, Uncle," he whispered. They descended into the cavern and wove through the stalagmites to the far side, examining the walls. Spade bent, tracing his hands over the rock. "I remember them being here somewhere," he muttered. "I'm certain of it . . ."

"A small stone staircase," Ember agreed, feeling around the boulders with Malachi. But after several minutes passed, none of them had found anything. Spade crouched, frustrated, and a sharp jolt of pain traveled up his leg. They were so close! And after all this work, they couldn't find the bloody stairs.

An icy hand of fear curled its way around his chest. What if the Woegan had gotten to the dungeons first? Or worse, what if—

Ash's low croak rang out, echoing across the cave.

Spade froze. They raised their eyes.

"Well, I'll be," Malachi said. "He's found something."

The raven sat perched on a narrow ledge of rock, a

series of ledges trailing upward, barely visible to the naked eye—small stone steps leading to a little hole in the cavern wall. Relief poured through Spade.

"Clever Ash!" Ember exclaimed.

They gathered just below the lowest step, Malachi giving Ember a boost up. "Careful now, watch yer step."

Ember clambered up onto the lowest ledge, reaching down for Spade's hand, when the sound of bootsteps rang out in the cave.

Everyone froze. Then Ash took to the air with a rasping croak.

Slowly, Spade turned. Malachi held up his lantern.

The lanternlight washed over a tall, muscled figure, arms crossed over his chest, a red stone shining at his belt.

"Hello, Royal Miss." Henchcliff descended into the cavern, gaze fixed on the three of them.

"Henchcliff." Ember's voice was cold and authoritative, princess-like, despite her mud-covered dress and filthy hair. "I know you've come to retrieve me, but we haven't got time to waste. I demand that you take us directly to the queen."

The captain's eyes flashed, his mouth pressed in a firm scowl. "I'm afraid that isn't possible. The queen is indisposed."

"Well then," said Ember, "bring me to Spinniker. I will talk with him until my aunt's headache has passed."

"I'm afraid I cannot do that, either, Royal Miss," Henchcliff said.

A flash of unease crossed Ember's face, and Malachi shifted, wary.

"What are you talking about, Henchcliff?" Ember demanded. "Of course you can . . ." Her voice trailed off as the queen's guard slowly raised his hands.

Spade stared at the man, then at his belt, as the ruby stone in the buckle sparked to life.

A hint of something—regret, maybe?—lingered in the man's gaze, as the stone seared bright.

And then Spade understood.

"Uncle! Ember!" he yelled. "Duck!"

A rumble spread through the cavern, and chunks of rock broke free from the ceiling, stalactites crashing to the floor.

Ember screamed and hurled her body behind a stalagmite, Spade landing beside her. Ash circled high above, cawing, while Malachi hunched beside them, trying to shield them with his body.

"He—he's trying to kill us!" Ember cried.

More stalactites fell, shattering and covering them with bits of debris. Ash dove and dodged the falling rock, nearly crushed beneath a jagged chunk.

"The ruby," Spade hissed. "It's magic."

"Magic . . ." Ember's lips whitened. "Spade! When Spinniker went to check on the deepstones every day . . ."

They met each other's eyes, and Spade knew they were both thinking the same thing. "Henchcliff was there," he finished. "Guarding him. He's likely observed Spinniker for years and learned how to get in."

They ducked their heads as more rock cascaded down around them, and Ember caught her breath, fists curled into balls. "This whole time, Henchcliff's been the Woegan's master. He must be planning to steal my aunt's throne."

Malachi looked between them, and slowly, comprehension dawned in his eyes. He swiveled his gray head, studying the man, and then turned to Ash, who circled above them. He winked at Ash, and the bird cawed in reply.

"I may not have my youth," he whispered. "But I'm still a Joolie. You young'uns wait for my signal, then run."

"I can't leave you, Uncle," Spade hissed as they shielded their heads, rocks raining down around them.

"No arguing. I'll be fine. Benji's waiting an' he doesn't have much time."

Before Spade could reply, Malachi stood from behind the boulder and walked out to the middle of the cavern.

Spade peered around the rock and saw Henchcliff's gaze narrow on the old man.

In one quick movement, he threw the lantern at the wall, signaling to Ash. The lantern exploded into flames, then went out, leaving them in pitch-black except for the red glow of Henchcliff's belt. But the belt had dimmed—he'd used some of his power.

"Where's Malachi?" Ember whispered. "I don't hear him."

"That's 'cause he's a Joolie," Spade murmured. "You never hear 'em coming."

"Arrggh!"

Henchcliff cried out in the dark, and then they saw the red glow of the ruby moving, flying through the air, as if Henchcliff had grown wings.

Spade blinked, then understood. Ash had the belt and was flying straight for them. Malachi must have slipped it off the guardsman in the dark.

"Ash!" Spade cried. The light dipped, then dropped into his hands, and a moment later Ash's talons dug into his shoulder.

"Run, boy," Malachi shouted, and he heard Henchcliff snarl in pain.

"Where are you, old man?" the guard rasped.

Spade tucked the belt in his jacket to try and smother the glow. "Let's go," he said in a voice lower than a whisper. "We've gotta get this stone far away from him." Ember held on to his arm and they scrambled up onto the rock ledge.

They pulled themselves up the first stair, then the second. *Where's Uncle?* Spade thought, feeling for the third stair, then the fourth. *He should be here by now.*

A weathered voice cried out in the dark, a groan of pain.

Spade jerked his head around as a match flared to life in Henchcliff's hand. He stood over Uncle Malachi, who lay hunched over on the ground, breathing hard.

Ash screeched and took to the air, bolting for the guard, but Henchcliff drew a dagger from his belt. "Don't you dare," he snarled at the bird.

"No—wait!" Spade cried. "Don't hurt him!"

"I'll give him to you in exchange for the belt." The guardsman tilted his head, waiting.

Spade stared at his uncle. He knew the moment Henchcliff got the belt, he'd kill them all.

"Don't be foolish, Spade," his great-uncle rasped. "Run!"

The matchlight wavered in the guardsman's hand, and the cave went black.

And then something rippled through Spade's pocket, a heat searing up his leg. He reached down and plucked the pebble out of his pocket, its glow spreading across through the cavern.

He stared at it, his heart slowing. Maybe . . .

You got no idea how to use it, he reminded himself. *Remember last time.*

Henchcliff's eyes widened, his gaze fixed on the pebble.

Spade clutched the deepstone in his fingers, raising it high in the air. A tremor snaked down his arm.

Gritting his teeth, he closed his eyes.

CHAPTER 38
INVISIBLE BENJI

The heat struck him first. One moment, he was holding the deepstone up, a spark coursing through his fingers, and the next, a fire wrenched down his arm, ripping through his insides. He gasped as several faint black wisps streaked out of the deepstone and curled around his wrist. The wisps writhed around his fingers, then spread, sweeping across the cavern to Henchcliff, where they latched onto the guardsman's hand.

Henchcliff's eyes widened in fear as the tendrils sprang up his arm. Malachi shuffled backward, mouth parted in surprise.

Black wisps swept over the guard's torso, twisting up his neck and into his nostrils, and he began to sputter. "Stop," he commanded, voice hoarse.

"Not so strong without yer murdering pet, are you?" Spade said.

"Wait," the guardsman hacked, hunching over. "I can explain . . ."

"An' you'll take just long enough to let your beast find us, I'm betting. Not on yer life." Spade held on, pushed harder. Anger spun through him. This man had tried to kill them, had threatened his great-uncle. His creature had taken dozens of villagers, had caused people to live in fear for years.

The magic grew thick, choking the air between them. Spade's fingers began to tremble, then his arms and legs.

"Don't," Henchcliff's voice came again, but this time it was weaker. Spade groaned with the effort, the tips of his fingers seared around the stone. A strange thrill coursed through him—he was the hunter now, instead of the hunted.

"Please." The guardsman's voice came out in a choked whisper as he toppled forward.

"Spade!" A sharp voice came from far away. "Spade, let him go!"

The voice reached out from a distance, tugging at him through the fog. Something grabbed his arm, but he wrenched it away and lashed out. A shriek sounded.

A flutter of wings, and then a sharp pain stabbed his ear, and he cried out. Another sharp pain in his hand, and a rough caw. The stone slipped from his grasp.

He blinked. Ash. His vision cleared slowly—Henchcliff on the boulder, slumped. Ash perched on his own boulder, eyes winking black in the dark, the stone clutched in his beak.

The bird muttered deep in its throat, a sound that Spade had never heard. A groan sounded beneath him. He jerked his gaze down, past the rock ledge. Ember lay on the bottom stair, panting and stricken, Malachi beside her, propping her up. "You—you began to change," she gasped.

She stood slowly, clutching at her knee, the skin blackened in one spot. Spade looked between them, awareness dawning. "Did . . . did I do that to you?"

A shadow crossed Malachi's face, and Spade saw the fear in Ember's eyes.

"That you did, boy. Or at least, yer pebble did," Malachi said.

"I'm sorry," Spade said. "I—I didn't mean to . . ."

He stared at the stone in Ash's beak. The raw power in it . . . the surge that had ripped through him . . . he'd forgotten where he was, if only for a moment.

"That stone may just have a mind of its own," Malachi said slowly, as Ash croaked and hopped onto Spade's lap, dropping the pebble into his hand. Spade looked at it a moment longer, and when he looked up, he noticed Ember and Malachi watching him. He shoved it back in his pocket.

Ember stood silent for a moment, then shook her head.

"Let's go," she said. "We've got a guardsman to tie up."

Henchcliff lay unconscious while they bound his legs using Spade's belt under the dim light of a couple of glow-slugs that they'd plucked from a fallen stalactite. Spade drew the guard captain's belt out of his jacket and pried off the buckle, the ruby embedded in its center. "The third deepstone," he murmured, and an idea started forming in his head.

"We've got two stones now," Ember said, catching his excitement. "All we need is to get the Moor Mage's emerald ring from my aunt. And if we can find out where she's been keeping the ruby during the day, we'll find the miner's tool there too. We need to find the queen!"

Malachi slid the key ring off a loop at Henchcliff's waist and handed it to Spade. "You'll need these," he said.

Spade stared at his uncle. "Yer coming with us, right, Uncle?"

Malachi glanced up at the ceiling of the cavern, and Spade noticed a long fissure running its length, a steady stream of water trickling from it. "The cave's unstable. If we leave the captain, he'll likely be killed by falling rock."

"But we don't have time to haul him with us," growled Ember. "And besides, I don't really mind if he gets squashed."

A sparkle winked in Malachi's eyes. "Maybe so, but that wouldn't make you much different than him, would it? An' I can tell you ain't like him, Royal Miss. That's why you'll be a good leader someday."

Ember snorted, but she smiled reluctantly. "Fine. And I suppose this way, he'll be served justice."

"Still, Uncle," Spade said, glancing along the massive cavern. "You can't carry him out on yer own."

Malachi looked at Spade. "I still have some strength in these old bones, boy. Leave the guard to me. Now go," he said. "Go free yer brother, an' find the queen."

They ran by the light of a couple of glow-slugs, holding them up high as they raced through the tunnels. At last the tunnel veered off and climbed upward, and they slipped through a narrow entrance into a stone corridor. They'd reached the dungeons.

Spade's heart raced. He'd used the pebble, and that meant the Woegan wouldn't be far behind them.

Benji. He had to get to Benji.

They rounded a corner into a wide corridor and a pungent smell hit them in the face.

The creature had been here.

Prison cells loomed before them, the reek of the Woegan so strong Spade's eyes watered while Ember coughed and sputtered.

"Benji!" Spade cried, limping down the passage. Then he spotted the cell at the end of the row. He recognized the small cot with the thin blanket, books crammed in the stone nook.

"Where is he?" Ember panted, peering through the bars.

Fear filled Spade as he gazed at the empty cell. Had the queen decided not to wait?

"Spade?"

The familiar voice wavered in the air. Spade spun around as a faint glow of orange appeared in the dark of the cell, and something flickered on the blue blanket atop Benji's bunk. A misshapen lump appeared, shifting from bright blue to a mottled gray. Grubble stood to his feet, unwrapping his arms from around a boy. Benji.

"I makes him invisibles, like me," the lumpskin said.

"Benji! Grubble!" Spade exclaimed, and he sagged in relief against the prison door. "Grubble, I thought you were—"

"Killeds? No, Grubbles is fast."

Ember pulled out the keys, trying each one while Benji explained what had happened.

"The Woegan passed by, sniffing the air deep. An' I knew it was looking fer you. It stopped right outside the cell. I think it smelled Grubble's finger magic, an' it got confused, couldn't figure out which magic to follow."

Ember breathed out in relief. "Brilliant, Grubble," she said. "Your quick thinking bought us time."

The lumpskin nodded. "It is Grubbles honors to protects Benjini." He paused. "But Grubbles wonders . . . can you tells him about Fidgets?" His voice wavered slightly. "My brothers and sisters have not founds him."

Spade swallowed and looked down, a hard rock in his throat. "I'm sorry, Grubble. He died protecting us."

The lumpskin looked down at his finger, and the light flared brighter. "Grubbles knows it, deeps down inside." He sighed. "Grubbles feels their magics in him now, and he has the feeling Fidgets is gones."

Eyes burning, Spade shook his head. "It was my fault, Grubble," he whispered. "I couldn't run fast enough with this leg."

"No, Spades," the lumpskin said, and he laid a clammy hand on top of Spade's own. "The lumpskins knews just what theys were doings." He paused, and pride rippled across his wrinkled face, his chest puffing out. "Fidgets was cleverly. He was stoppings the creature to makings sure yous could escape."

They stood in silence for a long moment, until at last Ember broke the silence, and held up a key. "I think I've found it," she said, quiet.

Grubble slipped through the bars, and together, the three of them hefted and pulled aside the heavy metal bar-lock.

Benji's face crumpled with relief when the cell door creaked open at last. He stepped out and then bent over, coughing.

Grubble's worried gaze went to the boy. "Benjini has a colds," he said. "Benjini is not mades for dark and damps like lumpskins is."

"It's nothing," Benji wheezed, regaining his breath.

"Maybe you should rest a minute, Benj," Spade began, but Grubble stiffened suddenly, his eyes darting to the tunnel, his ears twitching. "No time for restings," the lumpskin whispered. "We must hurries. The creature lumbers up the stairs, headed straights for the castle."

CHAPTER 39

HUNTING A BEAST

The dungeon's main door clicked open with Henchcliff's key, and they stumbled through into the castle's west corridor. Spade led the way, then froze. He held up his hand, ushering them to silence. A young pimply-faced guard walked by, footsteps echoing in the hall. He'd nearly passed when Benji coughed.

The guard-boy whirled, and his startled gaze fell on their ragtag group.

"Royal Miss," he garbled. "What—where—" His face paled as he took in the mud and dirt on her dress. "Captain Henchcliff and the kingdom have been searching for you for two days—"

But Ember didn't wait. "The queen!" she hissed. "Where is she? In the throne room?"

"Th-the queen?" the guard-boy stammered. "No one's seen her all day, young miss. You know how she is at Harvest Moon."

Ember drew in a quick breath, her face pale. "Of course. I'd forgotten! It's the last day."

"What happens on the last day?" Spade nudged her, leaning in. Only then did the guard seem to notice him and the others. The guard's eyes narrowed. "Wait, now," he began, "isn't that the traitor spy—and his brother? And what is . . . ?" He tried to peer around them at Grubble.

"Of course not. These are my footmen." Ember pretended to look offended. "And that is . . . my dog."

The guard's brows furrowed. "That is the ugliest dog I've ever seen, if you don't mind me saying, Royal Miss." He bent and peered closer. "Are you sure that's a—"

"*Run*," Ember hissed at Spade and Benji. They lunged forward, bowling the young man over, as Spade slid the man's sword out of his sheath with deft fingers.

"Halt!" the guard screamed, but Spade held the sword to the boy's chin. "Into the dungeon!" he commanded.

The guard backed into the dungeon entryway, and Grubble snatched the boy's keys from his belt. They slammed the door and locked him in, then ran.

"Stop!" the guard yelled through the bars, his face red. "Royal Miss!"

"Footmen?" Spade groaned as they ran.

"What?" she panted. "It was better than wanted criminals."

They raced down the corridor and around a corner. "I'd almost forgotten. It's the anniversary of the day the princess Wren died," Ember explained as they ran. "No one sees the queen on last day of Harvest Moon, not even her servants." Spade glimpsed her face, tight with fear.

The queen'll be all alone in her room, exactly what the crea-
ture wants, he thought. He pushed through the pain of his
limp, forced himself to move faster.

Ember sprinted down a small corridor. "I think we can
get to her rooms through here," she called over her shoulder, and they rounded a corner, then ground to a halt. Two
guards stood at the end of the hall. They turned, catching
sight of the strange group. "Halt!" they cried.

"Quick," Spade barked, and they ducked down another
corridor, nearly crashing into three kitchen maids, serving
dishes in hand. The maids dropped the dishes, mouths falling open at the sight of their ragtag group, one of them
screaming when she spotted Grubble.

They veered around the splattered food and past the
maids, bursting out into the main foyer and startling another
guard as the two guards chasing the group bolted out of the
corridor behind them.

Grubble took one look at the royal guards and vanished,
his color blending into the floor.

Spade skidded to a stop, eyes darting around the room—
they were surrounded.

Ember straightened, fixing them all with her most commanding look. "We need to see the queen," she ordered. "I
don't have time to explain."

Sharp footsteps clattered over stone and the queen's
thin advisor appeared in the doorway.

"Miss Ember!" Spinniker sputtered. "Thank gems
you've been found!" His eyes narrowed, sweeping over

Spade and Benji. "Are you harmed? Guards, arrest this boy at once for kidnapping the royal niece, and we will let Henchcliff deal with him when he returns—"

"No, Spinniker," Ember interrupted, firm. "He didn't kidnap me! He is not the one you should be after; it's Henchcliff. He's a traitor to the queen." She pointed up the spiral staircase to the royal chambers beyond. "And we may already be too late. You must check the queen's rooms!"

Spinniker stiffened. "Now, Miss Ember, that is a very serious accusation. Henchcliff has been dutifully looking for you all this time."

"To try and kill us!" Ember sputtered. "He's the Woegan's master. We can prove it, Spinniker, I swear it! But we're wasting time—we need to find the queen!"

The old advisor paused, his eyes darting up the stairs. He turned to the guard at the foot of the stairway. "The rooms have been carefully watched since Her Majesty went in, have they not?"

The guard straightened. "Of course, sir. A sentry is stationed outside of her rooms. No one has been up or down this staircase, save the servants, for several hours."

"No one that you know of," Spade said.

Spinniker turned on him, expression fierce. "What do you mean by that, boy?"

"There are other ways in an' out of her room."

"It's true," Benji piped up. "I seen the Woegan itself creeping through the dungeons. It's using the secret tunnels!"

"Spoken like true thieves," the advisor said, though a shadow crossed the gaunt man's face, and he glanced at the guard stationed at the base of the stairs.

"I've seen nothing, sir," the guard insisted, "save the queen herself, entering her rooms several hours ago. It would be impossible for a monster as large and rank as the creature to sneak into the castle, and I've never heard of these tunnels."

The mention of the Woegan seemed to unnerve the other guards, who shifted uncomfortably, casting their gaze about.

"Then let us show you," Ember demanded. "We're wasting time!"

Spinniker pressed his fingers to the bridge of his nose. "You are overtired, Royal Miss, and I fear this kidnapping ordeal has been too much for you. Let's talk more of this tomorrow, after you have had a rest in your rooms." He turned to the guard behind her. "Escort the royal niece upstairs, please, and take these thieves and their bird to the dungeons."

The advisor whirled to the stairs, and the guard gently took hold of Ember. "No!" she cried, as the second guard disarmed Spade of his sword, while another grabbed Benji. Ash circled, squawking, a guard chasing after him. Spade's hands were pulled behind his back, and he was marched toward the door, past the castle tapestries.

Spade blinked. One of the tapestries fluttered as if blown by a breeze, and yet the grand doors were shut.

A flicker of gray appeared behind his guard, and Grubble reached out with a glowing finger, poking the guard in his buttocks.

"Filthy demon—" the guard hissed, and whirled to find his attacker. But Grubble had already vanished, and a moment later, the guard holding Ember yelped, then the guard holding Benji tripped.

Grubble appeared near the wall with the tapestry. The guards whirled toward him, but Ash dropped from the ceiling, divebombing them as Ember, Spade and Benji sprinted for the tapestry and ducked behind it. Spade's fingers skimmed the wall, finding a latch. He pressed it, and Ash swept to his shoulder.

It swung inwards, even as the guards shouted and raced for the billowing tapestry.

The wall of stone shifted, revealing a dark tunnel behind. A cold wind streaked out of the opening and cut across the room, carrying with it a particular smell.

A smell that was earthy and rotten, a smell of decay and stench.

The guard closest to them stumbled back, the whites of his eyes showing as fear rippled across his face.

But Spade, Ember and Benji leaped forward, into the darkness.

They crept along the corridor, Ember's and Benji's quick strides coupled with Spade's awkward *cl-clump*, while Grubble led the way.

They turned in the direction of the queen's rooms, but the lumpskin paused, his flat nose wrinkling. "Grubbles smells perfume . . . peonies and lilacs."

"It's the queen's," whispered Ember. "She's been in the tunnel!"

Grubble looked nervous. "But it is not goings to her rooms. It wispies down the other way."

They whirled the opposite direction, moving faster now, and the stench of the Woegan grew stronger, overpowering the perfume. "The creature follows Queenie," Grubble whispered.

A faint tinge of blue appeared ahead, speckled with bright dots and a glowing, round orb. The night sky, Spade realized. Grubble's small silhouette paused at the tunnel opening. He signaled and they stepped out into the night. Tall grass brushed up against their legs, a sharp wind buffeting them.

Spade looked around, surprised. Hills of grass dotted the landscape and thin gray tree trunks snaked out of the ground, the earth sloping downward gently. He turned to see the castle's western wall towering dark behind him, and it took him a moment to place where they were. Peering through the spindly trees, he spotted the twisted pathway weaving between the hills, curving down to a pair of ornate wrought iron gates.

The Royal Cemetery.

"Of course she'd go here," whispered Ember, coming to stand beside him. "I can't believe I didn't think of it earlier."

Grubble sniffed the air, his wrinkled face pale. "The creature is waitings somewheres close."

Ember sucked in a sharp breath. "The Woegan knew she'd come to the cemetery, somehow." She turned to them, voice trembling. "It's set a trap."

Benji looked pale. "Are you sure we should go in there?"

"We're forgetting something," Spade said, forcing confidence into his voice. "We know something it doesn't:

that we found its master, an' we have his ruby, plus the pebble."

"Right," Ember said, squaring her shoulders. She turned to look down at the cemetery as an evening mist rose from the ground and swirled between the trees. "Let's find the queen."

Ash uttered a hoarse croak on Spade's shoulder.

Spade jerked his chin at the cemetery. "Lead the way, Ash."

The raven spread its wings and soared upward, over the graveyard gate.

CHAPTER 40
THE WREN

The wrought iron gate swung inwards on silent hinges and they crept forward, careful to be quiet. Spade's breath puffed out in small wisps of cold, hanging on the air, while Ember looked around nervously at the mist all around them.

Benji was breathing hard from all of the running, his eyes lined with dark circles. He bent forward, trying to suppress another deep cough, his shoulders shaking. Grubble stood beside the boy, supporting him with his lumpy head, his wrinkled face creased with worry.

"Benj," Spade whispered. "I need a watch at the gates, alerting us to any guards coming down the path—or the creature itself, should it try an' sneak out. Yer the best for the job."

Benji met Spade's gaze. "You don't think I can help you fight the monster," he rasped, his voice quiet.

"Benj, yer a great thief an' spy, but the truth is, yer sick. An' I won't have you end up in that dungeon again 'case anything goes wrong."

Benji's eyes flickered, but Grubble reached up, placing a lumpy hand on his arm. "Brother Spade is right, Benjini. It is better we stays here."

The boy scowled, but at last, he nodded. "Fine. But you'd better come back in one piece."

"'Course. I'm a thief, remember?" But even as Spade said it, he brushed away the sense of foreboding that washed over him, stuffed it deep down inside.

Benji melted into the dark, a silent shadow that stood guard by the gate, Grubble's small figure beside him.

Ember shot him a look. "Ready?" she whispered.

Ash perched on a tombstone in the dark, waiting silently up ahead. The raven hopped from tombstone to tombstone, quiet as the night, leading them deeper into the graveyard. The familiar drooping branches of the wendigo trees hung over the winding path, and Spade and Ember slipped between the trunks, following the raven. The path turned once more, and Spade spotted the baron's tomb, the one he'd tried to rob all those nights ago. It seemed like a lifetime since then—the night he'd first met the queen.

He uttered a prayer, a whispered mutter. What were the chances they'd find her alive?

A sound rose in the mist ahead, muffled, and Spade froze.

It grew louder. A snarl, then a low whine. A pungent musk swirled toward them, and the gloom parted, revealing a monstrous figure bent over a broken bench, a smashed deer statue beside it.

The same bench where he'd first met the queen.

It turned slowly, straightening to its full height. Moonlight washed over its wrinkled, drooped muzzle. The Moor Mage's emerald ring glittered on its claw, and something wet glistened on its gnarled hands, across its matted chest. The statue beside it was smeared with the dark stuff, the ground splattered. Blood.

Ember let out a low, unearthly moan. "Filthy creature!" she screamed. "You killed her, didn't you! You killed the queen!"

The creature snarled and whirled on her. Spade lunged forward and grabbed Ember's arm. "Ash!" he cried.

The raven tore through the air, claws outstretched, and the Woegan screamed.

Spade yanked Ember out of its path, and they ducked as the Woegan tore across the graveyard toward them, toppling tombstones. They crawled and scrambled behind statues and gravemarkers, trying to get out of its line of sight.

The creature was wearing the emerald ring. Spade forced away thoughts of what it might have done to the queen. All he knew was that they needed that stone.

"C'mon," he wheezed, and they raced down the hill, Spade limping with every step, willing his leg to move faster. They darted through the graves, crouching and twisting, and then he spotted it: the stone mausoleum with the strange handles and the carvings etched into its walls, the one he and Benji had seen that day they'd attempted to rob the baron's grave. Crawling behind it, they gasped for air.

Silence filled the graveyard.

Where was the Woegan?

Spade pressed his back up against the cold stone of the building and the strange engravings, Ember beside him, her breath short and fast. The pebble in his pocket pulsed, its light illuminating the wall behind them.

A shudder ran through him, as it had the first time he'd seen it when he'd dug up the tax collector. They crouched in tense silence, and he glanced up at the wall, the unusual artwork on it.

And then Spade froze. He peered closer. Amidst the strange shapes and designs, he spotted men coming out of a hole in the ground, the mountain rising behind them . . . and they carried pickaxes.

And suddenly he knew why the mausoleum felt strange, why it felt haunted.

"It's here," he whispered.

Ember's gaze darted to him. "What are you talking about, Spade?" she hissed.

"The place where the miner's tool is. It's in the mausoleum."

Spade and Ember crouched in the darkness, holding their breath.

A low snarl broke the stillness, very near the mausoleum. A sharp caw sounded above. A warning from Ash.

The sound of lumbering feet drew near, followed by a deep, low whine.

"I need a distraction," Spade whispered. "We have to get that ring."

Ember nodded. "I have an idea."

She edged behind the mausoleum, grabbing a dead branch.

Spade glanced up, locating Ash perched atop the small building. The raven met Spade's eyes with his beady black ones, ready.

Steeling himself, Spade limped out into the open, shoving his hand into his pocket to grasp the pebble. The stone surged to life, heat coursing through his fingers.

The Woegan twisted around, instantly drawn by the scent of the awakened pebble.

"I know what yer afraid of," Spade called out, raising the pebble high in the air, remembering what he'd seen in Lyrica's stream. "An' I know why you want this. You think it'll set you free from yerself." The creature's eyes widened, and its long claws paused, frozen in midair.

It was what he'd hoped for.

Ember stood up from behind a tombstone, lighting her branch aflame. The Woegan snarled and shielded its eyes, blinded.

Spade curled his fingertips out, thrusting the power across the tombs. Tendrils spread and twisted, grasping at the Woegan.

The creature roared, stumbling backward. Its own tendrils shot out, amassing in a black swarm. They writhed toward Spade, focused on him with hungry ferocity as Ash dove, talons outstretched.

The Woegan looked up too late. Ash lit down on its outstretched talon, latching on to the gem on its claw. With one maneuver, the raven plucked the emerald stone from the ring, then swept into the air.

The Woegan's coils faltered. It snarled and swiped at the air, but Ash wheeled and dodged out of its reach, dropping the emerald into Spade's hand.

The emerald seared bright, and a fire filled Spade's veins, a furious power that trilled through his muscles, echoed in his bones. The power surged up his wrist and Ember gasped from somewhere behind him, still holding her burning branch.

He hurled the power at the creature and watched as it fell to its knees. It opened its massive jaws and groaned, but it was no longer a match for the deepstones.

Something dark and heavy filled Spade, a feeling of rage, of want. He twisted the magic in his fingers, gathering it, and the muscles in his leg seemed to strengthen, the ache disappearing. The magic called to him, and he felt agile, swift. Powerful.

Lifting his arms, he thrust the magic back at the creature. It fell forward, clutching at its throat.

"Spade!" The voice sounded in the recesses of his mind, faint.

He pushed it aside, power rippling through him as he crossed the graves toward the creature. Its call pulled at him, slipped its fingers through his mind. He couldn't quite remember anything other than the pulse of magic thrumming through him.

"Spade!" The voice called out again, sharper now, full of fear. Familiar. Faintly annoying.

The power of the deepstones surged into his hands, and the voice faded away. He reached out for the Woegan, tightening the tendrils around the creature.

Something hit him hard in the side, something flat and heavy and metal, and he tumbled backward, somebody thin and bony landing on top of him.

He looked up into Benji's face, saw the shovel in his hands.

"Benji?" he muttered, the fog of his brain slowly clearing. "What are you doing here? Yer supposed to wait at the gate!"

"I heard Ember screaming." Benji gulped. "An' Ash shrieking. I came running, an' then I saw you—you were changing, Spade." Benji's face was pale. "The stones were doing something to you: yer skin was turning all black, an' you weren't walking with a limp anymore. I had to stop it . . ."

Spade shoved him off, and they looked over at the crumpled Woegan, lying on the ground, still.

"What were you thinking, Benj," Spade hissed. "I was stopping that creature—"

But Benji shook his head, fierce, his lip trembling. "You weren't stopping it, Spade, you were killing it. An' something was happening to you. I didn't recognize you."

Spade crawled to his feet, angry. "For once in yer life, Benj, I wish you'd just do what yer told."

Benji stared at him, hurt flashing across his face.

A pang of guilt hit Spade, but he whirled on Grubble and Ember. "Is it dead?"

"I think it's breathing," Ember said quietly, her face ashen. "But hurt. Badly."

Spade grit his teeth, ignoring Benji as he stood, silent. "We've wasted enough time. We've got a mausoleum to break into."

The door had no lock, the wood old and worn, the curved handles rusted beneath Spade's touch. Ingenious, he thought. It gave the place the look of unimportance. In fact, he remembered thinking it was abandoned when he and Benji first saw it that night by the baron's grave.

Spade stepped up to it, taking hold of the handle.

"Please be careful, Spades," Grubble said. "Lumpskins does not like this place."

Several feet away, Benji sat perched on a crooked tombstone, his back to them. He watched over the Woegan's still body, silent.

"He was just trying to help, Spade," Ember whispered, catching his glance. Spade sighed. Maybe he'd been unfair, but his brother didn't know how it had felt, for that brief moment, to be free from his leg for once. To be on the winning side of the fight, instead of the losing. Benji refused to look over, his shoulders slumped, but Spade dragged his gaze away. "I'll fix things after," he said. "There's no time right now."

Ember pursed her lips and sighed, then turned to the doorway. "I've read all about booby traps in *A Common*

History of Castle Ensnarement," she whispered. "Pass me your glow-slugs. I'll go in first."

Spade frowned. He was supposed to be the Joolie, after all. But she was right. She probably knew far more about the traps designed by her strange ancestors than he would. Reluctantly, he reached into his pocket and pulled out the little sack of glow-slugs.

Ember took it and shoved it into her dress pocket, then ducked low and crawled through the door. Spade waited for a long, tense moment for her to reappear.

"Ember?" he whispered.

Another moment passed, and she reached a finger out of the door, beckoning him in.

Darkness enveloped him, and the smell of musty air filled his nostrils as he ducked inside. The floor was made of smooth cobbles, the walls of stone.

He moved forward, following the faint sound of Ember's breathing, and then he heard her fumble in the dark.

She drew in a sharp breath. "Oops," she said. Then, "Duck!"

Spade dropped to his belly, the air knocked out of him as something whizzed overhead and clattered against the far wall.

"What was that?" he demanded.

"Oh dear . . . I think I released a spring-loaded arrow. By accident, of course. I should've read that chapter a little more closely."

"At least I still have my head," Spade grunted. He heard Ember shuffling around in the dark.

"I've disarmed it now," she said, and a dim green light flickered to life in her hand: the glow-slugs.

They stood in front of several ancient carvings engraved in the walls, elegant tombs laid between them. A bronze bowl sat on a pedestal in the far corner of the room, an inscription etched below it.

"A stone that gives such power to the living, must be guarded by those whose hearts are dead," Ember read, and shuddered.

Spade looked up. Two stone grim reapers overlooked the crypt, scythes crossed high over the bronze bowl. Several plaques lined the left wall, the remains of the cremated dead behind them. But other than that, the crypt was bare.

Inching along the wall, he approached the bowl. He reached out, feeling along its base, but he didn't find any latches or levers, no loose flagstones. The room spanned only the length of two men, and he reached the far end without finding anything. Slowly, he made his way across to the opposite side, tracing every nook and cranny, but still there was no sign of the miner's pickaxe.

"Wait," Ember murmured. "Those whose hearts are dead . . . maybe it doesn't mean corpses."

He followed her gaze to the two grim reaper statues, and noticed that something seemed off with the one on the left, but what was it? Perhaps it was angled differently . . . Spade crossed the room and moved to stand before it when his toe landed on a loose cobble.

A sound like a chisel dragging across slate filled the room, and a dark hole yawned open, giving away beneath his feet.

"Aaargh!" he yelled, as Ember lunged and wrenched him to the side, sending them both tumbling against the wall.

Breathing hard, Spade stared at the hole where they'd just been standing, his heart thudding in his chest.

"Thanks," he croaked.

A smile tugged at the corners of her mouth. "Not a problem. Can you get off me now?"

Heat filled his cheeks. "Right . . . sorry." He scrambled to his feet.

Grubble appeared in the doorway. "Is Spades and Royal Miss okay?" Spade stared at the reaper. Booby traps meant you were close.

"We're fine," he said, and then he saw it.

"Ember," he whispered. "Look at the reaper on the left."

Ember followed his gaze to the curved scythe in the statue's hand. "Wait a minute," she murmured, and peered closer. "That's not a scythe—it's a pickaxe!" Spade reached up to the reaper and pulled, and the handle slipped out of the statue's frozen grip, the tip steel-edged.

The miner's tool.

"Benji!" Spade yelled. "We've found it!"

Hands trembling, Spade pulled out the ruby belt buckle, then the Moor Mage's emerald ring, and last the pebble. Placing them together beside the tool, Spade watched as the pebble and the emerald ring flared to life with a brilliant light. Ember and Grubble drew a breath.

But the ruby remained dull, lifeless. The other two deepstones emanated heat, pulling at his gut, but the ruby lay cold.

Spade stared at it as a horrible thought slowly sank into his brain.

It wasn't possible. Couldn't be.

"It's not a deepstone," he whispered. "Henchcliff's not the master."

They stared at each other, silence permeating the tomb.

And then Spade looked up, noticing something. "Where's Benji?" he asked.

Grubble whirled, ears twitching.

"Benji!" Spade called.

His voice rang out in the stillness, echoing around the room. He shoved the stones into his pocket and scrambled to his feet.

"Benji?"

Then the sound of a garbled gasp from outside the crypt.

And ice trickled into Spade's veins.

The night air blasted him in the face as Spade hurtled out of the crypt, his heart dropping at the sight that greeted him.

The Woegan turned to meet his gaze, Benji dangling from its grip, its claws wrapped around his thin neck.

"Benji!" Spade shoved his hand into his pocket and groped for the pebble. How could he have been so stupid! It was his fault Benji had stayed alone outside.

Tendrils of the Woegan's magic wrapped around his brother's body, writhing over him.

Spade met the creature's dark eyes and the pebble's power surged up his wrist. But even as he thrust his hand into the air, the Woegan's black cords tightened, causing his brother to choke.

"Stop," Spade pleaded. "Let him go!"

The Woegan tilted its head, eyes narrowed on the pebble, and Spade knew what it wanted.

The stone's power coursed through him, calling him, and he felt the magic fill his veins. He wanted to use it. It clawed at his mind, but he caught sight of his brother's eyes, his eyelids fluttering closed. With all his strength, he grit his teeth, thrusting the power back down.

With his other hand, he reached into his pocket and drew the emerald out. He thrust both stones at the creature. "They're yours," he choked, holding them out, and heard Ember suck in a sharp breath. "Just let him go."

The Woegan loosened its grip, and Spade limped forward slowly.

The creature's rank odor was even more overpowering up close, and its tendrils snaked out, encircling his waist, squeezing the breath out of him.

Slowly, the creature uncurled its claws. Benji sank to the grass, choking.

"Run, Benj," Spade whispered.

His brother looked at him, eyes widening, and then Spade turned to the Woegan. Several tendrils sprang out of the creature and took hold of Spade's arms and legs. He held his hand up, palm open as it reached down with two curved claws, grasping the stones.

His brother cried out, flung to the side as the creature threw Spade to the ground. Something sharp and pointy dug into his hip as his leg crumpled beneath him, the breath torn from his lungs. Ash cawed from somewhere above him, frantic.

"Spade!" Ember ran for the creature, the miner's pickaxe in her hands. Its dark lips twisted in a grin, and she was thrown against a tombstone, her head smashing into the rock, the pickaxe landing somewhere in the grass. She sagged forward, moaning.

"No!" Spade yelled. The Woegan bent over him, its putrid breath in his face.

Ash dove for the creature, talons extended, but the beast whipped another tendril, and the bird was hurtled through the air.

Raising a long, terrible claw, the Woegan stared at Spade, its eyes burning into him. Spade grasped for something, anything in the grass that he could hurl at it, and he remembered the sharp object digging into his leg. He reached into his pocket and pulled it out, lifting it up.

The little wren figurine.

Not much of a weapon, but all he had. He pulled his fist back, the figurine clutched in his fingers.

The creature froze.

Claws poised in midair, its gaze fixed on the little wren. Spade blinked. Why didn't it attack?

It leaned forward, and something glittered in its hair, enmeshed in its tangled, blood-matted throat. Spade glimpsed a blue pendant.

The creature's black-orbed gaze met his, and the breath in Spade's chest stilled.

Wait . . . he knew that gemstone, that necklace. He'd seen it before . . .

The clear blue sapphire that hung around the queen's neck.

First the Moor Mage's ring, now the necklace. But what would the creature want with the necklace?

And then he knew.

A wave of shock met him as he looked into the creature's eyes, even as the Woegan's gaze wormed its way into his mind, trying to wrap around his thoughts. But this time he pushed back, clinging to the sudden idea that washed over him, taking hold. Agony contorted the beast's face.

"Spade! Look out!" Ember appeared behind the creature, staggering forward with a burning stick in her hands, Grubble holding another.

They lunged for the creature.

The Woegan reared up, claws extended.

"No, wait!" Spade screamed. "Stop, Queen Carmelia!"

CHAPTER 41

A GREAT SORROW

The creature froze, its entire body rigid, mist swirling around it. Time slowed as it turned its scarred face toward Spade.

Hands trembling, Ember lowered the burning branch. "Wh-what?" she sputtered. She stared at the Woegan, jaw working, and an awful understanding bloomed across her face. Horrified, she gazed at the creature, looking for something, anything resembling her aunt, the queen.

A deadly stillness filled the graveyard. Then a slow, piercing wail tore from the Woegan. The scream built to a deafening roar, reverberating off the tombstones.

Bits and pieces of thoughts ricocheted across Spade's mind, shards tearing through his brain. Quick flashes of memory surged upward: the queen, pale, with headaches. The funny, stale smell around the castle and the guards rarely seeing the creature itself. The untouched royal bedroom, the queen's things covered with a fine layer of dust.

She hadn't been in her rooms, he realized. She'd been out hunting.

Its eyes fixed on his, then something broke through the din in his head. A clear, desperate voice.

Let me go.

It was a voice he recognized, a voice he'd heard many times before.

Queen Carmelia.

When they'd come upon the creature it had been standing by a broken bench, a bloody wound on its head. Could the queen know what she'd become, somehow? Was she trying to break free?

The pool at Lyrica's cottage whirled into Spade's mind. *"Deepstones are a way to make you forget,"* she'd said. *"But friendship and love, that's a whole different kind of magic. They help you remember who you are."*

An idea took hold, and his hands began to shake, sweat beading on his forehead.

He'd have one chance.

In one swift movement he sank down before the creature, inches from its razor-sharp claws. Spade swallowed hard and held its gaze, hoping Carmelia could hear him somewhere in the rasping, grotesque form that had taken over her body. "You've got fears, Majesty. But we all do. An' I see you for who you are, an' Ember does too. You weren't always this way."

Behind the creature, he glimpsed Ember, still as a statue, watching. Benji began to stir, Grubble helping him to his feet.

Spade held up the little stone wren in shaking hands, its shining blue eye catching the moonlight. "You let the sadness take you over," he whispered, pleading. "You let the feeling that you wanted to be someone else fill you up."

The Woegan reared back, gaze locking on the wren. Its lips drew back and it snaked an arm out, curling its claws around his neck.

He choked as it stared down at him, its obsidian eyes churning. His frantic mind spun as he fought for air. "Maybe we can't change what's happened, Majesty," he croaked. "But we can choose to do something good with it."

The creature blinked, something flickering in the depths of its gaze. Blood rushed to Spade's head, and stars began to fill his vision. He thought of Benji, of Malachi and Ember. His family.

"Please, Carmelia," a low, gravelly voice called out from somewhere in the graveyard. Spade recognized it through the dim fog in his oxygen-deprived brain, though he'd never heard it like this, desperate, pleading.

Henchcliff crossed the cemetery and fell to his knees in front of the creature. "Remember who you are," the guard pleaded. "This creature isn't you."

Ash soared over the tombstones behind him, and Malachi hobbled up the path, cane in hand. Ash must have gone for help, Spade realized, even as his vision went dark.

He could feel his body shutting down, his heart slowing. The wren dropped out of his hand and bounced across the ground.

The Woegan hissed, a deep shudder snaking through it.

"Spade!" he heard Benji scream.

And then Spade was falling. He hit the ground hard, heaving air into his lungs.

His vision sparked to life as he lay there, wheezing. He looked up as the creature bent, grasping at the stone wren.

The creature stood quiet above him, gaze fixed on the little songbird. Slowly, the darkness in its eyes changed, glimmering to life in a familiar shade of pale blue, and Spade glimpsed the queen looking down at him.

"Take it," she whispered in a terrible voice, a whining mix of both the creature's and her own. He blinked as her words sank in.

"Quickly," she hissed. She dropped the emerald and the pebble into his hands and exposed her neck, the words garbled. "Before it returns."

Spade struggled to his feet, aching all over. He reached for the sapphire necklace and yanked it free from her neck. It seared him, burning his fingers, and she cried out. "Hurry," she groaned, and he saw her eyes flicker in pain, her face contorted against the internal battle inside her grotesque body.

Then Ember stumbled up beside him, a bloody gash on her cheek, her arm bent at a funny angle. But she clenched her jaw and clutched the creature's massive, hoary paw. "Hold on, Aunt," she whispered.

Spade scanned the grass, desperate, searching for the miner's tool.

"There," Malachi cried, pointing, and Benji lunged for the silver glint, then froze. Henchcliff stood in front of it. He met the boy's eyes for a long moment, while everyone held their breath.

Then the guard swept it up, tossing it to Ember. Taking a deep breath, Spade inspected the sapphire pendant and the Moor Mage's emerald stone, bringing them together. A small notch lay empty at their center, just large enough for the pebble. He held his breath and fit the smallest deepstone into place. They flared with a brilliant light.

Ember lifted the miner's tool above them, looking up at the queen, then gasped.

Spade followed her gaze to the queen's blue eyes, only they were no longer blue. They'd darkened, red seeping into the irises.

"No, Aunt!" begged Ember, as the creature's long, curved claw sliced through the air. It ripped the pickaxe from her hands and smashed it down on the bench, breaking it in two.

A wave of magic blew them back, and the metal seared orange, then red, and burst into flame. A charred remnant of metal remained, twisted into a blackened lump.

Spade's gut wrenched.

The Woegan stood to its feet. Its power swirled, amassing around it.

Sucking in a breath, Spade grabbed the stones and scrambled backward. He and Ember threw themselves behind a tombstone near Benji and Grubble. Malachi edged toward them, Ash shrieking above.

Spade looked down at the sapphire necklace deepstone in one hand, the emerald and pebble in the other.

"You can't," Benji whispered. "We'll lose you to the magic, with all three of 'em together. It'll be too much."

But the deepstones pulled at him. And it was the only way to stop the creature.

Ember's face paled and Malachi's eyes flickered as Spade

reached for the sapphire deepstone, lifting the chain up to his neck.

Something tugged at his tattered jacket. He looked down to see Grubble standing beside him, his bright eyes determined.

"Mr. Spades," the lumpskin whispered, holding out his hand. "The deepstones. Gives them to Grubbles."

Spade stared at the little creature. What could Grubble possibly do?

"The stones, quicksies," the lumpskin warbled as the Woegan lurched toward them. "You must trusts me."

There wasn't time to think.

Spade thrust the sapphire necklace and the emerald ring at Grubble, grasping the pebble in his other hand. But something deep and ferocious rang through him, and he found himself curling his fingers around the small deepstone.

"Spade," Benji pleaded. "Please."

The Woegan, stumbling toward them, unsheathed its claws. Spade ducked, landing hard against a statue, Grubble beside him.

He grit his teeth, hands shaking, and shoved the pebble at the lumpskin.

Grubble's pinky flared bright as the pebble touched his skin. The little lumpskin raised his eyes to the skies. "Brother and sister lumpskins," he whispered. "Lends Grubbles your glows."

The tip of his pinky continued to blaze, and a brilliant light swept down his finger. A glow radiated from Grubble, and he thrust his finger down on the three deepstones.

The beast roared, a terrible, haunting sound. It sank to its knees, burning eyes riveted on the stones as a black wall of magic rose up from them. Spade was knocked flat onto his back as the magic rippled over him, consuming the graveyard in a thick fog. It choked the air, drowned out the moon and stars, cloaked everything in its path. Ash's caw echoed somewhere in the dark, but Spade couldn't make out a single thing.

And then slowly, the smoke dissipated into the evening, revealing several shocked faces. Spade blinked and sat up.

Ember stood from where she'd crouched by a large gravestone, and Benji leaned shakily against a stone nearby. They all stared at the small figure of Grubble, a weak smile on his wrinkled face. A pile of dust lay at his toes.

A few feet away, Henchcliff knelt before the still figure of a woman lying on the ground.

The queen's golden hair stirred in the wind, her face as pale as a ghost's, her lips a cold blue. She clutched the wren sculpture in her limp hand.

Henchcliff bowed his head, his shoulders stiff. Spade held his breath, and it seemed the whole graveyard stood quiet, waiting with him. Ash dipped down from the sky, landing quietly on Spade's shoulder.

A slight breeze blew through the graveyard, and then with a soft sigh, the queen's chest rose. Faint color appeared in her cheeks, and her fingers twitched.

Henchcliff released a shuddering breath, and Ember gasped in relief.

Queen Carmelia opened her eyes.

CHAPTER 42

TO TELL THE TRUTH

The silence of the night settled deeply over the cemetery, and the queen looked at each of them in turn as she told her story, her eyes haunted and dark.

"So you see," she whispered. "After my husband's death, and Wren's, I . . . I began to change. Because always, the loss was there." She paused. "When my father died, I went down to the crypt to see the stone I'd inherited. It had a strange effect on me, and I was able to forget who I was, if only for a few minutes."

The memory of the stone's power swept through Spade as he listened, quiet. He'd felt the same draw.

"I found myself going down to the crypt more often, late in the evenings," she continued. "Until I couldn't remember going down one day, and my mind began to feel . . . foggy."

Henchcliff, silent until now, moved forward. He bowed before her, his head dropped. "It is my fault, my lady," he choked out. "I should have guarded you more closely. But I did not figure it out until it was too late. And by then, I did not know what to do . . . and so I followed you, and I tried to stop all who would discover you."

The queen looked at the silent guard for a long moment, something akin to a realization on her face, as if seeing him for the first time.

"If only I had found the stone before you," the guard muttered, fierce. "I would have found you something else to ease your grief." And then Spade knew what she saw too. The guard loved her.

Carmelia lay a quiet hand over the guard's. "No, Henchcliff. There is nothing you could have done. The choice was my own." The guard fell silent, his heavy face worn.

"An' what about yer own stone—the ruby?" Benji asked after a moment, having sat quiet on a tombstone until now. "Where'd it come from?"

Henchcliff met his gaze. "When I realized what the deepstone had done to Her Majesty, I went in search of a stone of my own. One that could enhance my protection over her and help me track her, even transformed as the Woegan. At last I found one. It was owned by a Joolie who agreed to sell it to me, though it cost me all I had."

A Joolie. Spade should have known. Joolies were never far from a deal that smelled of gold.

A sigh rattled the man's chest. "I wasn't prepared for the effect of the ruby's magic," he murmured. "It was so great that it blinded me to all else except the need to protect."

Carmelia wavered, the cloth pressed tight to the gash on her head. The guard halted his story and he and Ember reached out to steady her, but the queen raised a hand.

"Henchcliff was unable to stop me by then. In rare flashes, I realized what I had become, and I tried to break free, to find a way out. But the Woegan had become too strong. It had taken not only my memories of pain, but of who I was. When I awoke each morning, I knew something terrible had happened, but I couldn't remember what."

She paused and drew a deep, ragged breath. "Until last night. Perhaps it was the harvest moon, but I felt more clear-headed than I had in months. So I started to go to the cemetery, to the place where my husband and our daughter are buried. I thought perhaps I could regain some of my memories there."

A deep sadness etched across the queen's face. "I don't recall what happened after that, but I must have transformed. Everything was a blur until you held up the little wren figurine, Spade, and I recognized you. In that moment I discovered what I had become, and it is thanks to you."

Spade flushed. "I shouldn't have stolen the wren, Majesty. But I'm glad that it came in handy. An' I'm also glad you didn't eat me," he admitted.

Her hands trembled. "What a mess I have made," she whispered, and her gaze lingered on Grubble, who sat quietly on a tombstone, listening.

The sound of the cemetery gate creaking open interrupted them, the din of footsteps clattering over the stone walkway.

"My Queen!" Spinniker appeared, six guards beside him. "Captain!" He paled, his jaw dropping open as he took in Carmelia, broken and fragile-looking, then Spade, Ember, Malachi and Grubble. He froze upon spotting the broken bench and deer statue, the black blood marring the ground. "Where is the creature?" he demanded. "Did it escape?"

"Spinniker," the queen stood, swaying, her thin fingers white as she gripped Ember's offered hand. "I have something to tell you."

She gestured to the guards to leave, all except Henchcliff. Then she and her advisor turned away, walking to a quiet spot in the graveyard, where the queen spoke in a hushed voice. Henchcliff followed quietly behind, ever her stoic protector. The other guards looked around the graveyard in stunned disbelief, shooting strange looks at the motley group of Joolies, royal niece, and lumpskin, then left, quiet and sober.

A piece of rubble lay at Spade's feet and he bent, lifting it, seeing a pile of ash and dust beneath it. The remains of the three deepstones.

He brushed the dust aside, then stopped, startled. Something caught his eye: a slight glimmer nestled in the pile.

A piece of the pebble.

He bent down and carefully picked it up. Silence greeted him. Then, from somewhere in the depths of the stone, a faint pulse echoed up his fingers.

Ember, Benji and Malachi whispered in hushed tones together, picking up pieces of the rubble, while Grubble warbled quietly to Ash, the two of them sitting on a tombstone near the wendigo trees. None of them looked Spade's way.

He slipped the pebble into his pocket, then went back to work.

CHAPTER 43

UNLIKELY FRIENDS

Faint rays of sunlight peeked over the castle walls, chasing away the shadows from the night before. Spade walked along the parapets while Ash soared above, dipping and chasing bugs. Spade had left Benji and Malachi sleeping quietly in his small castle room, hoping to let Benji rest.

Grubble had remained with them until the early hours of morning, and when the dawn approached, he'd slipped back into the tunnels with the promise to find them again soon someday, when the moon was full.

A few sleepy guards watched them go by, but no one stopped him. Instead, they tipped their helmets as he passed, and it felt odd. In one single night, he'd gone from hated thief to respected royal spy, Woegan-killer.

"Spade?"

He turned. Ember stood from behind a parapet, pulling her hood down off her face. She must have been sitting there for a while.

"What are you doing up so early?" he asked, surprised.

"I couldn't sleep." She smiled, but there were dark circles under her eyes. "The whole your-aunt-was-actually-a-demon-monster thing, you know."

He nodded and walked over to sit down beside her. "Yup. It don't get much weirder. But you haven't met my family. Grandma Flint does a pretty good demon impression."

She laughed, her flaming hair blowing wildly in the wind. "I'd like to meet them some day."

He raised his eyebrows. "Careful what you wish for."

Her laugh died a little. "I know, you probably want to get out of here as soon as you can."

"I dunno about that," Spade said. "I seem to have pretty interesting adventures when I'm here. An' the chocolate pie is the best in the land."

"Watching Spinniker's face turn red is pretty fun too."

"An' running through secret tunnels."

A groan interrupted them, and the old advisor himself appeared at the end of the parapet, looking flustered after climbing the stairs, his white hair askew, coattails flapping in the wind.

"Most inconvenient," Spinniker muttered when he laid eyes on them. "The Royal Miss should not be wandering about the parapets . . ."

He teetered toward them, then stopped in front of Spade. Rigidly, as if it pained him, the old advisor executed a slight bow. "The queen has requested your presence," the advisor said. Spade glimpsed the weariness in his eyes, his shoulders stooped even further than usual. Spade imagined that being the advisor to a queen was no easy task, especially one that had secretly devoured citizens of the kingdom in her alter-ego as a dark-magic beast.

"Miss Ember, the cook has laid your breakfast out," he said stiffly. "It would please her if you would eat it."

Ember sighed. "All right, Spinniker."

The old advisor turned to Spade. "Follow me, Joo—er, ahem. Royal Spy." He whirled on his heel without even a glance to see if Spade was behind him.

"I guess I gotta go," Spade said.

Ember nodded. "I'll see you later?"

She said it quietly, almost as if she expected she might not.

Ash chose that moment to fly down and perch on her shoulder and give her a fond nudge with his beak. "'Course," Spade said. "Especially seeing as Ash has got a new best friend."

Spinniker frowned, overhearing, and muttered under his breath. "Quick now, boy," he said. "The queen shouldn't be kept waiting." He turned and tottered down the stairs, leading Spade across the courtyard to a small gate that led to the hedge gardens. The advisor reached out, fingers on the gate's iron handle, then paused.

"How did you know?" he asked, his voice low, defeated. He turned to face Spade, his stern face haggard.

Spade knew what he meant, but before he could say anything, Spinniker continued, his jaw tight. "I spent every day in her presence. *Every day.* And yet, I did not see it. I never imagined it was her, all along."

"I guess . . . she had a certain kinda sadness." Spade

glanced down. "The kinda sadness I know about . . . wanting to be something or someone else."

The old man considered Spade for a long moment. "I see," he said at last. He nodded once, and for the first time, Spade thought he detected a glimmer of respect in the thin man's eyes. Spinniker turned and opened the gate, and bright sunlight poured in. "The queen is waiting for you in the garden."

Queen Carmelia sat on a bench beneath a wendigo tree that overlooked the castle grounds. She sat so still that servants and gardeners might never notice her if they passed by. For a brief moment, Spade wondered if he should slip away. What could she possibly want from him now?

But she lifted her head, casting a cool gaze across the gardens, and he knew she'd seen him.

He barely recognized her as he approached. Her dress was plain, a simple brown fabric, and her fingers and neck were bare of jewelry, except for one small piece—a little silver wren that hung on a thin chain around her neck.

Her hair was drawn up beneath a wide-brimmed hat that cast her face in shadow, though many of her golden strands had turned to silver. When she tilted her head, he saw that her skin was pale, but the circles beneath her eyes had faded. Her gaze was clear, startling, and she met his with a sort of determined look.

"You came," she said quietly. "I did not know if you would." She gestured for him to sit down beside her, but he remained standing.

Spade took a breath. "If I can, Majesty, I came to ask if you'd consider letting my debt be paid, an' if you'd release my brother an' me."

The queen's eyes moistened. "Not only have you fulfilled our bargain, but you've freed my kingdom, defeated the Woegan and saved my life."

Spade felt a blush creep up his cheeks. "I had help, Majesty," he said. "I'd be dead without Grubble, Benji an' Ash, an' it was Ember who solved most all the puzzles."

A small smile spread across her lips. "I don't doubt it," she said, then released a long sigh. "I've been blinded in more ways than one." Her eyes flickered. "I've misjudged not only you, but my own niece. And all along, her capabilities were more than that of my entire royal guard." She looked up. "Which brings me to a favor, Spade."

Spade stiffened at the words, wary, but the queen shook her head. "Don't worry, I'm not asking you to do any more creature-hunting, Spade. I am no longer the queen."

Spade blinked, her words sinking in. "Pardon, Majesty?"

She looked past him as if straight through the walls of the castle, in the direction of the mountains to someplace he couldn't see. "I could never be the queen of this kingdom after all that's happened," she said. "Some things cannot be undone.

"I could tell them the truth, of course," she continued, "but that would erode their trust in the Wyndhail royal family, and I can't bear to do that when the kingdom is so unstable. Especially if a new queen will sit on the throne—one who has proven herself a better candidate than any in our family's history. Though she is young, she is honest to a fault, courageous, clever and compassionate."

Spade stared at her. "Ember?"

She nodded. "She will be the youngest queen in our history, but Henchcliff will act as regent until she is of age. I know you may doubt him, but Henchcliff is truly the best protector she could have. He did not know what the deepstones could do, nor that his own stone would take over his reasoning. But that is why he will make a better regent than all others. He will be more prepared for the deceptive power of Wyndhail's magical stones than anyone else."

She had a point, Spade realized. "An' what do you want with me?"

A flicker of hope crossed Carmelia's face. "Ember will need a friend. I realize I have no right to ask you this, but would you consider staying on at the castle? Becoming the castle's royal spy, and . . . traveling magician? The lumpskin and your pet raven would be very welcome, of course. You see, the castle . . . it's a very lonely place, at times. I know this better than most."

Spade gazed at the beautiful gardens. He thought of the meals, his comfortable room. She was offering him a way to remake himself, a life where he might be seen differently, more than just a Joolie.

He looked up to see Ash soar overhead, circling the thick castle walls, before flitting over them and beyond into the farmland, no doubt hunting for bugs. And suddenly he missed the stars in the night sky, the sparks of a Joolie fire and simmering meat on sticks. He missed Malachi's crooked laugh, and the snores of his family.

"I'll think about it," he said at last.

She nodded, her face falling only slightly. "That is all I can ask." She looked toward the castle gates. "And I haven't forgotten my promise to you. Before you leave, the gate guards will deliver your horse."

"My horse, Majesty?" Spade looked at her, stunned.

"Ember wishes that Pronto be yours," the queen said. "You'll need him to carry your reward home."

His throat swelled tight, and he attempted an awkward bow. "Thank you, Yer Majesty," he rasped in disbelief.

Humor glinted in the queen's eyes, and a slight ripple of sadness. "You've earned it."

"An' where'll you go, Majesty?"

"I'm not sure." Her gaze moved past him once more, in the direction of the mountains. "I will travel and make amends where I can. Perhaps I will live as the Joolies do." A ghost of a smile turned the corners of her lips.

Spade pictured the queen as a Joolie and chuckled, shaking his head. She stood and drew a plain cloak over her shoulders, and he spied a pack behind the bench.

"Aren't you gonna say goodbye to Ember?" he asked. "To Henchcliff? Spinniker?"

She shook her head. "Not this time. They would try to stop me, and I couldn't make them see reason. I've left them all notes, and perhaps one day they'll understand. But think on what I said?"

He swallowed. Nodded. Watched her head down the

path and duck under the thick branches. She'd almost disappeared from sight when she paused.

"Spade?" she called. "Thank you."

He paused. "May yer adventures make a new day fer you, Majesty," he returned, a Joolie blessing. It felt right.

She nodded, then bent beneath the brush, and was gone.

CHAPTER 44
A JOOLIE RETURN

The smell of campfire wafted through the air and the sound of a guitar reached Spade as he and Benji rode up to the camp on Pronto, Malachi behind them on a fine mare they'd been gifted by Ember. The familiar rickety carriages came into view, and Spade was glad to be home.

Both horses' saddlebags bulged with Spade's reward, more gold than he had ever seen. And his pockets were filled with buns from the castle cook, Ash eyeing them from his shoulder.

Benji clambered off his horse and went running as Joolie tent doors flapped open and his family poured out. His mother uttered a shriek of delight and strangle-hugged Benji, then turned and planted a big rouge-lipped kiss on Spade's cheek. "Yer both skin an' bones! And the heart spasms I've had! My poor nerves!"

She swept up to Malachi, fixing him with a beady-eyed glare. "Shoulda known you'd go looking fer trouble," she scolded, then softened. "But I got a feeling those boys are thankful fer it." She turned, and her gaze latched on to Pronto's bulging saddlebags. "An' maybe a little trouble ain't a bad thing, once in a while."

Spade's Grandma Flint wrapped him in a bony hug, even while checking his pockets for valuables. Then her gaze followed Opalline's to the saddlebags and she cackled, pinching both his cheeks. "Knew you had it in ya," she croaked.

His uncle and aunt joined the fray, his uncle slapping him on the back while his aunt demanded he sit and eat, asking a hundred questions of the queen and the castle: Are the queen's chambers as opulent as they say? Does that big guard truly carry a ruby the size of a fist in his belt? Did you happen to get a glimpse of the treasury?

A familiar rumbling voice cut above the rest and his father parted the crowd, big hands taking Spade by the shoulders as he whirled him around. He looked Benji up and down, relief flashing across his face before he covered it with a quick grin.

"Didn't I tell you all?" he crowed. "The queen's cemetery—the gig of a lifetime! An' here the boys are, the talk of the whole town, safe an' sound after defeating the nasty Woeg—"

"Shush, Garnet! Don't say its name, for gems' sakes," Opalline interjected. "Heaven knows it'll resurrect an' devour us all in our sleep—"

"Like I was saying." Garnet leveled a stern glare at his wife. "Not only does Spade here defeat the wily beast, he manages to wheedle himself the disguise of being the queen's royal spy, frees his brother an' returns with a nice little fortune! Now that's a true Joolie if I ever did see!" He winked at Spade, while the others cheered.

Spade fought an inward sigh. His dad was his dad, as usual.

Garnet sobered and looked him over, a cunning gleam in his eye. "No doubt you learned lots of interesting things 'bout the castle, huh, son?"

"Maybe," Spade said. "But that information's not up for grabs."

His dad winked conspiratorially. "Still playing spy, I see." He turned to the others and raised his voice. "The boys just need a rest, 'course, a moment to breathe, before we get down to the nitty gritty of the Stone Queen an' her castle secrets—"

"Queen Carmelia ain't the queen anymore."

The chatter died down, and even Grandma Flint paused in her rifling through Spade's pack. All eyes turned to him, including Benji's—he hadn't had a chance yet to tell his brother about the queen.

Benji straightened from leaning against their mother.

"What's this now, dear?" Spade's mother asked. "What's happened to the Stone Queen?" She rubbed her hands together, and Spade could see her thoughts whirling. "She didn't get in a blood feud over her jewels, did she? Perhaps an assassination?"

"No," Spade said. "It's, uh—a long story. But there's gonna be a new queen." He took a deep breath. "An' she's my friend." His voice was firm and confident, and it surprised him.

His dad coughed, and his mother looked aghast. "A new queen? Yer friend?"

"Yup," Spade said. "An' I've been offered a job."

"A job!" Garnet sputtered, cheeks puffed out. "A Joolie with a job! Let's not get carried away, son. Us Joolies, we're not the steady-work type."

Something in Spade rose up at the words, something he'd shoved down for a long time. He squared his shoulders and took a deep breath. "But maybe we're not all the same, Dad." He glanced at Benji, whose eyes were wide. "And maybe I can choose what I wanna be."

Garnet stilled, and the rumblings and chatter of the family fell silent, for once. His dad's brow furrowed, eyes flashing. "Now, son—"

"The boy's probably starving," a voice rose above Garnet's, cutting through it. Malachi hobbled over to them. "Let's give him some breathing room. Ain't it time we celebrated?"

Garnet frowned, but nodded, his shrewd eyes staring hard at Spade. "Of course, of course," he said. "My boy's likely so hungry he can't think straight. It's high time we had a Joolie feast!"

Later that evening the fire died to embers, and Spade sat quietly under the stars. He was stuffed to the brim with roast chicken, bread and corn, all bought with the reward money. Well, except for the corn, which his father had stolen from a farmer's harvest fields. "Hard to break old habits," Garnet had said sheepishly.

Bats dipped and reeled across the sky now, the night deep in darkness. Malachi slept in his chair. Benji curled by the fire. His chest rose and fell, deep and slow, and his pale skin had gained some color, Spade noted with relief. Ash slept perched atop his great-uncle's chair like a watchful guardian, his beak buried in his feathers.

Spade leaned back, exhausted. Each family member had visited him in private throughout the evening, some trying to extract some information out of him about the layout of the castle, others curious about who the Woegan's master was. He hadn't said much to any of them, of course. He knew better than to tell the others the queen's secrets— secrets were never safe in the hands of his Joolie family unless you wanted them to rob you blind.

It was a relief when they'd finally all gone to bed, and he and Benji had got to sit by the fire in peace with Malachi. They'd murmured together deep into the night, until Benji's eyes had drooped and Malachi had given a great yawn.

But Spade sat awake.

He gazed up at the stars in the velvet-black sky, his mind turning. Reaching into his pocket, he drew out the piece of the pebble and turned it over in his palm. The strange ache returned, a small spark at his fingertips, sending a shudder down his spine. The magic slipped just beneath the surface, and Spade longed for the feel of it.

A low whistle caught Spade off guard, directly behind him.

He whirled to see his father standing there, having approached quieter than the dead—Spade had forgotten what it was like to live with Joolies.

"Seems we both can't sleep tonight, my boy," Garnet chuckled, peering over Spade's shoulder. He stilled, then bent closer. "That's quite a stone you got there, son, glowing like a night star." He scratched his chin. "In fact, reminds me a bit of a ruby I sold long ago to a royal guard—had that same sorta glow."

Spade stared at his dad, and then Henchcliff's voice was in his head. *It was owned by a Joolie who claimed it had magic,* the guard had said. *It cost me all I had.*

"It was you," Spade whispered. "You sold Henchcliff the stone."

"What now?" Garnet's thick, dark eyebrows raised. "I didn't know the man, of course." He grinned. "He had deep pockets, though."

Spade shook his head in disbelief. "You sold it to the captain of the guard, an' he . . ." Spade stopped. "Never mind. It doesn't matter."

Garnet frowned. "Well now, the man was wearing a dark cloak, and I couldn't see his face. Though he did have a beautiful horse. Could have fetched a pretty penny on the black market." He sighed, and scratched his chin. "I always did regret selling that stone. The miners told me wasn't worth much, but I always wondered if it didn't have a little magic to it."

Spade sighed. He should have known Garnet would have been the one to sell the ruby to the guard.

"Don't go looking so glum, son." Garnet watched him, nervous now. "I never meant fer anyone to get hurt. I suppose I saw a deal . . . it's the Joolie way, right? Speaking of which, that stone of yers is one of a kind, ain't it? The things we could do, boy! If you'll just let me see it, I can figure a good price for it on the black market . . ."

Crud. Spade should have been more careful, shouldn't have taken the pebble out in plain view—

"Ahem."

They whirled to see Malachi awake in his chair, cane in hand, a stern look fixed on Garnet.

"I think the owner of the stone should decide what's to be done with it now, Garnet," Malachi said in a low voice. "An' that's the boy. Especially seeing as how getting it nearly killed him."

Garnet scratched the back of his neck, glancing at Malachi, whose immoveable stare narrowed.

"Of course. The lad's a man now." Garnet tore his gaze from the pebble as Spade slipped it back into his pocket, relieved to tuck it out of sight.

"Listen, Spade." Garnet cleared his throat, and it creaked with a sort of roughness Spade had rarely heard. "Truth is, we're real glad to have you back. An' well, I'm proud of ya."

In a rare show of affection, he reached out to pat Spade on the back. Then, whistling a low tune, he walked away, hands shoved in his pockets. Spade shook his head and watched his dad go, a small smile on his face despite himself.

Benji and Ash remained asleep, so Malachi gestured at the fire, and they settled down by it. "You've had quite the adventure, boy," his old great-uncle commented, leaning back to look up at the black expanse of the night sky, stars bright above them. "Interesting how the creature the whole kingdom feared had a fearful heart itself, isn't it?" Malachi paused. "We all have our fears, though," he added, his voice soft. Without realizing it, Spade had slipped his hand back in his pocket and was fidgeting with the pebble.

Flushing, Spade pulled his hand out of his pocket, but his great-uncle had turned to Ash, perched on the back of his chair. He scratched under the bird's beak, and the raven crooned, one eye half-open.

Spade stood, a strange heaviness sweeping over him. "I'm gonna take a walk, Uncle."

Malachi nodded and Ash blinked awake, spreading his wings, but Spade gently shook his head. "Not this time, Ash. I need to go alone."

The raven watched him walk away, a low croak in his throat, but Spade didn't look back. He didn't want to see the shadow in Malachi's eyes.

He'd reached the edge of camp when he heard swift footsteps behind him. "Where you going, Spade?" Benji's voice was thick, his hair wild from sleep. "I heard you an' Uncle talking."

Spade turned, meeting his brother's curious gaze. "Fer a walk. I've gotta figure something out, Benj."

Benji regarded him with his big green eyes, and Spade feared he'd ask to come with him.

But the boy simply looked past Spade, over his shoulder and into the dark night. "You still got it, don't ya? The pebble. I can see it in yer eyes."

A tingle of warmth sparked in Spade's pocket, and he hesitated.

But his brother crossed his arms, resolute, and Spade knew he couldn't lie. "Yeah. I still got it."

Benji set his jaw, his brow creased. "Well," he said at last. "You'll always be my brother, no matter what you do with it."

A lump rose in Spade's throat at the words.

"'Sides," Benji continued. "I'm thinking there's a reason you found it."

"You do?"

"Yeah. I've always thought so. Yer the best one to know what to do with it."

Spade swallowed, his throat raspy. "Thanks, Benj."

He watched his brother turn and walk back across the field. Before he disappeared into the dark, Spade heard the low hoot of Benji's barn-owl call. A farewell.

Spade looked after him for a moment. He returned the call, then slipped into the night.

CHAPTER 45

GRAVEDIGGER

The cool wind whispered over the gravestones at the Wyndhail cemetery, which lay just as he remembered it: perched above the town with the crooked elm at its center, the lonely guardian of the dead. At the gate, he turned and spotted the dark silhouette of the castle to the west.

It didn't take him long to reach the bench. It seemed like a year ago when he'd dragged the heavy thing all the way up the hill for Lyrica. He sat down and reached into his pocket, his fingers brushing the pebble as he drew it out, glowing soft in the moonlight. A current of power rippled just beneath its smooth surface, calling to him.

And he wanted it. Badly. He craved the power it had given him, the feeling of being strong, capable. Free from his damaged leg.

His fingers trembled as he gazed down at it, and he pictured himself running fast and unhindered. He stood, fingers shaking, and the stone slipped out of his sweaty grip, landing on the bench.

He bent to pick it up, then paused. He'd never noticed the sides of the bench were carved with ornate ivy, familiar somehow . . . and then he remembered. He closed his eyes and saw the Woegan queen in his memory, and the bench in the royal cemetery, blood marring the stone: the twin of this one.

He picked the pebble up and turned it over in his hand.

Caw-caw! Caw-caw!

The sound jerked his gaze upward. Ash swooped out of the night and soared above him, then perched on a fresh headstone near the big, twisted elm. He croaked, long and deep, and Spade grinned despite himself. "Stubborn bird," he muttered.

He looked up at the golden moon that hung in the sky, then gazed out across the tombstones, the landscape silent in the way that only a cemetery can be.

There's strength in weakness, Lyrica had said, and he looked down at his crooked leg. He'd had to ask for help, and he'd made a friend because of it, something he'd never done before. And despite his leg, they'd outwitted a mage, met the lumpskins, defeated a monster and he'd been named a royal spy. Maybe Ember was right—maybe he was more than just a gravedigger.

He glanced over at Ash once more, perched on the tombstone, and then he saw it: a shovel, leaned up against the crooked elm.

Of course, being a gravedigger did have its upsides.

Could be quite useful, in fact.

Spade walked down the path and picked up the shovel. He hefted it over his shoulder and turned to Ash and the tombstone.

Bagman Grute, it read. Tax Collector, Wyndhail.

And he knew what to do.

The sun broke over the hill, faint light streaming across the gravestone when he'd finished the last shovelful.

He leaned back, breathing hard, then patted the loose soil down atop the grave. Wiping his forehead, he straightened and gazed out across the cemetery. As he did so, he saw a flicker of orange dart between the tombstones, then leap atop a crooked stone angel across from the grave.

Spade chuckled. He had wondered when he'd see that cat again. The tabby blinked its big green eyes and twitched its tail, then jumped down and disappeared between the graves, into the morning mist.

Ash crowed behind him, drawing him back to the present. Spade leaned the shovel against the gravestone and wiped his hands on his empty pockets.

He'd returned to Bagman Grute what once belonged to him, for who better to watch over a stone like this one than a man that could never use it? *No one keeps secrets like the dead*, Garnet liked to say. And for once, his dad was right.

Ash croaked in approval, and Spade swung the shovel over his shoulder and walked out of the cemetery, turning his steps toward Wyndhail castle.

ACKNOWLEDGMENTS

A special thanks to my agent, Naomi Davis of BookEnds Literary, who inspires me and stands by me, and who always reaches for the moon.

Thank you to my editor, Samantha Swenson: your discerning eye saw right to the heart of this story, and I'm so grateful we share the same love of sandwiches, pie and ornery yaks.

To the team at Tundra, you have talent in spades! Shana Hayes, Copyeditor Extraordinaire, you never miss a thing, and I'm so grateful. Endless thanks to illustrator Kristina Kister for turning this story into an image that breathes.

Theresa, Noelle and Christine, my amazing writing trio: your fine-tuned notes helped to shape Spade's adventure and your friendship continues to encourage me.

To authors and writers Swati Chavda, Brenda Johnson, Patti Nielson and Liz Grotkowski: you are the ones who understood and persisted in helping me find the threads.

Boundless thanks to author P.J. Vernon for challenging me to grow.

To photographer Owen Belanger: thank you for running from bears with me and sneaking through graveyards in the dead of night. You are the best co-thief a writer could ask for.

To my first classrooms at Airdrie Koinonia and the students of Webber Academy: your support has made all the difference.

To Mrs. Deboo: thank you for handing me the book that began my love of reading.

Thank you to my mum, for raising an explorer.

To my family, Jaxson, Chantz, and Adaleigh, for your kindness to me and your belief in this book. I love you.

Finally, thank you to my husband Michael: your indomitable spirit and encouragement is a great gift to me.

And to God, who has blessed me richly, and given me a reason to write.